T‾‾ ‾‾‾‾ ‾‾‾‾ ‾‾‾‾‾‾
SECOND CHANCE CAT MYSTERIES

"A surefire winner."
—*New York Times* bestselling author Miranda James

"An affirmation of friendship as well as a tantalizing whodunit, *The Whole Cat and Caboodle* marks a promising start to a series sure to appeal to anyone who loves a combination of felonies and felines."
—*Richmond Times-Dispatch*

"Ryan kicks off the new Second Chance Cat Mystery series with a lot of excitement. Her small Maine town is filled with unique characters. . . . This tale is enjoyable from beginning to end; readers will look forward to more."
—*RT Book Reviews*

"Cozy readers will enjoy the new Second Chance Cat series."
—*Gumshoe*

"If you enjoy a cozy mystery featuring a lovable protagonist with a bevy of staunch friends, a shop you'd love to explore, plenty of suspects, and a supersmart cat, you'll love *The Whole Cat and Caboodle*."
—*MyShelf.com*

"Enjoyable. . . . Remember—everyone has a secret, ev‾‾‾ ‾‾‾‾ ‾‾‾‾‾‾‾‾‾‾ ‾‾‾‾‾‾ *Magazine*

"I‾ ‾‾‾‾‾ ‾‾‾‾‾‾‾‾‾‾ ‾‾‾‾‾‾‾‾‾‾ The cast of ‾‾‾‾‾ ‾‾‾‾‾‾‾‾‾‾ ‾‾‾‾‾‾ minute of ‾‾‾‾‾ ‾‾‾‾‾‾‾‾‾‾ ‾ *Meows*

The Second Chance Cat Mysteries

The Whole Cat and Caboodle
Buy a Whisker
A Whisker of Trouble

A WHISKER OF TROUBLE

A SECOND CHANCE CAT MYSTERY

Sofie Ryan

AN OBSIDIAN MYSTERY

OBSIDIAN
Published by New American Library,
an imprint of Penguin Random House LLC
375 Hudson Street, New York, New York 10014

This book is an original publication of New American Library.

First Printing, February 2016

Copyright © Darlene Ryan, 2016
Excerpt from *Curiosity Thrilled the Cat* © Penguin Group (USA), Inc., 2011

For more information about Penguin Random House, visit penguin.com.

ISBN 978-0-451-41996-5

Printed in the United States of America
1 3 5 7 9 10 8 6 4 2

Penguin
Random
House

Acknowledgments

Thank you to my editor, Jessica Wade, for finding all the leaps in logic and holes in the plot. Thank you to my agent, Kim Lionetti, who keeps my professional life running smoothly. And thanks as well to John, who answered my questions about wine and never laughed at my ignorance. Any errors are mine, not his.

Chapter 1

Elvis regarded breakfast with disdain. "Oh, c'mon," I said, leaning my elbows on the countertop. "It's not that bad."

He narrowed his eyes at me and I think he would have raised a skeptical eyebrow if he'd had real eyebrows instead of just whiskers—which he didn't, since he wasn't the King of Rock and Roll or even a person. He was just a small black cat who *thought* he was a person and as such should be treated like royalty.

"We could make a fried peanut butter and banana sandwich," I said. "That was the real Elvis's favorite."

The cat meowed sharply, his way of reminding me that as far as he was concerned he was the real Elvis and peanut butter and banana sandwiches were not his favorite breakfast food.

I looked at the food I'd pulled out of the cupboard: two dry ends of bread, a banana that was more brown than it was yellow and a container of peanut butter that I knew didn't actually have so much as a spoonful left inside, because I'd eaten it all the previous evening, *with* a spoon, while watching *Jeopardy!* with the cat. It wasn't my idea of a great breakfast, either, but there wasn't anything else to eat in the house.

"I forgot to go to the store," I said, feeling somewhat compelled to explain myself to the cat, who continued to stare unblinkingly at me from his perch on a stool at the counter.

Elvis knew that it wouldn't have mattered if I had bought groceries. I couldn't cook. My mother had tried to teach me. So had my brother and my grandmother. My grandmother's friend Rose was the most recent person to take on the challenge of teaching me how to cook. We weren't getting very far. Rose kept having to simplify things for me as she discovered I had very few basic skills.

"How did you pass the Family Living unit in school?" Charlotte, another of Gram's friends, had asked after my last lesson in Rose's small sunny kitchen. Charlotte had been a school principal, so she knew I'd had to take a basic cooking class in middle school. She'd been eyeing my attempt at meat loaf, which I'd just set on an oval stoneware platter and which I'd been pretty sure I'd be able to use as a paving stone out in the garden once the backyard dried up.

I'd wiped my hands on my apron and blown a stray piece of hair off my face. "The school decided to give me a pass, after the second fire."

"Second fire?" Charlotte had said.

"It wasn't my fault." I couldn't help the defensive edge to my voice. "Well, the sprinklers going off wasn't my fault."

"Of course it wasn't, darling girl," Rose had commented, her voice muffled because her head had been in the oven. She was cleaning remnants of exploded potatoes off the inside.

"They weren't calibrated properly," I told Charlotte, feeling the color rise in my cheeks.

"I'm sure they weren't." The corners of her mouth twitched and I could tell she was struggling not to smile.

Tired now of waiting for breakfast, Elvis jumped down from the stool, made his way purposefully across the kitchen and stopped in front of the cupboard where I kept his cat food. He put one paw on the door and turned and looked at me.

I pushed away from the counter and went over to him. I grabbed a can of Tasty Tenders from the cupboard. "Okay, you can have Tasty Tenders and I'll have the peanut butter and banana sandwich." I reached down to stroke the top of his head.

He licked his lips and pushed his head against my hand.

I got Elvis his breakfast and a dish of fresh water. He started eating and I eyed the two dry crusts and brown banana. The cat's food looked better than mine.

I reached for the peanut butter jar, hoping that maybe there was somehow enough stuck to the bottom to at least spread on one of the ends of bread, and there was a knock on my door.

Elvis lifted his head and looked at me. "Mrrr," he said.

"I heard," I said, heading for the living room. It wasn't seven o'clock, but I was pretty sure I knew who it was at the door.

And I was right. Rose was standing there, holding a plate with a bowl upside down like a cover. "Good morning, Sarah," she said. She held out the plate. "I'm afraid my eyes were a little bit bigger than my stomach this morning. Would you be a dear and finish this for me? I hate to waste food." She smiled at me, her gray eyes the picture of guilelessness.

I folded my arms over my chest. "You know, if you don't tell the truth, your nose is going to grow."

Rose lifted one hand and smoothed her index finger across the bridge of her nose. "I have my mother's nose," she said. "Not to sound vain, but it is perfectly proportioned." She paused. "And petite." She offered the plate again.

"You're spoiling me," I said.

"No, I'm not," she retorted. "Spoiling implies that your character has been somehow weakened, and that's not at all true."

I shook my head and took the plate from her. It was still warm. I could smell cinnamon and maybe cheese?

There was no point in ever arguing with Rose. It was like arguing with an alligator. There was no way it was going to end well for you.

"Come in," I said, heading back to the kitchen with my food. I set the plate on the counter and lifted the bowl. Underneath I found a mound of fluffy scrambled eggs, tomatoes that had been fried with onions and some herbs I couldn't identify and a bran muffin studded with raisins. Rose was a big believer in a daily dose of fiber.

It all looked even better than it smelled, and it smelled wonderful.

Rose was leaning forward, talking to Elvis. She was

small but mighty, barely five feet tall in her sensible shoes, with her white hair in an equally sensible short cut.

I bent down and kissed the top of her head as I moved around her to get a knife and fork. "I love you," I said. "Thank you."

"I love you, too, dear," she said. "And thank you for helping me out."

Okay, so we were going to continue with the fiction that Rose had cooked too much food for breakfast. "Could I get you a cup of . . ." I looked around the kitchen. I was out of coffee and tea. And milk. "Water?" I finished.

"No, thank you," Rose said. "I already had my tea."

I speared some egg and a little of the tomatoes and onions with my fork. "Ummm, that's good," I said, putting a hand to my mouth because I was talking around a mouthful of food. Elvis was at my feet looking expectantly up at me. I picked up a tiny bit of the scrambled egg with my fingers and offered it to him.

He took it from me, ate and then cocked his head at Rose and meowed softly.

"You're very welcome, Elvis," she said.

"Why don't my eggs taste like this?" I asked, reaching for the muffin. Scrambled eggs were one of the few things I could make more or less successfully.

"I don't know." Rose looked around my kitchen. Aside from the two crusts of bread, the empty peanut butter jar and the mushy banana on the counter, it was clean and neat. Since I rarely cooked, it never got messy. "How do you cook your eggs?"

I shrugged and broke the muffin in half. "In a bowl in the microwave."

She gave her head a dismissive shake. "You need a cast-iron skillet if you want to make decent eggs." She smiled at me. "Alfred and I will take you shopping this weekend."

I nodded, glad that my mouth was full so I didn't have to commit to a shopping trip with Rose and her gentleman friend Alfred Peterson.

It wasn't that I didn't like Mr. P. I did. When Rose had been evicted from Legacy Place, the seniors' building she derisively referred to as Shady Pines, I let her move into the small apartment at the back of my old Victorian. Mr. P. had generously made a beautiful cat tower for Elvis as a thank-you to me. He was kind and smart and he adored Rose. I didn't even mind—that much—that Alfred had the sort of computer-hacking skills that were usually seen in a George Clooney movie and he was usually using them over my Wi-Fi.

It was just that I knew if I went shopping with the two of them, I was apt to come home with one of every kitchen gadget that could be found in North Harbor, Maine. Rose had made it her mission in life to teach me to cook, no matter how impossible I was starting to think that was. And Mr. P. had already—gently, because he was unfailingly polite—expressed his dismay over the fact that I didn't have a French press in my kitchen.

Rose smiled at me again. "Enjoy your breakfast," she said. "I need to go clean up my kitchen."

"Do you want to drive to the shop with me?" I asked. "Or Mac and I can come and get you when we're ready to head out to Edison Hall's place."

Rose worked part-time for me at my shop, Second Chance. Second Chance was a repurpose shop. It was part antiques store and part thrift shop. We sold furniture, dishes, quilts—many things repurposed from their original use, like the teacups we'd turned into planters and the tub chair that in its previous life had actually been a bathtub.

Our stock came from a lot of different places: flea markets, yard sales, people looking to downsize. I bought fairly regularly from a couple of trash pickers. Several times in the past year that the store had been open, we'd been hired to go through and handle the sale of the contents of someone's home—usually someone who was going from a house to an apartment. This time we were going to clean out the property of Edison Hall. He had died over the winter and clearing out the house had turned out to be too much for his son and his sister.

Calling the old man a pack rat was putting it nicely. Rose and Mac were going with me to get started on the house, along with Elvis, because I'd heard rustling in several of the rooms in the old place and I was certain it wasn't the wind in the eaves.

"Why don't I just come with you?" Rose said. "That will save you having to come back and get me."

"All right," I said, picking up a piece of the muffin and wishing I had coffee. "Does half an hour give you enough time?"

She smiled at me. "It does."

I put down my fork to walk her to the door, but she waved one hand at me. "Eat," she ordered, already heading for the living room. "I can see myself out."

I stuffed the bite of muffin in my mouth and waved over my shoulder as the door closed behind her.

I finished my breakfast, sharing another bite of the

scrambled eggs with Elvis. He followed me into the bathroom, washing his face while I brushed my teeth. When we came out of the apartment, Rose was just coming out of hers.

"Perfect timing," she said, bustling over to us, as usual carrying one of her oversize tote bags.

Ever since I'd seen the movie *Mary Poppins*, I'd thought that Rose's bags were like the magical nanny's carpetbag. You just never knew what was going to be inside. This one looked as if it had been made from the same blue-striped canvas as a train engineer's hat.

"I have coffee just in case we're out," Rose said, patting the side of the carryall with one hand.

"Just coffee?" I asked as I picked up the canvas tote at my own feet. Mine was filled with a stack of thrift store sweaters that I'd brought home and felted for my friend Jess.

"And some tea bags." Rose held the door so Elvis could go out first.

I looked at her, raising one eyebrow.

"And a coffee cake." She followed Elvis outside. "Don't make that face, Sarah. We all work better after a cup of tea and a little taste of something."

"If I keep on having a 'little taste of something,' I'm going to turn into a big something," I said, pulling out my keys and pushing the button to unlock the SUV.

"Nonsense," Rose said, making a dismissive gesture with one hand. "All that running you do, you'd be skin and bones if I didn't feed you." She set her bag on the floor of the passenger side of the vehicle and climbed inside. Elvis had already jumped in and settled himself in the middle of the backseat. I set my bag and my briefcase next to him.

"Are those more tablecloths?" Rose asked, half turning in her seat and pointing at the canvas tote.

I slammed the passenger door and slid in behind the wheel. "No. It's a bunch of sweaters I felted for Jess."

Rose's gray eyes lit up. "Is she going to make more slippers?"

I nodded as I stuck the key in the ignition.

Jess was a master at recycling and upcycling clothes. Her latest project was making slippers out of felted wool sweaters. We were going to sell them at Second Chance. She'd made me a red pair of slipper "boots" that I'd worn at the shop most of the winter. So many customers had asked about them that Jess and I had scoured area thrift stores over the weekend looking for sweaters that would felt well. I had done the actual process in my washer and dryer, and Jess was coming by the store to pick up the soft, shrunken sweaters.

"Do you think she'd make a pair for me?" Rose asked. "And for Alfred? They'd be lovely to wear around the apartment."

"I'm sure she would," I said. I concentrated on backing out of the driveway and tried to push away the image of Alfred Peterson, who generally wore his pants up under his armpits, in a pair of bright felted boots halfway up his calves.

Second Chance was in a brick building from the late eighteen hundreds located on Mill Street, where it curved and began to climb uphill. We were about twenty minutes by foot from the downtown, and easily accessed from the highway—the best of both worlds for catching the tourists. We had a decent side parking lot and an old garage, which we were working on turning into work and storage space.

Tourists came to North Harbor during the spring and summer for the beautiful Maine seacoast. In the fall and winter it was the nearby hills with the autumn colors and skiing that drew them in.

I parked close to the back door because we'd need to load some empty boxes and garbage bags in the back of the SUV. I'd already arranged to have a Dumpster for the garbage and a bin for everything that could be recycled delivered to Edison Hall's house.

It looked as though spring was going to be a busy time for us between the influx of tourists eager to get away from the city after a cold winter that had stretched all the way from the Atlantic Canadian provinces down to Virginia, and the work I was planning on the old garage. I wouldn't have said yes to clearing out Edison Hall's house if it hadn't been for my grandmother. She'd known Edison's sister, Stella, since they were, as she put it, captains of opposing Red Rover teams on the playground.

"Please, do this for me," Gram had asked when she called from South Carolina. She and her new husband, John, were working their way back to Maine after almost nine months of an extended honeymoon traveling around the country and working on several housing projects for the charity Home for Good. "I know what I'm asking, believe me. I was in that house a couple of years ago and it could only have gotten worse."

I'd pictured her shaking her head, lips pressed together.

"I'll call Stella," I'd told Gram. I couldn't say no to her, which was why both Rose and Charlotte were working for me. And how bad could Edison Hall's old house really be? I'd reasoned. Very bad, I'd discovered. The man was a pack rat.

I followed Rose and Elvis into the workroom at the back of the store. I could smell coffee. The morning was getting better and better. I set the bag of felted sweaters on the workbench that ran along one wall of the work space and headed into the shop. Mac had just come downstairs. He was carrying a heavy pottery mug and he held it out to me. His title, on paper at least, was store manager, but he was a lot more than that. He was my colleague, a second set of eyes and sometimes the voice of reason I needed to hear. And more and more he was the person I turned to when I needed someone to talk to. It had started the past winter when I was almost killed in my own house. It was Mac I'd called, Mac who I'd shared with how scared I'd really been. Our friendship had only deepened in the following months.

"You read my mind," I said, dropping my briefcase at my feet and taking the cup from him. "Thank you."

As good as Rose's breakfast had been, this was one of those mornings when I needed a nudge of caffeine.

Mac smiled. "You're welcome."

This past winter the building where he had rented an apartment had been sold. So we'd renovated part of the second-floor space above the shop and now Mac had a small self-contained apartment up there and I worried a lot less about security for the store. Not to mention that most mornings the coffee was on when I arrived. It seemed to be working out well for both of us.

Rose and her furry sidekick, Elvis, were disappearing up the steps to the second-floor staff room. I knew she'd be back in a couple of minutes with a slice of coffee cake for both Mac and me.

Mac walked over to the cash desk where he'd set his own coffee mug. He was tall and lean and the long-sleeved gray T-shirt he wore showed off his muscles very nicely. He had light brown skin and kept his black hair cropped close to his scalp.

I took a sip of my coffee and pushed a stray piece of hair back off my face. Usually I wore my brown shoulder-length hair down, but I'd pulled it back into a ponytail, since we were going to be working for most of the day on the old house. "I saw the boxes you left by the back door," I said. "Thank you."

"There's more under the stairs if you think we need them," he said, walking back over to me. He studied my face. "Are you having second thoughts about taking the Hall estate on?"

I shook my head. "No. The numbers are good. We both checked them. We'll make a nice little profit and I think the price is reasonable as far as what Stella Hall will have to pay. The house just makes me a little sad, piled full of . . . well, boxes of junk that no one else wants." I ducked my head over my cup and gave him a sidelong glance. "If I tell you something, do you promise not to laugh?"

His brown eyes met mine. He put a hand over his heart. "I promise."

"The first time we went out to look the place over—when we were trying to decide what to charge Stella—when I got home that night I cleaned out two closets." Mac smiled. "Just between you and me, I came back here and put two boxes of old parts in the scrap-metal recycling bin."

"And how much did you pick back out the next day?" I teased.

"No comment," he said, taking another sip from his cup.

I laughed.

Mac could fix just about anything. About eighteen months ago he'd left his high-powered job as a financial planner to come to Maine and sail. I had no idea what had prompted him to make such a dramatic change in his life. I'd asked him once and he'd very skillfully evaded the question.

I hadn't asked again.

During the sailing season he spent every spare minute crewing for pretty much anyone who needed an extra set of hands on deck. Wooden boats were Mac's passion. There were generally eight windjammers tied up at the North Harbor dock during the season, along with plenty of other boats, so there were lots of opportunities to get out on the water.

I knew eventually Mac wanted to build his own boat. He worked for me because, he said, he liked the satisfaction of having something tangible to show for his efforts at the end of the day. There wasn't anything he couldn't fix, as far as I'd seen. Second Chance was successful as much from his efforts as from mine.

"It probably wouldn't hurt to take a few extra boxes," I said, walking over to the front window to straighten two quilts that were hanging on a wooden rack. "According to Gram, Edison was a collector of—well, a lot of things. Maybe some of his collections will turn out to be something we can sell here or in the online store."

"We have some of those plastic bins out in the garage," Mac said. "Do you want to take maybe half a dozen?"

I nodded. Rose came down the stairs then, still trailed by Elvis. She handed me a slice of coffee cake on a blue-flowered napkin.

I smiled. "Thank you."

"You're very welcome." She smiled back at me.

Elvis looked up at me and blinked his green eyes.

"No," I said, breaking off a chunk of coffee cake. "Don't think I don't know Rose already fed you a piece."

The cat made a huffy sound and headed for the workroom.

Rose handed a piece of coffee cake to Mac. "I left half of the cake for you upstairs in the blue tin," she said.

"Thank you," he said. "I fixed your iron. It was just a loose connection. It's on the workbench."

Rose clapped her hands together. "Aren't you wonderful?" she exclaimed.

Rose's steam iron was probably as old as I was. It gave off copious amounts of steam, surrounding her in a cloud as if she were standing in a fogbank. And it was as heavy as an anvil. But she liked using it and when it had stopped blasting steam a few days ago, Mac offered to see what he could do. I wasn't surprised he'd been able to fix it.

"I may as well go do those last two lace tablecloths," Rose said. "I can probably get them done before Charlotte gets here."

"Thank you," I said. "I think we'll put the bigger one on that table." I pointed to a long farmhouse kitchen table that sat about three feet from the back wall of the shop. Mac had sanded it for me and I'd whitewashed the top and painted the legs black. It had turned out even better than I'd hoped. With the lace tablecloth and several place settings of vintage china, I knew it would make customers think of happy meals shared with family and friends.

Charlotte arrived about five minutes to nine. Her cheeks were rosy and her white hair was a little mussed.

"Did you walk?" I asked. "I could have picked you up."

"Yes, I did," she said. "It was a lovely morning for a walk." She pushed her glasses up her nose and looked down at me. Even in flats Charlotte was at least an inch taller than I was. She had perfect posture—it seemed she was incapable of slouching. And she still had the steely glare of the high school principal she'd been before she retired.

"I'll just go put my things upstairs and you can head out to Edison's." She hesitated for a moment and then reached out and gave my arm a squeeze. "Thank you for taking this on, Sarah," she said. "I've been in that house." She shook her head. "I know Stella tried to get Edison to keep the place up, but he acted like running a vacuum cleaner around would kill him. The dust bunnies have probably taken over."

"I have Mac and Rose *and* Elvis in case there's anything with more than two legs," I said. "We'll be fine."

"Nicolas is using this against me, you know," she said, pulling the soft cotton scarf from her neck and tucking it into the pocket of her jacket. "He says my garage is in danger of looking like Edison's."

Nicolas Elliot—Nick—was Charlotte's son, a former EMT who now worked as an investigator for the medical examiner's office.

"Did you suggest that maybe he should come and clean it out?" I asked. I'd known Nick since we were kids. In fact, when we were teenagers I'd had a huge crush on him. I'd seen him butt heads with his mother over the years. I'd never seen him win.

Charlotte shrugged. "No. Although I did point out that about ninety percent of the boxes in there belong to him." A smiled played at the corners of her mouth. "That was the last I heard about the garage." The almost smile turned into a grin as she started for the stairs. "I'll be right back," she said over her shoulder.

By quarter after nine we were on the road, with Mac riding shotgun and Rose and Elvis in the backseat. I'd been serious when I told Charlotte that I was taking the cat along to deal with anything that had more than two feet. While I believed that all living creatures had the right to life, liberty and the pursuit of the animal equivalent of happiness, I didn't really want most of the four-legged ones sharing my space while they were doing it—Elvis excluded, of course.

Before I'd acquired Elvis, or maybe more accurately,

before he'd acquired me, the cat had spent some time living on the streets around the harbor front. I wasn't sure if that was where he'd honed his skill as a rodent wrangler, or if that particular ability came from his previous life, whatever that had been.

Edison Hall's house was a small white bungalow on the outskirts of town. It was usually a short trip over to Beech Hill Road, but a water main had broken on the street a few days earlier. Now it was being repaved, down to one lane for traffic. When it was our turn to go, I tried not to wince as the tires threw bits of pavement up against the undercarriage of the SUV. Elvis sneezed at the sharp smell of tar and when I looked in the rearview mirror he was making a sour face, despite Rose stroking his black fur.

There was a single-car garage at the end of the short driveway at the Hall house. I was happy to see the Dumpster I'd ordered sitting on a patch of gravel to the left of the garage. As I backed in, I caught a glimpse of the smaller recycling bins against the long right wall of the garage, on the old stone patio by the path to the back door, exactly where I'd asked Aaron Ellison to put them.

"Do you want to leave everything here and take another look around, maybe make a plan of attack?" Mac asked as he undid his seat belt.

I nodded. "Remember all those wine bottles that were in the basement?"

"Uh-huh."

"Apparently Ethan moved them up to the kitchen. Stella left me a message saying they were supposed to all be moved out yesterday, but I want to make sure."

I had told Stella that we didn't have the expertise to

handle her brother's wine collection. She'd said that Edison's son, Ethan, was planning on hiring someone to put a dollar value on the bottles so they could be sold.

Rose had already picked up Elvis and was getting out of the SUV.

I pulled the keys Ethan had given me out of the pocket of my jeans and climbed out as well.

I noticed the smell the moment we stepped in the front door. Mac looked at me and frowned. "Rat?" he asked.

I made a face. "Maybe." It wouldn't be the first time we'd shown up at an empty house and found a dead animal. A couple of times it had been mice, once a raccoon and once a seagull that appeared to have fallen down the chimney.

Elvis squirmed in Rose's arms. She looked at me and raised an inquiring eyebrow.

"Let him go," I said. "It's the fastest way to find whatever it is that crawled in here and died."

The cat was already making his way to the kitchen. There seemed to be a path more or less through the stacks of boxes. One thing I could say about Edison Hall: The house wasn't dirty. Charlotte was right about there being dust bunnies everywhere, but there were no bags of garbage, no muddy footprints or bits of spilled food. The place was piled, but I had the same thought I'd had the first time I was in the house with Edison's sister, Stella: The old man had had some kind of system for the boxes that were piled everywhere. The problem was, I had no idea what that system was.

Elvis meowed loudly. I couldn't see him, but from the sound he was in the vicinity of the kitchen.

"I'll go," Mac said.

I shook my head and stuffed the keys back in my pocket. "It's okay. I'll go."

The cat gave another insistent meow. "I'm coming," I called. I made my way in the direction of the kitchen. There was a path through the boxes, although it was a bit like being in a tunnel made of cardboard.

"I'll get the shovel and a couple of garbage bags," Mac said.

The path widened at the kitchen doorway. Elvis had somehow climbed up onto a stack of cartons about shoulder height. He was looking down at the floor, but he turned his head and his focus to me as I reached the doorway.

"Mac, forget about the shovel," I said, raising my voice so he'd be sure to hear me.

"What do you need?" he asked.

I hesitated and after a moment he appeared behind me.

"What do you need?" he asked again.

I moved sideways so he could see that the body lying on the kitchen floor didn't belong to a mouse or a raccoon.

"I think we need nine-one-one," I said.

Chapter 2

I reached for Elvis. I didn't need to get any closer to tell that the man lying on his side on the brown-and-gold-cushion flooring was dead. There was a dark stain on the collar of his jacket and what looked to be dried blood matted on the back of his head. I was guessing he'd been dead for hours, certainly not as long as a day. He looked to be in his early forties, dressed in a dark wool jacket and good-quality black trousers. There was a wide smudge of white on one leg of the pants and bits of black asphalt stuck to the soles of his leather shoes. A wine bottle lay on its side about a foot from the body.

Mac and I backtracked to the living room, being careful not to touch anything.

A half wall to the left, just inside the front door, made a bit of an entryway. Rose was waiting there, her face pale. "It's not Stella, is it?" she asked.

I shook my head and a bit of the color came back to her face. "It's a man," I said. "I've never seen him before."

"Maybe someone who was homeless," she said. "Maybe he came in looking for somewhere to sleep."

"Maybe," I said.

Mac and I exchanged glances. The dead man was wearing what looked to me to be nice clothes and expensive shoes. I doubted he was homeless.

We went back outside. I handed Elvis to Rose. "Would you put him in the car, please?"

"Of course," she said.

Mac had taken a couple of steps away from us and pulled out his phone, calling 911, I guessed. Now he came back to stand beside me. "Police are on their way."

I sighed and rubbed one shoulder with the other hand. "Have you ever seen that man before?" I asked.

He shook his head and put the phone back in his pocket. "Never."

I glanced over at the SUV. Rose and Elvis were in the back and she was feeding the cat something, probably something it would be better I didn't know about.

"He wasn't homeless," Mac said. "Those shoes he was wearing? They set him back more than a thousand dollars."

I didn't ask how he knew. Instead I asked the next most obvious question. "What's a man in thousand-dollar shoes doing in Edison Hall's kitchen?"

He didn't say anything at first. "It wasn't an accident, Sarah," he said finally, looking over his shoulder at the house.

I took a deep breath and let it out slowly, thinking about the dried blood in the dead man's hair. Mac was right. However the man had died, it wasn't accidental.

A patrol car, the ambulance and a dark blue car all arrived a few minutes later. I walked across the grass toward the car.

The driver got out and gave me a half smile across the roof of the car. "Hi, Sarah, what's going on?" she asked.

Detective Michelle Andrews was tall and slender in jeans, a shirt the color of chocolate pudding and a tan jacket. As usual, her red hair was pulled back in a sleek ponytail.

The patrol officer was already going up the front steps.

"Edison Hall's sister, Stella, hired us to clean the place out," I said as Michelle came around the car to stand next to me. "This morning was our first day." I stopped to clear my throat. "I could . . . uh, smell something as soon as I unlocked the door. I thought it was a mouse. It was a man, dead on the kitchen floor."

Michelle's green eyes narrowed, but other than that, nothing changed in her expression. "Do you recognize him?"

"No," I said. "He's not from around here, at least as far as I know."

Mac was still standing at the edge of the driveway.

"Anyone else here with you besides Mac?" Michelle asked.

"Rose and Elvis," I said. "They're in the car."

"I'm going to have a look inside the house." She fished a pair of plastic gloves from one of her jacket's pockets. She looked at me for a long moment without speaking. "You know how this works," she finally said.

I nodded. "We'll stay right here."

Michelle started across the grass and I walked back

to Mac. "We can't go anywhere, not for a while at least," I said.

He shrugged. "It's not cold and it's not raining." He looked over his shoulder at the small white bungalow, then turned back to me. "There are worse places to be." His gaze slid past me. "Sarah, Nick's here," he said quietly.

Out on the street a black SUV had pulled over to the curb at the end of the line of police vehicles. Nick Elliot got out, carrying a boxy silver case, which I knew held all the gear he needed to do his job. He'd been working for the medical examiner for months now. He started toward us in his usual uniform of navy windbreaker and black pants.

"I'll be right back," I said to Mac.

I cut across the lawn and met Nick at the curb. "Hi," he said. "What's going on?"

"We found a body in the kitchen."

"Anyone you recognize?"

I shook my head. "No one I know."

Nick made a face. "I know there've been problems with drifters breaking into some of the summer places."

"I don't think this was a drifter," I said.

I looked up at him. He was just over six feet tall with broad shoulders and sandy hair he wore much shorter than when we were young. He was even more handsome and charming and funny than he'd been at fifteen, but sometimes when I looked at him, all I saw was the boy I'd had a crush on when we were teenagers and not the man he was now. And sometimes I caught myself falling into the teasing relationship we'd had back then in which we didn't talk about anything directly.

"What do you mean you don't think this is a drifter?" he asked.

I cleared my throat, wishing I hadn't said anything, but it was a little late now. "You should see for yourself, but the man doesn't look like a drifter. He's wearing what looks to be very expensive shoes and a nice jacket."

Nick had explained to me once that it was his job to figure out what had happened at a potential crime scene; had a crime actually been committed or not? It was up to the police to work out the who, how and why.

"Was the door locked when you got here?"

"The front was," I said. "I don't know about the back."

Nick patted one of his jacket pockets. Checking for gloves? I wondered. Or his phone? "Did you notice if anything was disturbed in the house?"

I rolled my eyes. "You've been inside that house, Nick. You can't exactly tell if a box is out of place."

He nodded and grimaced. "Yeah, good point." Then he looked over at the house. "Is Michelle inside?"

I nodded.

"I take it she asked you to wait."

"She did," I said, suddenly feeling more than a little uncomfortable. This was the third time I'd found myself connected to a case Nick and Michelle were investigating.

"Okay, so you and Mac found the body," Nick said.

"Strictly speaking, Elvis found the body."

He raised an eyebrow and didn't completely manage to keep a smile back. "I'm going to need to ask him some questions."

"I'll tell him not to leave town."

Nick did smile then. "I should get to work," he said.

"I'll need to talk to both you and Mac later, though. You'll both be at the shop?"

I nodded, shifting my weight from one foot to the other. "We can't do anything here. As soon as Michelle says we can leave, we'll head back. I'm going to have to call Stella at some point. This is going to move our timeline back."

Nick looked over his shoulder at the house again. "I'm guessing she and Ethan want to get the house on the market as soon as they can."

I knew that Nick and Ethan Hall—Edison Hall's son—had played hockey together in high school. I wasn't sure whether they'd reconnected when Nick moved back to North Harbor.

"I think it's been a bit overwhelming for Ethan," I said.

"The old man was never one to throw anything away," Nick said. "I was in the garage a few times back when Ethan and I were in school. You couldn't fit a car in it—that's for sure." He gave his head a slight shake at whatever memory had just slipped into his mind. "Anyway, I'll talk to you later." He started for the front door, raising a hand in hello to Mac as he cut across the lawn.

I walked up the driveway to rejoin Mac. He was standing by the front fender of the SUV. "Nick will have some questions later," I said.

"I thought he would," Mac said. He inclined his head in the direction of the car and lowered his voice. "You know Rose is going to see this as a case they can investigate."

I sighed. "I know."

They included Rose, Alfred Peterson, Charlotte and Liz French, another of my grandmother's closest friends. They called themselves Charlotte's Angels, a play on the movie and the television show *Charlie's Angels*. Since Rose, at least, saw them as the three detectives—she'd dubbed herself Farrah Fawcett because she had the best hair—that meant Alfred was Bosley. And since they'd set up their detective office in my sunporch, where they used my Wi-Fi and drank my tea, by default I was Charlie. When I pointed out to Rose that, since they were Charlotte's Angels, Charlotte should be Charlie, Rose had just smiled sweetly at me and said, "She's Kate Jackson, dear. She can't be Charlie, and you own the building."

I didn't even try to argue with her logic.

The Angels had been involved in two of Nick's cases since he'd taken the medical examiner's job. He'd explained how dangerous it could be for them to be mixed up in a criminal investigation. He'd pointed out that they weren't detectives, that they had no training in law enforcement. He'd even threatened to have Michelle arrest them all. They'd pretty much ignored him.

"You didn't tell Nick that Rose is here," Mac said, narrowing his dark eyes as he studied my face. The corners of his mouth twitched.

"He didn't ask," I said. "And do you want the two of them to get into it yet again over the Angels getting involved in this case?"

Mac gave up trying to stifle the smile. "So, who were you trying to protect? Him or her?"

I leaned sideways and gave him a long, appraising look. "Isn't it obvious?" I said. "Nick's built like a hockey enforcer. He works in law enforcement. She's barely five feet high in her sensible walking shoes and she's blind as a bat without her bifocals."

Mac looked at me, unblinkingly, the way Elvis did sometimes. "Her, then," he said.

"Obviously." I rubbed my left shoulder with my other hand, trying to work out a knot that had settled in when Mac reminded me that Rose was going to look at this dead body as an invitation for the Angels to investigate. "I should talk to her before she gets any ideas."

Something caught Mac's eye and he looked past me. "Sarah," he said, a note of caution suddenly in his voice.

I turned to see what he was looking at.

A small silver car had just parked at the curb. I could see Ethan Hall behind the wheel. "What's he doing here?" I said.

Mac touched my arm. "I'll go."

I shook my head. "It's okay. I'll do it."

He inclined his head in the direction of the SUV. "Talk to Rose," he said. "I've got this." He started for the street before I could argue the point anymore.

I walked around the side of the SUV, opened the driver's door and slid behind the wheel, turning to face Rose and Elvis. The cat straightened up and licked his whiskers. I knew it was pointless to ask Rose what she'd been feeding him.

"Can we leave now?" she asked.

"Not yet," I said. "Michelle and Nick are taking a look around inside. But it shouldn't be much longer."

She leaned sideways to look past me. "Is that Ethan Mac's talking to?"

"Uh-huh." I turned back around and flipped down the sun visor.

The cat craned his neck as though he were trying to see what Rose was looking at. She patted her lap and her climbed up on her knee. "What's he doing here? Did you call him?"

"He probably came to see if he could get a better idea of how long it's going to take us to clear everything out." I pulled the elastic out of my ponytail and raked my fingers through my hair. Then I looked at her in the mirror. "This is not a case, Rose," I said.

She reached forward and patted my arm. "Has Nicolas gotten his knickers in a knot, dear?" she asked.

"No. I didn't tell him you were here." I didn't add that I didn't see the point in the two of them having the same argument they'd already had at least half a dozen times. Nick was dead set against his mother—and Rose and Liz, whom he thought of as family—investigating crimes. Rose was just as fixed in her opinion that it was none of his business.

I understood why Nick worried, but I could also see Rose's point of view—which meant a couple of times they'd been arguing I'd managed to get on the wrong side of both of them.

She smiled. "Thank you, Sarah. That was probably for the best." She smoothed her white curls with the hand that wasn't stroking Elvis's fur. "He's such a worrywart. I'd say he's such an old woman about things, but really, none of us are anywhere near that bad."

Elvis gave a soft murp of agreement.

"I think in this case, what he doesn't know won't hurt him," Rose continued. "Thank you for having our back, sweet girl."

Both she and Elvis were smiling at me and I wasn't

exactly sure how we'd gotten from me warning Rose to stay out of this investigation, to me having her back.

Mac and Ethan Hall had started up the driveway. "I should go talk to Ethan," I said.

"Of course," Rose said. "Elvis and I will stay here."

I saw the cat's green eyes dart over to Rose's bag. I was pretty sure I knew how Elvis, at least, would be passing the time.

I got out of the car and met Mac and Ethan in the middle of the driveway. Ethan Hall was easily six feet tall with deep blue eyes that seemed to lock on to your face when he spoke to you, and blond hair in a modified brush cut. He looked over at the house. "Sarah. Do you know what's going on?" he asked.

"The police are inside," I said. "Detective Andrews should be out in a minute."

His mouth twisted to one side. "How could someone have gotten into the house?"

I didn't think he was looking for an answer. His gaze came back to me again. "You didn't recognize the . . . you don't know who it is, do you?"

"No," I said. But I described the body, including the expensive clothes.

"Wait, was it a dark brown wool jacket?" he said slowly. "Three-quarter length?" He made a chopping motion just below his hip.

"Yes," I said.

"Do you know who that is?" Mac asked, lines tightening around his mouth and eyes.

Ethan swallowed hard and swiped a hand across his chin. "Maybe . . . yes. I'm not sure."

Before I could say anything Michelle came out the

front door. She looked around and started over toward us.

"I'll be right back," I said to Mac. I intercepted Michelle on the worn brick walkway.

"What is it?" she asked. She must have seen something in my expression.

I gestured over my shoulder. "That's Ethan Hall," I said. "I don't know if you know him. This is—was—his father's house." I cleared my throat. "I think he might know who . . . the body is." I made a motion in the general direction of the house behind her.

Her gaze never left my face. "Why do you say that?" she asked.

"He asked about the dead man. When I mentioned the jacket he wanted to know if it was dark brown and hip length."

"Okay," she said. "Thanks." She walked over to Ethan and I followed. "Mr. Hall, I'm Detective Michelle Andrews." She kept both hands in her pockets. "Sarah says you may know who our victim is."

Ethan shrugged. "I'm not certain, but it's possible it's a man named Ronan Quinn."

"Can you describe him to me?" she asked.

"He's, um . . . maybe a couple of inches shorter than me and his hair's dark with some gray in the front." He made a sweeping gesture in the air with one hand. "Like I told Sarah, the last time I saw Ronan he was wearing a dark brown jacket."

Michelle nodded. "And when was that?"

"Here. Yesterday afternoon."

"What kind of business did you have with Mr. Quinn?"

Ethan shifted from one foot to the other. He seemed a little uncomfortable. "He's a wine expert I hired to value my father's collection of wine so it could be sold. There were a couple of bottles he wanted to take another look at. That's why we were here yesterday."

"Would you be willing to come take a look at the body and see if it is Mr. Quinn?" Michelle asked.

Ethan hesitated, closed his eyes for a second and then nodded without speaking.

Michelle looked at Mac and me. "You can come, too."

We followed her back into the house. Nick was in the kitchen taking photographs. I saw a flash of surprise in his eyes when he caught sight of us, but he didn't say anything.

Michelle stuck out her hand, stopping us in the doorway to the kitchen.

Ronan Quinn—if that was who the dead man was—was lying half·on his side, half on his back as though his legs had just collapsed underneath him. I kept my eyes on the bottom half of his body. I'd seen the battered back of his head once, and that was enough.

Ethan swallowed and turned away. "That's him," he said. His face was pale. "That's Ronan."

Nick looked up from his camera. "Wait a minute. The guy you hired to appraise the wine collection?"

Ethan nodded. "From Boston, yes."

"Did Mr. Quinn stay behind yesterday?" Michelle asked.

Ethan shook his head. "No. We left together, maybe three thirty, quarter to four. Ronan said he had some calls to make."

"Do you remember if he had a cell phone with him?"

"Yes. An iPhone. And he had a briefcase. The old-fashioned kind with a flap and buckles." He looked around. "I don't see it."

"We'll look for it," Michelle said. "Thank you."

Mac and Ethan were already on their way back outside. Michelle and I followed them. Ethan stood at the bottom of the steps. He had one arm crossed over his midsection and he was running the edge of his thumb repeatedly over the ends of his fingers.

"This is my fault," he said. "It's my fault Quinn is dead."

"What do you mean?" Michelle asked.

"I told you my father had a wine collection." He pressed his lips together for a moment before he continued. "He had a lot of collections. You've seen the house. But he told me the wine was worth a lot of money. He spent a lot of money on it—more than I realized. It turns out the whole collection is fake—cheap wine in bottles with fake labels and fake provenance."

"You think these fakes had something to do with Mr. Quinn's death?" Michelle asked.

Ethan nodded. "I . . . I pushed him to find as much evidence as he could about the phony bottles so we could go after the people who conned my father. When Quinn asked me to meet him here yesterday, he said he was onto something, but he wouldn't say what." He let out a breath. "I should have let it go."

Nick had come out onto the front steps. "This isn't your fault," he said.

Ethan looked up at him. "I set it in motion, Nick," he said. "I was so damn mad when I found out the whole thing—those bottles of wine—was a con job. You know the old man was no wine connoisseur. He was a couple-of-beers-on-a-Saturday-night type of guy. Quinn said he'd seen this kind of thing before. He'd been involved in several other cases just in the past year and a half. He told me that we might be able to sue in civil court if we could find who sold all the fakes to my father. He said even if the law can't get them, then at least we can hit them in their wallets."

He smoothed one hand down over the back of his head. "The worst part is the whole wine collection thing? It was for me and Ellie and the kids. He wanted to leave something to us. How many times did I tell him it didn't matter? You know what he was like. When he got his mind set on something, there was no point talking to him."

Nick nodded. "I know. And if you had screwed up, he would have been the first person to tell you to man up and take responsibility, but this isn't your fault."

Ethan just shook his head.

"How did you come to hire Mr. Quinn?" Michelle asked.

Ethan laughed, but there was no humor in the sound. "There was an article in the *Boston Globe* about the trend in buying wine as an investment—and, ironically, about the dangers of getting scammed. Ronan Quinn was quoted as an expert. I got in touch with him. He's . . ." He paused for a moment. "He *was* one of just three people in New England qualified to properly appraise a collection."

"How did he know the bottles were fake?" Nick asked.

"Inconsistencies in the documentation, problems

with the labels. In the case of one of the bottles that was opened, the quality of the wine made it pretty clear." He shook his head again. "I can't believe this is happening to me."

"Mr. Hall, could you come down to the station?" Michelle pulled her cell phone out of her pocket, glanced at it and then looked at Ethan. "Anything you can tell us about Mr. Quinn could help."

"I want to help," Ethan said, "but could it wait? My wife is having a very small procedure at the hospital. I've been there since"—he glanced at his watch—"quarter to six. I just came over for a moment because I forgot to give Sarah the key for the garage." He slid a hand back over his hair. "I really need to get back. I've been gone for way too long already."

"All right," Michelle said. "Go back to your wife." She handed him her card. "Once you get home, please call me."

"Thank you," Ethan said. "I will." He turned to me. "I'm sorry, Sarah. I should have done a better job of keeping you in the loop as far as the wine and everything was concerned." He made a helpless gesture with one hand.

"We'll talk in a couple of days," I said. "Don't worry about this." I indicated the house behind us. Stella was our client and in the end, what happened next would be up to her.

Mac walked Ethan to his car. They shook hands and Ethan left. Michelle looked at Nick. "Keep an eye out for the victim's cell and his briefcase."

"I will," he said. He glanced at me, almost smiled and then went back inside the house.

"You can go now, Sarah," Michelle said. "But I'll need

to talk to both you and Mac"—she glanced over at the SUV—"and Rose."

"We'll be at the shop for the rest of the day," I said. The crime scene van pulled in at the curb then.

"I'll talk to you later, then." She touched my shoulder and then headed across the lawn toward the van.

I joined Mac. "We can leave," I said. I pulled the car keys out of my pocket. "When Stella asked us to clear out this place, this wasn't what I was expecting."

"It'll work out," Mac said, one hand on the passenger door of the SUV. "The guy is a stranger. They won't have a client. They're not going to get involved this time."

In the backseat Rose was writing furiously in a small notebook while Elvis craned his neck, seemingly trying to read what she was writing.

I looked at Mac. "I think there's half a jar of Charlotte's cucumber relish in the refrigerator at the shop," I said.

He frowned. "And why would I want Charlotte's cucumber relish?"

I gave him a tight smile as I reached for the driver's door handle. "Because I'm pretty certain you're going to have to eat your words."

Chapter 3

I was coming down the stairs carrying a stack of three cardboard boxes—the top one wobbling precariously—when Stella Hall walked into Second Chance, stopping to wipe her feet on the rubber welcome mat by the front door. It had been more than a week since I found Ronan Quinn's body. The police and the medical examiner's office were still investigating, so the house was still off-limits. Both Michelle and Nick were staying tight-lipped.

Stella was a tiny dumpling of a woman, short and solid in a blue slicker and green rubber boots. "Hello, Sarah," she said.

"Hi, Stella," I replied, waggling an elbow at her before I stopped, midstep, to lean a shoulder against the teetering boxes trying to steady them. "How are you?"

Rose had spotted me coming down the stairs and was on her way over from the cash desk to rescue me.

"Mad as a wet hen," Stella said flatly. "I want to hire you."

"Um . . . you already did that," I said. The side of my face was against one box, and my voice was a little muffled.

"I know that," she said. "I was talking to Rose."

I forgot all about my tipsy load and leaned sideways to look at her.

Rose was at the foot of the stairs. Stella had pushed back the hood of her slicker and her soft white hair was mussed a little. The look on her face was pure determination from the set of her jaw to the gleam in her blue eyes. "I want to hire you, all of you," she said. "I want you to find out who killed that man, Ronan Quinn."

The top box of my stack fell and bounced down the steps to land at Rose's feet, followed by the second one. Luckily they were full of old pairs of jeans and nothing breakable.

I scrambled down the stairs still holding the third box. Rose picked up the one that had landed directly at her feet. The other had come to rest just to the side of the last riser. I set the box I was carrying on top of it and took the one Rose was holding from her.

She smiled at me. "Less haste, more speed, my dear," she said softly.

I put the third box on top of the other two—in a less unsteady pile than I'd been carrying—and turned to face Stella, pasting what I hoped was a warm, non-judgmental expression on my face. "The police are investigating Ronan Quinn's murder," I said.

"And taking too bloody long at it," she retorted. "Pardon my language." She looked from me to Rose. "Ethan said he told you that Edison's so-called wine collection was nothing more than a bunch of swill."

I nodded.

"Ethan hired that man to appraise all those bottles of wine. He was killed in my brother's house. I don't believe it was a coincidence." Stella's voice was edged with anger.

"Neither do I," Rose said.

"I want you to find out who killed Mr. Quinn. I'm sure it's the same people who cheated my brother," Stella said vehemently, two splotches of color appearing on her cheeks. "I want them punished!"

Liz had just come in the front door, stopping to shake her umbrella. She was wearing a trench coat with the collar turned up and a tan fedora.

"Why?" she asked, walking over to join us.

"Hello, Liz," Stella said. "What do you mean, why?"

"I mean why do you care?" Liz said. "You don't even know that so-called expert your nephew hired and no offense, but you and Edison weren't exactly close when he was alive." She took off her hat and smoothed her blond hair into place. As usual her nails were perfectly manicured, today in a soft shade of coral that matched the coral-and-turquoise scarf at her throat.

Rose's eyes widened. "Liz!" she hissed.

Stella waved one hand in the air. "It's okay. It's a valid question." She focused her attention on Liz. "You're right. Edison and I always had a prickly relationship—right back to when we were kids. But he was my blood and no one had the right to take the money he earned with his own two hands."

"Fair enough," Liz said.

"Do you want to hear the rest?" Stella asked.

One perfectly groomed eyebrow rose slightly. "If you want to tell us."

"You may as well know the whole story before you say yes or no," Stella said. She stood, feet apart, hands shoved in her pockets. "I'm hoping there's some way to recover at least some of the money my dang fool brother spent on all those worthless bottles for Ethan and Ellie."

Ellie was Ethan's wife, a kindergarten teacher and mother to their four small children.

"This stays between us," Stella continued, her expression grave. "But Ellie needs an operation on her back."

"What's wrong?" Rose asked immediately.

Stella gave her head a shake. "I don't understand all the medical mumbo jumbo, but I can tell you that it's getting harder for her to walk without falling and if she doesn't have the surgery, eventually she'll be in a wheelchair."

"Don't they have health insurance?" Liz asked.

Ethan was an associate professor of political science at Camber College.

Stella made a face. "They won't pay because the surgeon wants to use some new technique—he says it'll give Ellie the best outcome—and the insurance company calls it experimental."

"I'm so sorry," Liz said softly.

"Ellie was good to Edison and Lord knows he could be a cantankerous old coot sometimes. But he would have wanted to help her." She sighed. "I was hoping there'd be some money from his estate, but it turns out he'd borrowed against the house. I don't know what he was thinking."

Out of Stella's line of sight, Liz rolled her eyes. When I'd agreed to take on the job of clearing out Edison's house, Charlotte commented that we never would have gotten in the door when the old man was alive. He'd gotten even more prickly and suspicious in the last couple of years.

Liz had countered that she'd seen Edison at the bank, arguing loudly with the manager. "I'd thought about giving him a nudge out the door with the toe of my best red pumps," she'd said.

The shoes she'd been talking about had a sharply pointed toe that looked as lethal as an ice pick. I'd tried not to grin at her comment while Charlotte shook her head and frowned at Liz over her glasses.

"I said I thought about it," Liz had said, not the slightest bit contrite. "I didn't say I did it."

Stella looked from Rose to Liz now and I could see the determination in the set of her jaw and her squared shoulders. I could also see worry for Ellie etched in the lines on her face. "Ethan and Ellie made a lot of sacrifices the last few years because of Edison. If there is any money to be gotten, they deserve to have it."

"Of course we'll help you," Rose said. She put her arm around Stella's shoulders. "Come back to the office. I have a little paperwork for you." She glanced over her shoulder at me. "You don't mind if I take my break now, do you, Sarah?"

"Um, no," I said, because what else was I going to say? I gave her what I hoped was a supportive or at least positive smile and they started for the sunporch.

Liz took a couple of steps closer to me, leaned in and kissed my cheek. "Thanks, toots," she said. Then she followed Rose and Stella.

Mac had come from somewhere, probably the garage, based on the bits of dirt and dried leaves on one leg of his jeans. He'd made himself busy by the cash desk, but I knew he'd heard most, if not all, of the conversation. He smiled at me as he crossed the floor of the store. I waited for him to say something, but all he did was pick up two of the three boxes I'd stacked at the bottom of the stairs.

I tipped my head back and stared at the ceiling. There were no answers up there. I looked at Mac, rubbing one temple because it suddenly felt as if the Seven Dwarfs had started mining the left side of my head. "You said this would all work out," I said to Mac, glaring at him because he had told me that, and because there was no one else to make a cranky face at. "You said they wouldn't have a client."

"I'm sorry," he said. "But I thought you said you were going to stay out of the Angels' business, anyway."

I pushed a stray piece of hair off my face. "I was . . . I mean I am." I sighed. "It's pretty hard to stay out of what they're doing when their office is in my sunporch and when I end up driving them everywhere because the state of Maine—very wisely—no longer allows Rose to drive."

"Maybe it's not such a bad idea," Mac said. He raised a finger before I could ask him what color the sky was in his world. "Between the three of them—Rose, Liz and Charlotte—they know pretty much everyone in town, and more important, they know everyone over the age of sixty-five. Who do you think those people are more likely to talk to? The Dynamic Trio or the police?"

He was right, but I wasn't quite ready to concede the point. "You're forgetting that all those little old ladies would just love talking to Nick. He does that boy-next-door thing that they all like."

Mac laughed. "All they're going to do is feed him cookies and try to set him up with their granddaughters."

"Feed who cookies?" a voice said behind us. Nick was standing just inside the front door.

"Horse pucks," I muttered under my breath. Why did he have to show up now? It seemed as though the confrontation I'd been trying to circumvent between Nick and Rose was going to happen no matter what I did. "What are you doing here?" I asked.

"My mother sent you a meat loaf," he said. "I'm not exactly sure why. She just asked me to drop it by." For the first time I noticed the vintage harvest gold casserole dish he was holding.

"It's a long story," I said.

He raised an eyebrow.

"Let's just say my last cooking lesson didn't go so well and leave it at that."

"Got it," he said, handing me the Pyrex dish. "So, who are you feeding cookies to?"

Mac put down the boxes he was holding. "He knows, Sarah," he said.

"I know what?" Nick asked.

He did a pretty good poker face, but as I studied

him I realized Mac was right: Nick did know that the Angels had a case.

I sighed. "Seriously, Nick?" I said. "You really think you're going to come over here and convince Rose and Liz to stay out of your investigation?" I knew that he cared about all of them, not just his mother, but going caveman wasn't going to get them to go back to having bake sales to buy books for the library.

"They have no business getting involved."

I glanced at Mac, whose expression gave away nothing about what he was thinking.

"They don't think so," I said, struggling to keep the frustration that was tightening in my chest out of my voice. "How many times now have you had this conversation with them? Give it up." I was aware of the irony of me defending the Angels taking on a new case when it was actually the last thing I wanted them to do.

"This is the last time," Nick said, holding up both hands in a gesture of surrender.

I looked at Mac again and held out the dish of meat loaf. "Would you put this in the fridge for me?"

He set the boxes down again and took the container from me. "Sure," he said. He looked from me to Nick. "Yell if you need reinforcements." Then he turned and headed up the steps.

"Let's go," I said to Nick. "Rose and Liz are in their office. If Stella is still with them, can you at least wait until she's gone before you pounce?"

"I'm not going to pounce," he said, with just a touch of indignation in his voice.

"You're not going to win, either," I retorted as we got to the workroom door. "I don't want them involved in anything dangerous any more than you do, but they're adults, and as they like to point out, they changed both our diapers."

Avery was just coming in the back door of the building. "Is it lunchtime already?" I asked.

The teenager shook her head and the dangling earrings she was wearing made a tinkling sound. "Nah, it's only eleven o'clock."

"So what are you doing here so early?"

"Water pipe burst," she said. "There's about a foot of water in the gym and the halls." She grinned. "We got evacuated. I figured I might as well come and work." The grin disappeared. "That was okay, right?"

I nodded. "Right now you can watch the cash for me. After that I have a project for you."

The smile came back, a bit more tentative than before. "I kinda have a project I'd like to ask you about, too."

I held up one hand. "I'll be about five minutes."

"No problem," she said, moving past us.

Rose and Liz were in the sunporch, which was the Angels' base of operations at least during the warmer months of the year. During the winter they had moved into a corner of the workroom. Stella Hall had left, but Alfred Peterson was at his computer sitting in the office chair that Rose had trash-picked and Mac had repaired.

"Hello, Nicolas," Rose said. There was just an edge of challenge in her voice. She clearly knew why Nick was at the shop. On the other hand, she hadn't come out swinging the way she had in the past.

Something was up and as usual I was the last one to know.

"Hi," Nick said, with a nod that took in Liz and Mr. P.

"What can we do for you?" Rose asked.

"Stella Hall is hiring you to look into Mr. Quinn's death." He said the words as a statement of fact, not as a question.

"Yes, she is," Rose said. She wasn't so much smiling as looking smug, rather like Elvis after he'd just eaten a particularly tasty bite of chicken. As I had the thought I noticed the cat was sitting on a chair next to Mr. P., seemingly settled in to watch whatever was going to happen, almost as if he, too, knew what was coming.

"Then what I'd like you to do is tell her you can't investigate," Nick said.

"Why on earth would we do that?" Liz asked. She and Rose exchanged a look and as Rose turned back to Nick, I saw a quick smile pass between her and Mr. P. It really did seem that everyone knew what was up except me.

"I'm sorry," Nick said. "Your agency is out of business."

"No, it isn't," Rose replied. "We just got new business cards." She took a couple of steps over to the table they were using as a desk, picked up a small cardboard rectangle and handed it to him.

"I'm sorry," he repeated, "but you're not a licensed private investigator. The state has rules."

For a moment I didn't know what to do with my hands because I was pretty sure I couldn't follow my first impulse for what to do with them, which was to slug him in the arm.

Rose moved closer to Nick and I took a step closer to both of them in case *she* decided to slug him, but all she did was pat his arm and give him a smile of pure condescension. "I know that, dear," she said. "But I don't own the agency. Neither does your mother. Alfred does. And he *is* a licensed private investigator."

Rose turned to Mr. P. and beamed and he beamed right back at her.

Nick's mouth gaped like a goldfish that had jumped too high and had suddenly found itself outside the fishbowl.

Liz caught my eye over the top of Rose's head and winked at me.

"I'm over twenty-one and I'm an American citizen," Mr. P. said, squaring his shoulders with just a bit of pride. "I have no criminal record and I passed the exam with flying colors."

"Alfred has an excellent memory," Rose added.

Nick pulled a hand across his mouth. "It's not possible," he said. "You don't have any experience in law enforcement."

"Chapter eighty-nine of the Maine Revised Statutes, section 8105, 7-A, experience, paragraph D," Mr. P. recited. "A person is qualified to be a licensed private investigator who possesses a minimum of six years of preparation consisting of a combination of: work experience, including at least two years in a non-clerical occupation related to law or the criminal justice system; and educational experience, including at least: an associate degree acquired at an accredited junior college, college, university or technical college in police administration, security management, investigation, law, criminal justice or computer forensics or other similar course of study."

"I told you he has an excellent memory," Rose said.

I wondered how long it had taken Mr. P. to commit that legalese to memory.

A flush was creeping up Nick's face from his neck. I'd been annoyed that he'd shown up planning to ambush Rose, but now I felt bad that he'd been the one ambushed instead. On the other hand, it wouldn't have been happening if Nick would just stop trying to make Rose and the others do what he wanted.

"I have a four-year bachelor's degree in computer science with a specialty in computer forensics," Mr. P. continued. He gave a sly smile. "I'm not just a pretty face."

I could see Liz smirking at me out of the corner of my eye, but I refused to look in her direction because I knew if I did I was toast.

"And I've been working with the Legal Aid free clinic for the last three years, doing research and computer work," he finished.

Nick's mouth worked, but no sound came out.

"And I'm Alfred's investigative assistant," Rose said. "In another sixteen weeks I'll have all my training hours completed." Her gray eyes met Nick's and there was a clear challenge in them.

Behind her Liz waved a hand. "I'm their executive assistant. Think of me as Della Street."

I figured it wasn't a good time to point out that Della Street had been secretary to Perry Mason, a lawyer, not a private investigator.

"So it's lovely of you to be concerned about us," Rose said. "But we're just fine."

Her hand had been on Nick's arm the entire time. Now she gave it a squeeze and let go. "Is there anything else you need, dear?" she asked.

"No. There isn't," he said, his words as tight as the muscles in his jaw.

Rose leaned around him and looked at me. "I'll be right out, Sarah."

"Take your time," I said. "Avery's here. There was some kind of water main break and the school flooded. They sent them home early."

"Please tell me that my granddaughter had nothing to do with that water main break," Liz said dryly.

"She didn't." I was pretty sure she hadn't.

I caught the back of Nick's jacket and gave it a tug. He turned and shot me a dark look.

"Rose, would you start on those parcels when you're ready?" I asked.

"Absolutely, dear," she said. She was being very gracious in her victory.

Nick followed me out. He didn't say a word as we walked through the workroom. It was as if there were a black storm cloud over his head. As we stepped into the shop, I bumped him with my hip. "As Jess would say, pony up, little buckaroo."

He glared at me. "Did you know?"

I shook my head. "No."

"Alfred Peterson is a licensed investigator. How the hell did that happen? You know he's worse than some teenage hacker."

"No, he's not," I said. "Mr. P.'s not stealing people's

identities or unleashing a virus that shuts down everyone's computers."

He made a face at me.

And I laughed. I couldn't help it. "They beat you," I said. "Liz, Rose and Alfred. And your mother. Three old ladies and a little old man who wears his pants up under his armpits beat you fair and square."

"Crap!" he muttered.

I gave him a push. "Go to work. Go to Sam's and have lunch."

"This is going to complicate your life just as much as it does mine," he warned, fishing his keys out of his jacket. The hint of a smile pulled at the corners of his mouth.

"Thank you for your concern," I said. "Go."

He went.

Mac had been on the phone. He hung up and walked over to me. "I'm guessing Rose looks better than Nick does," he said.

"She set him up," I said. "Short version?"

"Please."

"Nick tried to shut them down because they're not licensed by the state. However, it turns out Mr. P. has in fact become a licensed private investigator and is acting as Rose's supervisor, so everything is legal and aboveboard."

Mac grinned. "They planned this, didn't they?"

"For months, probably. Mr. P. even had the relevant section of the law memorized and he quoted it to Nick." I couldn't help it. I started to laugh, remembering the look on Nick's face as the older man had rattled off sections and paragraphs.

A customer checking out a sideboard along one end wall of the shop looked around for assistance.

Mac caught the woman's eye and nodded. Then he leaned in toward me. "Keep that positive attitude, Sarah," he said. "Because we're now sharing space with an honest-to-goodness detective agency."

Chapter 4

Mr. P. drove home with Rose and me at the end of the day. They were planning on working on the case for a while after supper.

"Did you make Alfred a cake?" I asked as I fastened my seat belt in the parking lot.

Beside me Rose looked a little confused. "No," she said. "But I have some oatmeal raisin cookies."

"They're my favorite," Mr. P. chimed in from the backseat. Elvis meowed his agreement.

"I meant, did you make a cake to celebrate him getting his investigator's license?"

Rose had the good grace to blush. "I'm sorry I didn't tell you."

I glanced over at her and then put the SUV in gear and started across the lot.

"That was my suggestion, Sarah," Mr. P. said from the backseat. "It's been a while since I was a student. If I hadn't passed the certification exam and we'd had to work under the radar, I wanted you to have plausible deniability."

"I appreciate that," I said. "Thank you." This wasn't the first time I'd hoped I'd have plausible deniability when it came to something the Angels were up to.

I looked both ways for traffic and then pulled out onto the street. When I stopped at the corner I held up my right hand, palm facing Rose. It only took a moment for her to get the significance. She high-fived me. I turned my arm and got a high five from Mr. P. as well.

"It's not that I don't love Nicolas," Rose said, hands folded primly in her lap again. "It's just that he seems to think because we're old we've taken leave of our senses. I suppose it was wrong of me to spring the whole license thing on him."

I shot her a quick glance. "Maybe just a little." I took my hand off the steering wheel long enough to hold up my thumb and forefinger about half an inch apart. "He loves you, too," I said. "That being said, I know that he can sometimes be a gigantic pain in the—"

Behind me Mr. P. cleared his throat.

"Neck," I finished. I glanced in the rearview mirror and Mr. P. smiled approvingly at me.

"Would you like to join us for dinner, dear?" Rose asked.

A loud meow came from the backseat. The meat loaf from Charlotte was in a canvas bag on the seat next to Elvis.

"Thank you," I said. "But as Elvis just pointed out, we have Charlotte's meat loaf."

"What are you having with it?" Rose asked.

"Ummm . . . ketchup probably." I did a mental run-through of the contents of my refrigerator. "Or mustard."

I was pretty sure there was a half-empty bottle in the door.

Rose sighed softly. That was the wrong answer.

"And salad," I added. There was at least one limp carrot and a couple of wrinkled grape tomatoes in the fridge, too. The two of them could be salad if I sprinkled a little of the fancy balsamic vinegar Liz had bought for me on top.

I pulled in to the driveway at home and Mr. P. climbed out and handed me the bag with Charlotte's casserole dish of meat loaf. Elvis jumped out, his green eyes never leaving the bag. I unlocked the front door and gestured for Rose and Mr. P. to go ahead of me into the hall, but Alfred moved behind me and put a hand on the painted wood.

"Go ahead, my dear," he said.

I smiled. "Thank you." Mr. P. was what most people would consider an old-fashioned gentleman, and while I was perfectly capable of opening my own doors, jars and shrink-wrapped packages, I was charmed by his thoughtfulness.

I set the tote bag and my briefcase by my front door. "Have a good night, you two," I said.

Rose reached up and patted my cheek. "You, too, dear."

They headed down the short hallway to Rose's apartment and I let myself and Elvis into my—our—place.

I'd owned the house for several years now. It was an eighteen sixties Victorian that had been divided into three apartments by a previous owner. The house had been an incredibly good deal, run-down but structurally sound and an easy walk to the harbor front. I'd been able to buy it before it went on the market, because the owner was interested in the tiny one-room cabin that I'd owned and that Jess and I had lived in and fixed up during our last year of college.

At first I'd told myself and everyone else that I'd bought the house as an investment. But the truth was, even though I hadn't grown up here, North Harbor felt like home to me and deep down inside I guessed I'd always known it was where I'd end up.

My dad and my brother, Liam, had done almost all the work on my apartment and the one on the second floor where my grandmother had lived until she remarried and went off on an extended honeymoon cum road trip around the country. Mom, Jess and I had foraged through every thrift store and flea market within about sixty miles of North Harbor to furnish and decorate the place.

I'd been working slowly on the third small apartment at the back of the house for close to a year. It had been livable—it was where my parents or Liam stayed when they came to visit. When Rose had been asked to leave her apartment at Legacy Place, the seniors' residence in the refurbished Gardener Chocolate Factory, I'd offered the little apartment to her and Mac had helped me get it ready.

I liked having Rose around. Once the snow had cleared, she and Alfred started working in the backyard. Mac had built a couple of planter boxes for them and I was looking forward to tomatoes and zucchini in late summer. I hadn't realized just how much I missed my grandmother until Rose moved in. I liked knowing there was someone else in the big house, other than Elvis, who at the moment was at my feet looking impatiently up at me.

I set the bag with the meat loaf on the counter and held up one hand. "Five minutes," I said to the cat. "And then we'll eat."

Elvis jumped up onto one of the stools, made a sound a lot like a sigh and sat, staring at the bag. I reached over and scratched the top of his head. "You'll live," I said.

I changed into leggings and a T-shirt and was retrieving the two tomatoes and the sad carrot from my fridge under the watchful gaze of the cat when there was a knock on the door. He looked at me and lifted one paw.

"No, no, you're all comfortable. Let me get it," I said.

He tipped his furry head to one side and almost seemed to smile at me. Sometimes I had the feeling that he did get sarcasm.

It was Mr. P. at the door holding a small bowl. "Rosie sent this," he said. The dish was full of steaming rice with onions, mushrooms and some kind of leafy green.

"Let me guess," I said, smiling at him. "She made too much food."

"That is her story," he said.

I took the bowl from him. "Tell her thank you and give her a kiss from me," I said.

He smiled at me. "It would be my pleasure." He headed back to Rose's apartment and I realized that he was wearing her fuzzy slippers.

I warmed up a couple of slices of the meat loaf in the microwave and settled at the counter with my plate and the bowl of rice. Elvis hopped back up on the other stool and I fed him a couple of bites of the meat.

"So, did you know that Mr. P. was getting his investigator's license?" I asked.

The cat stared at me for a moment and then licked his whiskers. I decided that could be a yes. Or a no. Or "more meat loaf." I gave him another bite just in case it was the latter.

The Angels spent the next day doing what Rose called "background work." That seemed to involve Mr. P. spending a lot of time on his computer using my Wi-Fi. I fervently hoped everything he was doing was legal.

"Would you like a ride home?" I asked Rose at the end of the day.

"Alfred and I were thinking about walking," she said.

I leaned over and kissed her cheek. "Think about driving. It's going to rain later. The walk might be a bit much for Mr. P.'s knees." I'd noticed Rose rubbing her left hip earlier in the afternoon when she thought no one was looking. She'd never admit the damp weather was probably making it ache, but I knew she'd agree to driving with me if I couched it in terms of being good for Alfred.

"You're right, dear," she said with a smile. "His knees have been sounding a lot like someone deboning a turkey lately."

Elvis sat in the back with Mr. P. and I could hear them having a murmured conversation all the way home. The cat didn't have a lot to say, but he made a few agreeable murps from time to time.

Elvis jumped down from the backseat of the SUV as soon as Mr. P. opened the car door. He followed me inside, but instead of stopping at our apartment door he headed down the hall behind Rose and Alfred.

"Where are you going?" I said.

Mr. P. stopped and looked back at me. "I'm going to Rosie's apartment," he said. "Is that a problem?"

I shook my head. "I'm sorry. I was talking to Elvis, not you."

At the sound of his name the black cat looked toward the door to Rose's small apartment, then turned to look back at me—almost as though he was saying that *he* was going to Rose's apartment as well.

Rose was already at her door, fishing for her keys in her voluminous tote bag. "Elvis is having dinner with us," she said. "I invited him."

"You invited my cat to dinner?"

"Yes," she said. "It's Thursday," as though that explained everything, which it didn't.

"Is Thursday Invite a Cat to Dinner Day?" I asked.

Rose crinkled her nose at me. "Don't get saucy with me, young lady. Aren't you going to Sam's for Thursday Night Jam?"

By Sam's she meant The Black Bear Pub owned by Sam Newman. Sam was like a second father to me. On Thursday nights his band, The Hairy Bananas, played, and anyone and everyone was welcome to sit in. Most Thursdays Jess and I were in the audience.

"Yes," I said.

"Well, Elvis was going to be all by himself." Rose looked at me as though the rest was self-explanatory.

I could have pointed out that we were talking about

a cat, but half the time the cat in question seemed to think he was a person anyway, and I knew if I tried to argue the point with Rose I'd be late meeting Jess.

"Okay," I said.

"I'll just let him in to your apartment when he's ready to come home, if that's all right," she said.

I nodded. "That's fine."

Liz had told me that I was out of my mind for giving Rose a spare key to my apartment, but Rose hadn't abused the privilege so far. Then again, I had her key and I was careful not to abuse that privilege, either. Seeing Mr. P. in her fuzzy slippers was all the information that I needed to have about Rose's private life.

Jess was at a table to the left of the stage when I got to the pub. She was wearing jeans and a plaid shirt with her long hair loose on her shoulders. Instead of bringing our usual basket of nachos, a waiter slid a bowl of Sam's chili in front of me as soon as I sat down. Jess was working on a plate of fries and an egg over easy.

"How did you know I didn't have supper?" I asked, snagging a french fry and dipping it in my chili before eating it.

Jess pressed two fingers to her right temple and squinted at me. "I'm getting an image of a dark, empty place. It's very cold . . . it looks like . . . the inside of your refrigerator!" She grinned at me, blue eyes sparkling.

I made a face at her. "What do I owe you?"

"You can get us some nachos at intermission." She looked around. "Is Nick coming?"

My mouth was full, so I shook my head.

"Still got his knickers in a knot over being bested by Rose and her crew of supersleuths?"

"It wasn't like that."

Jess raised an eyebrow.

I set my spoon down and gave her my full attention. "C'mon, Jess. Charlotte's his mother and Rose and Liz are like family. He doesn't want anything to happen to them, so no, he doesn't like the idea of them playing detective."

"From what I've seen they're not playing detective. They're actually pretty good at it." She speared a forkful of egg and two french fries and dipped the whole thing in ketchup. "So are you, for that matter."

"No, no, no," I said, shaking my head. "I am not getting involved in another one of their cases. Not going to happen."

"Famous last words," Jess said, blue eyes sparkling.

"Not-going-to-be-changing last words," I said firmly.

She laughed and we ate in silence for a couple of minutes. "He seemed like a nice man, you know," she said as I reached over to swipe another french fry from her plate before they were all gone.

I gave her a blank look. "Who seemed like a nice man?"

"Ronan Quinn."

"Wait a minute. You knew him?" I said. Out of the corner of my eye, I could see that there were almost no empty chairs now in the pub.

"I didn't know him, but I did talk to him. I was buying a bottle of wine for Josh. He helped me get that problem with the streetlight outside the shop fixed."

Josh was Josh Evans, a lawyer I'd known since we were kids. He'd helped the Angels more than once.

"And?" I prompted.

Jess shrugged. "And I know nothing about wine. I was standing there holding a bottle wondering how to tell if it was any good. Quinn was behind me. He said, 'Don't buy that.' I asked him why. He said wine was his area of expertise. It didn't seem as though he was trying to hit on me, so I got the bottle he suggested."

"When was this?"

"Last Monday afternoon, sometime just after four o'clock." Before I could say anything she held up a finger. "Yes, I know that's the day before he was killed and yes, when I saw his photo in the *Globe* this morning I called Michelle and told her."

"She's probably trying to put a timeline together," I said. Jess talking to Ronan Quinn confirmed what Ethan had said, that he and Quinn had left the house together the day before the murder.

Jess picked up her cell phone, which had been sitting on the table next to her now-empty plate. "I have a voice mail from Rose. She asked me to call her."

I couldn't help laughing. "How does she do that?" I said. Actually I was pretty sure that Rose had gotten her information via a certain geriatric computer whiz.

"You think Rose knows I saw Mr. Quinn just before he died."

"I can promise you she does." I took a deep breath and let it out slowly. "And it doesn't matter because I'm staying out of it."

The crowd began to clap and cheer as Sam and the rest of the band came from the back of the pub and made their way to the same stage. Jess smirked and said something that got lost in the noise. I was pretty sure she'd said "famous last words" again.

Elvis and I left the house early the next morning. I'd found him asleep at the top of his cat tower when I got home. Rose wasn't due in until lunchtime. I had no idea what time Mr. P. had left or if he even had. It was none of my business and since they were consenting adults and then some, I didn't want to know.

Elvis sat on the passenger seat watching the road. The cat was a backseat driver no matter where he was sitting, turning to look over his shoulder when I backed up and intently watching the lights when we were stopped. He'd even protested loudly when I ran a yellow light, much to the amusement of Jess, who'd been in the passenger seat that day.

We stopped at McNamara's Sandwich Shop to pick up the rolls for the elementary school's hot lunch program. Glenn McNamara was in the kitchen stirring a huge pot of soup. "Banana muffins just came out of the oven," he said, dipping his head in the direction of two wire racks on the long stainless steel counter. "Try one and tell me what you think."

I picked up a muffin, broke off a bite and popped it in my mouth. "Oh, that's good," I said after a moment. "Do I taste walnuts? And nutmeg, maybe?" As part of my cooking lessons, Rose was teaching me about spices and herbs.

Glenn grinned and nodded. "Very good. I was getting tired of the same old thing, so I wanted to change it up just a little."

"I'd buy them," I said, breaking off another piece. "And what do I owe you for this one?"

"Don't worry about it," he said, moving to the large sink to wash his hands. "I needed a taste tester."

"Thanks," I said.

"I heard you found a little more than you bargained for when you went to clear out Edison Hall's house," he said, reaching for a paper towel to dry his hands. "He was a nice guy, Quinn, I mean."

"You met him?"

"He was in here maybe half a dozen times altogether. Twice for lunch and the rest for coffee. He always took a table right in the center of the room and he'd sit there and work on his tablet." He leaned against the counter and crossed his arms over his white apron. "He knew a lot about wine, obviously, but the guy wasn't a snob. He got talking to Carmen about Feast in the Field and he made some suggestions for this year. She said they weren't all that expensive."

Feast in the Field was a festival of fine wine, food and spirits held in the fall, a fund-raiser for charity. We'd had tourists from as far away as Oregon. Hotels and bed-and-breakfasts were booked up months in advance. The festival got its name from the open field where it was staged, a place where local lore held that a farmer and his two sons had held off a British garrison with nothing but pitchforks and an ornery bull.

According to Charlotte, who had taught history among other subjects before she became a principal, the real story was that the farmer had found two British soldiers, no more than fifteen years old, who had somehow gotten separated from their comrades hiding in his barn, hungry and half-frozen from the early winter, one of them with an ugly wound on his leg.

The farmer's wife, mother to two boys close to the

same age, had insisted on feeding the two young men and bandaging the wound before sending them on their way.

"Did you ever see Mr. Quinn with anyone?" I asked Glenn.

He shook his head. "Aside from Ethan Hall, no. He made small talk with a couple of people while he was having coffee, but nothing more." He made a face. "It's hard to believe his old man got conned. Edison Hall wasn't a stupid man, you know. He only went as far as sixth grade in school, but he got a job with the railroad and worked his way up to supervisor." He shrugged. "He'd come in sometimes. He liked my coffee. Said it was strong enough to float an iron wedge."

"That's why I like it," I said.

Somehow I'd managed to eat the entire muffin. I brushed the crumbs off my fingers. "What was he like?" I asked.

Glenn gave a snort of laughter. "Edison Hall was a stubborn cuss, no doubt about it, but he was different when his wife was alive. After she died he didn't go out as much and he got kind of sour about people, about life, it seemed to me."

He pushed off from the counter. "I saw Edison just a couple of days before he died. He was moving a little slower, but hell, aren't we all?" He grinned at me and I thought how creaky my own back and shoulder had been when I got up.

"There was nothing wrong with his mind," Glenn said. "He was sharp as a tack to the end, so if someone managed to con him into buying all those bottles of wine that turned out to be worthless, whoever it was ran a pretty good con. Ronan Quinn said pretty much the same thing."

A timer buzzed then. "That's my cupcakes," Glenn said.

"And I better get going." I grabbed the bags of rolls. "Thanks," I said, heading for the back door.

I dropped the rolls off at the school office and then drove over to the shop. There was a light on in the old garage and I found Mac there sanding the arm of an old church pew.

"Good morning," he said, pushing his dust mask up onto the top of his head.

"Hi," I said. "How long have you been out here working?"

Mac shrugged. "A while. An hour, maybe" He gestured to the empty coffee mug sitting on top of an old wooden trunk. "That's my first cup."

"You want another one?" I asked.

He rubbed the side of his neck. "Please. Sanding these arms is turning out to be trickier than I expected."

The wooden pew was almost twelve feet long. It had come from an old country church that was being torn down. We were restoring it as a gift for a retiring Episcopal bishop who had begun his ministry in that little church. We didn't usually take on commissions like this, but the bishop's friends who were planning to surprise him with the pew had been persistent. They'd kept offering more and more money until it seemed silly to keep saying no.

Mac and I had wanted to leave the bench the way

it was and just strengthen and rebrace the bottom, but our clients had insisted the pew be stripped and refinished. They wanted it to look the way it did when it had first been installed in the church more than eighty years ago.

The wood was beautiful under several coats of paint and varnish, but I still wished we'd left the old finish intact. I walked the length of the piece, trying to imagine it being built all those years ago.

"What's the bishop going to do with this?" I said to Mac.

He got to his feet, brushing the dust off his jeans. Elvis made a face and took a couple of steps backward. "I don't know," Mac said. "Maybe he'll stick it in his living room and use it as a sofa."

"It doesn't look that comfortable."

"I don't think it's supposed to be."

I looked at the long expanse of wooden seat and the unyielding rolled armrests. "It needs Jess," I said to Mac.

He wrinkled his nose at me. "I don't know how we'd wrap her."

I made a face back at him. "I mean we need Jess to make some pillows and maybe some kind of long cushion to sit on."

"That's a good idea," he said.

"I'll call her later on and see if she can stop by later today or tomorrow." I yawned. "I'll go start the coffee and then I'll come back and give you a hand."

"Sounds good," Mac said. "Did Rose come with you?"

"She's not working until this afternoon. I think she and Mr. P. are working on their case."

"Did you talk to Nick last night?" Mac asked. He was wearing a long-sleeved, paint-splattered T-shirt and he pushed the sleeves up his arms, showing off the dark skin of his forearms.

I shook my head. "I called, but all I got was his voice mail and I didn't know what to leave for a message. 'Sorry you got bested by a bunch of senior citizens' seemed a little mean."

Mac laughed. "Has he always been such a . . ." He hesitated.

"Tight-ass?" I finished. I laughed. "Don't worry. I've called him that a couple of times to his face when he was driving *me* crazy."

"I was going to say responsible person, but I guess in some ways it's the same thing."

I stuffed my hands in the pockets of my red hooded sweater. "Yeah, he has. He was a kid when his dad died. It wasn't as though Charlotte had any expectation for Nick to be the man of the house. You know Charlotte. She's very capable."

Mac nodded.

"But Nick seemed to think he had to take on that role. He cares about people very, very deeply. And sometimes that comes across as though he's trying to tell us all how to live our lives." I felt a twinge of guilt. I'd been a bit hard on Nick lately.

"He wasn't going to college, you know," I said to Mac.

"I bet that didn't go over well with Charlotte."

I could still see Charlotte standing next to the dining room table in my gram's old house, back and shoulders rigid, hands clenched as Nick explained, at dinner to celebrate my brother Liam's college acceptance, that *he* hadn't been accepted anywhere because he hadn't mailed any of the applications.

I gave Mac a wry smile. "No, it didn't. Gram had a little sunroom on the back of the house. She marched the two of them back there, told them to work it out and then stuck the back of a chair underneath the doorknob so they had to stay in there and talk."

"I take it they worked it out," Mac said.

"They did. But that doesn't mean Nick is good at compromise."

Mac laughed. "Neither is Rose. And she's been at it a lot longer."

Elvis stayed out in the workshop while I went inside and got coffee. Mac and I spent about an hour working on the church pew. Finally I sat back on my heels and pulled off my dust mask. "I think that's it," I said.

"I'll get the dust cleaned off and I think I'll be able to do a coat of stain this afternoon."

"I'm going to go change my clothes. It's almost time to open."

"Yell if you need me," Mac said.

I stepped outside and rolled my neck from one side to the other to work out the kinks. Then I brushed the dust off my sweatshirt and old jeans. I'd covered my hair with a thin knit beanie and I pulled it off and gave it a shake.

I started for the back door of the shop and caught sight of Charlotte coming up the sidewalk. I detoured and met her at the bottom of the parking lot.

"Good morning," she said. She was carrying a large, crazy quilted tote bag. I took it from her and we started up the slight slope to the back door.

Charlotte had always had beautiful skin. This morning her cheeks were touched with a slight flush of pink from her walk and her brown eyes sparkled.

"Isn't this a beautiful day, Sarah?" she said, looking up at the cloudless sky.

Before I could answer she took in my dusty sweatshirt and jeans. "Have you been working already?"

"Yes and yes," I said in answer to her two questions.

"You work too much," she said with just a touch of reproach in her voice. "You know what you should do?"

"Meet a nice young man and make babies," I answered, holding the back door for her with my free hand. "I wonder where I've heard that before?"

Charlotte smiled back over her shoulder at me. "I was going to say you should take a morning off and sleep in, but if you'd rather not do it by yourself, that would be fine."

"Charlotte Elliot!" I exclaimed in mock outrage, putting one hand on my hip and frowning at her.

She gave a snort and rolled her eyes. "Isabel is never going to be a great-grandmother at this rate," she said. "And don't waste your time giving me that speech about staying out of your love life. You don't exactly have one, dear."

I put my arm around her shoulders. "I have all of you. Why do I need a man?"

She struggled to keep a straight face, but I could see a smile pulling at the corners of her mouth. "If you're asking that question, then you clearly weren't paying attention in your personal development classes."

I laughed and gave her a hug. She smiled back at

me, and then her expression grew serious. "Sarah, have you talked to Nicolas?" she asked.

"Not since he was here yesterday. Why?"

She sighed. "To quote Rose, Nicolas has his knickers in a bit of a knot."

"Did you know what she and Alfred were up to?" I reached over and flipped on the light switches as we stepped into the shop.

"Not for a long time, no," she said. "I just can't seem to get it through to Nicolas that we don't want to spend whatever time we have left just organizing bake sales and growing roses. He's hardheaded sometimes."

I smiled and set her bag down by our feet. "When he makes up his mind about something it is pretty difficult to get him to change course." I tipped my head to one side and studied her face. "I wonder where he got that?"

"It comes from the Elliots," she said, straight-faced. "They've always been a stubborn bunch."

Charlotte was wearing caramel-colored pumps with her dark brown skirt, which made her several inches taller than I was. I stood on tiptoe and kissed her cheek. "I love you and your britches are starting to smoke," I whispered.

She smiled and I started for the stairs.

"I'll open up," she called after me.

"Thank you," I said without turning around.

I changed out of my dusty clothes, touched up my makeup and went into the tiny staff room for another cup of coffee. When I went back downstairs, Charlotte had put on her apron and unlocked the front door.

"What do you want to do with the rest of these books?" she asked me.

I'd purchased a box of old hardcover books for two dollars at a yard sale to "stage" an old bookcase I'd bought from one of my regular trash pickers. We'd ended up selling half of the books, but we still had the bookcase.

"I don't know," I said. "What do you think?"

Charlotte cocked her head to one side. "What if I rearrange the remaining books and add a few other things?"

"Go ahead," I said.

"I'm going to take a look at the lamp shades that Avery got started on," I said to Charlotte. "If you get customers, call me."

I had Avery covering a collection of mismatched lamp shades with some old classroom maps that Charlotte had found in her basement. Avery had a good eye for detail and a surprising amount of patience for this kind of project. She'd covered one small and one large shade and done a meticulous job.

The bag filled with felted wool sweaters was still on the end of the workbench. It reminded me that I needed to call Jess. I pulled my cell out of my pocket and leaned against the side of the bench.

"Hey, Sarah, what's up?" she said when she answered. Her voice was slightly muffled.

"Those sweaters are ready for you and I need a favor."

She muttered something I didn't catch.

"What are you eating?" I asked. "You sound like you have a mouthful of marshmallows?"

"I'm not eating," she said. "I'm pinning."

"Tell me you don't have a mouthful of pins?"

She gave a small grunt and I pictured her leaning across her worktable. "Not anymore," she crowed.

When Jess was sewing she had a habit of sticking pins in her mouth for a moment instead of back in her pincushion—a purple octopus with sparkly false eyelashes and a black boa. I thought it made her look like Jaws from the James Bond movies.

"So, what do you need?" she asked.

I explained about the church pew.

"One cushion would be too long. You need at least two, or maybe three would be better. I need to see it before I can tell you." We agreed that she'd try to come by the shop late in the afternoon and I said good-bye.

I was just about to go back out front to help Charlotte when Mac came in the back door. He was carrying his coffee cup and walking quickly. "Don't laugh," he stage-whispered as he came level with me. There was a touch of urgency in his voice, but a smile played across his face.

Rose and Mr. P. came in the back door behind Mac. Rose was carrying one of her huge bags as usual. I knew there was a good chance that there was a cake or some ginger cookies inside. My attention, however, was totally focused on Mr. P. Now I understood why Mac had warned me not to laugh.

Alfred was wearing a toupee. It was the color of oxblood shoe polish, which meant it wasn't anywhere close to the color of real hair. And it was curly. What little natural hair Mr. P. still had was gray and straight.

"Oh my," I said almost under my breath. I couldn't look at Mac, because I knew if I did I would laugh.

"Good morning, dear," Rose said, bustling over to us. "I'm just going up to put the kettle on."

"I'll do that for you," Mac said. "I'm on my way upstairs."

"Oh, thank you," she said. She seemed a little frazzled this morning. The edge of her collar was caught in the neck of her jacket.

Mac disappeared into the shop.

"Hold still," I said, reaching over to fix Rose's jacket.

"Heavens," she said. "I'm a little addled this morning."

"What's going on," I asked. "Why are you here so early?"

"Elizabeth has an emergency board meeting," Mr. P. said.

Don't laugh, I told myself sternly as I turned to look at him. Up close his hairpiece was even more . . . alarming than it had been at a distance.

"Is everything all right?" I asked.

For many years Liz had run the Emmerson Foundation, a charitable organization started by her family, and she was still active on the board of directors.

"Yes," Rose said, unzipping her jacket. "They have a new offer from the developers for those buildings the foundation holds the mortgages on down on the waterfront and they need to discuss if they're going to accept it or not."

"That's good news," I said. Over the winter, there had been a development proposal for a section of the downtown waterfront. The deal had fallen apart after the death of Lily Carter, who had lobbied against the plan, but now a new group was floating a similar idea for retail units, a small hotel and some residential space built in an environmentally responsible manner. The first step was to secure all the property they needed.

Mr. P. nodded, which made his "hair" bounce gently on his head. "It is, but it means Liz won't be available to interview Edison Hall's neighbors with us."

"I know Ethan thinks Mr. Quinn's death is connected somehow to his father's wine collection, but we can't afford to get tunnel vision at this point in the investigation," Rose said.

"I agree," I said.

She turned to Mr. P. "Alfred, show Sarah your suit."

"Ah yes," Mr. P. said, unbuttoning the jacket he was wearing. "Rosie and I are having a bit of a disagreement about my tie. I'd like a second opinion."

"Um, all right," I said, wondering what was wrong with the offending piece of clothing.

Alfred's suit was dark gray with a fine blue check. His shirt was pale blue and the tie they were disagreeing about was a conservative blue stripe.

"What do you think, Sarah?" he said, tipping his head to one side, which made the hair slip a bit to the left as well.

I kept my gaze locked on his face. "I think it's fine," I said. I turned to Rose. "What's wrong with Alfred's tie?"

"Well," she sighed softly. "It's a little . . ." She hesitated.

"The word Rosie is trying not to say is dull," Mr. P. said.

"I just think Alfred should wear a tie that goes with his personality, something that has a little flare like he does."

They both looked at me.

Great. How was I going to get out of this without hurting someone's feelings?

I took a deep breath and hoped for the best. "Rose, I see your point," I said. "With the tie that Alfred has chosen, we don't get a hint of the more playful side of his personality."

She beamed at me.

I held up a hand.

"However." I made a point of clearly enunciating the word. "You haven't considered that perhaps today he wants to showcase his serious side."

Mr. P. gave me a small smile. "Exactly, my dear."

"I hadn't considered that," Rose said, her expression thoughtful.

He reached over and patted her arm. "I'll go up and make the tea for you."

"That would be lovely," she said. She handed him the oversize tote. "The oatmeal cookies are in the blue tin."

Alfred took the bag and headed for the shop. Once the door had closed behind him, Rose turned to look at me. "I suppose you think that thing on his head looks fine, too?"

"No comment," I said, doing my best to stifle a smile and pretty much failing.

"When I went to the door to let him in this morning, I was afraid for a moment that I'd had a stroke," she said. "My next thought was that a bird's nest had fallen on his head on the walk over."

A bubble of laughter escaped. "I'm sorry, Rose," I said. "It's just that I never thought Alfred was the type of person who felt the need for extra hair." I struggled to get the urge to keep laughing under control. "It's not that I think a hairpiece is a bad idea. I just didn't think being bald bothered him."

Rose played with the zipper pull on her jacket. "As far as I know, it doesn't. He's just gotten this idea that he should look a little younger, for professional reasons."

I rubbed the space between my eyes, trying to come up with something helpful to say. "Did you point out that in the investigation business being older equates with wisdom and experience?"

Rose's eyes lit up. "That's so true. Would you tell Alfred that, please? We already quarreled about his tie. I don't want him to think I'm criticizing all his choices."

I blew out a breath. "I'll tell him," I said.

She reached up and patted my cheek. "I don't know what we'd do without you," she said. She pointed back over her shoulder in the direction of the old sunporch. "I'll be in the office."

"I'll tell Mr. P.," I said.

Out front Charlotte was showing a customer a china tea set and Mac was lifting an upholstered slipper chair out of the front window.

I walked over to him. "Is Mr. P. upstairs?" I asked, keeping my voice low.

He set the chair down on the floor between us. "He's making Rose's tea and another pot of coffee."

I leaned over and brushed a bit of lint off the back of the chair. "Where did that hair come from?"

Mac gave me a half smile. "I'm not clear on all the details, but late-night TV and a credit card were involved. Be glad he didn't order something called the Blond Bombshell."

"Please tell me you're joking," I said.

"Sorry."

I shook my head. "Somehow Rose roped me into talking to him about it."

"What are you going to say?"

"I don't know," I said. "I guess he doesn't want to look old. I don't want him going out looking foolish instead."

Mac reached for the vintage teddy bear that had been sitting on the chair when it was in the window and set it back in place. "Did you know they're planning on walking over to Edison Hall's neighborhood to talk to people?"

I shook my head. "I knew they were going. I didn't know they were planning on walking."

Mac looked at me without speaking.

"No," I said.

"I didn't say anything."

"I'm not driving them. I said I wouldn't try to stop them from being detectives if that's what they want to do. But . . ." I held up both hands. "But I'm not getting involved. Not this time."

"Okay," Mac said.

"I'm serious."

"I believe you."

We just stood there for a moment. I gestured in the general direction of the stairs. "So I'm just going to go now," I said.

"I'll just put this chair over there," Mac said.

I found Mr. P. in the small staff room on the second floor. "I made a fresh pot of coffee, Sarah," he said. "Would you like a cup?"

"Please," I said. I was stalling. Alfred was a good

man, despite his propensity for hacking into other people's computer systems. He adored Rose. How could I tell him his hairpiece looked like a piece of shag carpeting from the nineteen seventies?

I took the mug he held out to me and added cream and sugar.

"Thank you for getting Rosie on my side over my tie," he said, reaching for a cup on the shelf over the counter. "Could I trouble you for your opinion on something else?"

"Of course," I said, taking a sip of my coffee. I was all for stalling a little while longer.

His chin came up. "What do you think of my new hair?"

So much for stalling.

"What made you decide to . . . invest in some new hair?" I asked. The lame question made me cringe, but Mr. P. didn't seem to notice.

"Rosie and Elizabeth and Charlotte put a lot of faith in me when they made me the de facto head of Charlotte's Angels," he said. "I don't want to let them down. I didn't want anyone to think I'm too old for the job."

I smiled at him. "You're not too old. You know your way around a computer better than Avery does and you can find things that no one else can find." I held up one finger. "And I don't really want to know how you do that."

He smiled back at me and a touch of color flushed his cheeks.

"I also think you're forgetting that in this case, being older, *looking* older suggests maturity, wisdom, experience."

He didn't say anything for a moment, but I could see that he was turning over my words in his mind.

I wrapped both hands around my cup. There was one more thing I wanted to say. "Rose and Liz and Charlotte all knew how old you were when they asked you to be the face of their agency. I've known them a long time and they have pretty good judgment."

Mr. P. raised a hand to his toupee and then dropped it. "I wouldn't want Rosie to think I was questioning her judgment," he said. He took a deep breath and slowly let it out. Then he lifted his hand again and grabbed the hairpiece to pull it off.

Except it didn't come off. He pulled harder, but the only thing that achieved was to show that the toupee had the stretching ability of a piece of Silly Putty.

"Sarah, I think I need a little help," he said.

In the end it took the two of us and some nail polish remover to unstick Alfred's new hair from his head. The "handy gripper pads" left red marks on his scalp, but I put a little antibiotic cream on them and arranged his own hair so it more or less covered everything.

"You look nice, very professional," I said. "Make sure you take a look at yourself in that cheval mirror Mac just brought in from the workroom."

"I will, my dear," he said. "Thank you." He patted my hand and then he picked up Rose's tea and went downstairs.

I went into my office. Elvis was sitting in my desk chair as though it belonged to him. "Up," I said, making a move along gesture with one finger.

The cat didn't so much as twitch a whisker.

"This is my office," I said.

Elvis looked all around the room and then his green eyes came back to me. It seemed, at least in his kitty mind, that there was some dispute as to whose office it was.

I picked him up, claimed the chair and set him on my lap. He made an elaborate show of getting comfortable.

"Rose and Mr. P. are going to talk to Edison Hall's neighbors," I told the cat, leaning back in my seat.

He didn't really seem interested. Instead he butted my hand with his head, cat for "scratch behind my ears." I began to stroke his fur and after a moment Elvis began to purr.

"I don't really have time to drive them," I said.

"Mrrr," Elvis said. That might have meant "sure you do," or it might have meant "don't stop."

"You know Rose has some arthritis in her hip and Mr. P.'s knees aren't good."

He didn't say anything other than to keep on purring.

I'd meant it when I said I didn't want to be involved in another one of the Angels' cases. Two was more than enough, thank you very much.

But.

"If I don't drive them I'll be worrying about them the entire time they're gone."

Elvis leaned into my hand and looked up at me, green eyes blissfully narrowed almost to two slits. I folded my free arm behind my head and stared up at the sloped ceiling over my head.

"On the other hand, if I take them it's a slippery slope down to getting pulled into their investigation. It's like sitting at the top of the Poseidon's Plunge slide at Splashtown water park. I'm going to end up barefoot and rump over teakettle, trying not to upchuck, asking myself what the heck I was thinking in the first place."

"Mrrr," Elvis said.

I picked him up, got to my feet and set him back in the chair. He shook his black furry head and made a face at me. I kissed the top of his head, just above the bridge of his nose. "I have things to do," I said. "Guard the office."

Rose and Mr. P. were in the sunporch office, their heads bent over the laptop. I knocked on the doorframe. They both looked up at me.

"Hi," I said. I hesitated. "I need a favor."

"Of course, my dear," Mr. P. said.

"What do you need?" Rose asked.

My head examined, was what I wanted to say. "I'd like to come with you," I said.

Rose looked at Alfred and then she got to her feet. "Why?" she asked, a challenge evident in her eyes. "Do you think Alfred and I aren't capable of talking to witnesses?"

"I think you're capable of talking to anyone about anything. I'd like to come because I think I owe it to Stella. We said we'd help her and I want to do that."

As I said the words I realized they were true. I liked the way Stella stepped up, first by hiring us to clear out her brother's house and make things easier on Ethan and his wife. And how she was still trying to help them, trying to somehow salvage some money from Edison's estate so Ellie could have the surgery she needed. It was the kind of thing my grandmother would do—had done more than once.

"She reminds me of Gram," I said.

Rose smiled then. "Yes, she does." She looked at Alfred.

He nodded.

"Of course you can come with us," she said.

I glanced at my watch. "Does half an hour work for you?"

"That would be lovely," Rose said.

Mac was at the workbench, searching through a container of metal wall hooks.

"I called Jess," I said, leaning against the bench. "She has some ideas for cushions for the bishop's pew. She'll probably be here sometime this afternoon."

Mac shook the Mason jar, made a face and then upended it onto the painted wooden surface.

"What are you looking for?" I asked.

"Those two brass hooks with the lion's face."

I looked up at the row of glass canning jars on the long shelf behind the workbench. "Try that one," I said. "Four from the end."

Mac reached for the container I'd indicated and unscrewed the lid. The two hooks he'd been looking for were on top. "Thanks," he said. "How do you do that?"

I put my fingers up to my temples. "It's my superpower."

"I thought your superpower was the ability to spot a decent piece of furniture under nine coats of old paint."

"That, too," I said with a grin. "Superpowers don't just come one to a customer."

Mac laughed. He put the lids back on both jars. "Are you leaving soon?" he asked as he leaned over and set them back on the shelf.

"What do you mean?" I said, feeling my face begin to get warm.

"Are you and Rose and Alfred leaving soon?"

I scuffed one foot against a small divot in the floor. "How did you know?" I shot him a sideways glance.

"You care about them," he said, dipping his head in the direction of the sunporch. "And you like Stella Hall. You gave her a good deal on clearing out the house."

"Gram asked me to help, if I could. She and Stella go way back."

"I saw your face the first time she came in here to talk about the job. You would have given her a deal whether Isabel was friends with her or not."

I sighed. "It's not much of a way to run a business, is it?" I said.

Mac picked up the two hooks and gave me a thoughtful smile. "I think it's a good way to run a life," he said. He turned and headed for the back door.

Mac and Charlotte were arranging different versions of our current chair collection around a long trestle table for a customer when I came downstairs with my coat and purse about twenty-five minutes later. I raised a hand in good-bye. Charlotte smiled and mouthed, *Good luck*.

Rose and Mr. P. were waiting by the back door. In his long jacket over his gray suit, he looked almost distinguished. Rose looked equally polished in a blue coat over a black skirt and jacket.

"What's the plan?" I asked as we walked across the parking lot to the SUV.

"We'd like to talk to the neighbors on either side of

Edison," Rose said. "As well as the people across the street."

"The police already talked to them and didn't come up with anything," Mr. P. said, "but I think it's worth a second conversation."

"As usual, I'm not going to ask how you know that," I said.

He gave me an enigmatic smile. "Sometimes talking to somebody other than the police is a lower-pressure situation and people remember things they didn't know they knew." He raised an eyebrow. "I know *that* from my psychology class."

"Remind me never to do anything illegal when you're around," I said.

Mr. P. gave the slightest of shrugs. "I'm afraid it's too late for that, my dear. You forget that I've driven with you more than once."

Rose started to laugh. I had a bit of a lead foot when I drove, although I tried very hard not to speed when I had anyone other than Elvis in the car.

It was a beautiful spring morning and I cracked the driver's window of the SUV just a little as we drove over to Edison Hall's neighborhood. I parked at the curb in front of the house. Maybe it was just knowing what had happened in the little bungalow, but the place seemed to have an air of sadness about it. I hoped that once the investigation was over and we'd cleared out the place, a family would move in and fill the little house with happy memories.

Rose was on the front passenger side and she turned to look at Mr. P. "Where do you think we should start?" she asked.

I shifted in my seat to survey the area. The houses were a mix of small bungalows and equally tiny Cape Cod–style houses and there were large trees along both sides of the narrow street. It was a beautiful neighborhood.

Diagonally across the street from us, a gray Cape Cod with sea blue shutters caught my eye. "May I make a suggestion?" I asked.

"Of course," Mr. P. said.

"I think you should start with the gray house across the street."

They both turned for a look and then Rose looked at me again. "Why there?" she asked.

"Because I just saw a man with a little kid head into the backyard and I'm pretty sure I know him."

"Splendid!" Mr. P. said from the backseat.

"I'm almost certain it's Paul Duvall," I said. "He was friends with Josh when we were kids. He'd be a couple of years younger than I am. He's a townie."

Josh was Josh Evans, a local lawyer who had helped us out a couple of times. He'd grown up in North Harbor just a few houses from my grandmother's, which was how we'd gotten to know each other, even though I was just a summer kid.

Rose frowned. "Tall and skinny? Delivered the newspaper?"

I nodded. "That's Paul."

"He had lovely manners as I remember," she said approvingly. She looked from me to Alfred. "Everyone ready?"

We climbed out of the SUV. Rose patted her white hair and smoothed the front of her skirt. She reached over to adjust Mr. P.'s collar, giving me a quick appraising look as she did so. I had changed out of my jeans into a pair of gray pants and my favorite black boots. Rose didn't say anything, so I assumed she'd decided I looked presentable.

We crossed the street and followed the interlocking brick path around the side of the house to the backyard. It was deeper than I expected, rimmed with evergreen trees that provided lots of privacy.

Paul was pushing a blond, curly-haired little girl on a swing. He frowned, squinting as he first caught sight of us, and then the frown turned to a smile. "Sarah?" he said.

I nodded, returning the smile.

He said something to the little girl, then came around the swing set and met me in the middle of the lawn.

"Josh told me you were living here now," he said. "The repurpose store about halfway up the hill—it's yours?"

"It is," I said. I had to look up to meet his gaze. He was easily a good six inches taller than my five foot six, towering over me even with the extra couple of inches my boots gave me. He was wearing glasses with thin wire frames, and his egg-shaped head was shaved smooth. He still had the same intelligent blue eyes behind those glasses.

I looked around. "How long have you been here? I thought you were in Oregon."

"We were," Paul said. "We've been back about three months and we moved into this house about six weeks ago." He half turned and smiled at the tiny blonde slipping off the swing. "That's Alyssa."

The preschooler ran over to us, stopping beside her father. She looked up at me, curiosity in her blue eyes that mirrored her father's. "My name is Alyssa," she said. "What's yours?"

I leaned forward and smiled at her. "My name is Sarah."

"Sarah and I were friends when I was a little boy," Paul told her.

"That's a long ago time," she said, the expression on her tiny face grave.

Paul laughed, smoothing a hand over his scalp. "That it was."

Alyssa turned her attention to Rose and Mr. P. "Are they your mommy and daddy?" she asked.

"No," I said. "They're my friends, Mrs. Jackson and Mr. Peterson." I looked at Paul. "Actually we were hoping you could answer a couple of questions for us about the house across the street."

Alyssa had let go of her father's leg. She walked over and looked up at Mr. P., tipping her blond head to one side. "Are you a papa?" she asked.

"Yes, I am," he said.

"Can you push me on my swing?"

"Alyssa," Paul said, a slight edge of warning in his voice.

She glanced back at her father for a brief moment. "Please?" she said. She reached for Mr. P.'s hand and gave him a smile that I knew I wouldn't have been able to resist.

"I'd love to," he said, clearly enchanted by her. He looked at Paul. "As long as your daddy says it's okay."

"It's okay," Paul said.

"I like to go high," I heard Alyssa say as she pulled Mr. P. across the grass.

Paul shook his head. "Sometimes I think she'll run the world someday."

"Then it will be in good hands," Rose said. She smiled at Paul. "You probably don't remember, but you were my paperboy a good many years ago."

"I do remember, Mrs. Jackson," he said, his blue eyes twinkling. "You made the best oatmeal cookies with raisins and walnuts. You used to leave a couple in a little bag on the doorknob for me every Saturday."

Rose beamed back at him. "And you never just threw the paper on the lawn. You always put it between the doors."

Paul laughed. "Well, I have to admit those cookies were a pretty good incentive." He looked over at the swings where Alyssa and Mr. P. were talking as he pushed her.

His gaze came back to me. "You said you had some questions, Sarah, about the Hall place across the street?" He swiped a hand across his mouth. "The police have already been here asking questions. You know someone found a body over there?"

I nodded. "I'm the one who found it."

His eyes widened. "You did? Wait a minute, you're the people who are going to clear out the house?"

"Yes. The family hired us."

He looked past us toward the street. "I didn't make the connection. I'm sorry."

"Paul, Rose and Mr. Peterson are private investigators. They're looking in to what happened."

If Paul was surprised, it didn't show.

"Did you see anything?" Rose asked. "Or anyone hanging around that you hadn't seen in the neighborhood before?"

Paul shook his head. "I'm sorry. We weren't even here most of that day. We drove down to Portland to see my sister and we stayed the night. My wife had a meeting."

"What about the week before? Did you see anyone then?"

"No, I mean except for Ethan Hall and the man who died—Quinn, I think his name was."

I nodded but didn't say anything.

"I saw them several times in the past couple of weeks." He ran his hand over his smooth scalp again. "I'm sorry I can't tell you anything that will help."

"It's all right," Rose said.

He looked over at his daughter and Mr. P. again. "It's a pretty quiet neighborhood. That's one of the reasons we bought this house. You could talk to Sharon Marshall, the blue house across the street. She's been around a lot more in the last six weeks. She had hip replacement surgery. I'm not sure if she's home right now. She has physio a couple of mornings a week." He bent down to pick up a lime green pail and shovel on the grass at his feet. "Although I think if she'd seen anyone around other than Ethan, Mr. Quinn or the recyclers, she would have mentioned it." He straightened up and smiled at us.

"Recyclers?" I said.

"That's what we call the trash pickers. It's just a nicer word. I don't want Alyssa to think reusing things is a bad idea."

Rose and I exchanged a look. "Who exactly are these recyclers?" I asked.

"It's just one, really," Paul said, brushing a clump of mud off the side of the little pail. "I saw her a couple of times the week before last, you know, when it was the spring-cleaning pickup."

Once a year North Harbor did a recycling and garbage pickup. There were rules about what could be put out at the curb, but in theory if two people could move it, the town would pick it up to be either recycled or taken to the landfill. In practice, most things didn't spend very long curbside and didn't usually end up at the recycling center or the landfill, either. People came from other towns to cruise around looking for freebies.

Mac and I had come across some great finds that week and had bought a few more from the pickers we regularly did business with.

"Can you describe her?" I asked.

Paul frowned and looked at me. "I'd say she's a bit shorter than you, swimmer's build—you know, wide shoulders and strong legs."

"Long curly hair?" I finished.

"You know her?"

"We do," Rose said.

"Her name is Teresa," I said. "I've bought some things from her for the store. Do you remember when you last saw her over at the Hall house?"

I shifted a bit uneasily from one foot to the other. I hated to think that Teresa Reynard might be involved in Ronan Quinn's death. I didn't know her well, but she'd always brought me good-quality items—no junk—and she'd always been fair in the prices she asked.

Paul blew out a breath. "Let me see. Four or five days before . . ." He paused. "Before, you know, what happened, I saw her with Ethan. She was putting a couple of concrete planters and a small concrete statue—I think it was a lion—in the back of her van. It's an old Volkswagen van. Blue."

It was definitely Teresa whom Paul had seen. She called her old van Mitch. It always made me think of the little clown cars at the circus when she started unloading it. She somehow managed to put far more inside than the laws of physics decreed should fit.

"Was that the last time you saw Teresa around here?" Rose asked.

"Actually no," Paul said. "That morning we drove down to Portland, I saw her van go by. Sometime before six." He glanced over in the direction of the swing. "Alyssa is an early bird. She was in the living room watching a video. I'd just slipped into the kitchen to make a cup of instant coffee." He rolled his eyes. "My wife thinks I drink too much coffee." His expression grew serious. "You don't think this Teresa person killed that man, do you?"

"Heavens, no!" Rose gave her head a slight shake. "But she might have seen something when she was in the neighborhood." Her eyes darted to me for a brief second. "We've taken enough of your time, Paul. Thank you."

"You're welcome," he said.

Rose looked in Mr. P.'s direction and raised a hand. He nodded, then said something to Alyssa before giving her one last push. He walked over to us.

"You have an enchanting daughter," he said to Paul.

"Thank you for entertaining her," Paul said.

"The pleasure was mine."

Alyssa was still swinging, pumping now with her legs to go higher. She waved at Mr. P., who waved back.

There was no one home at the blue bungalow that belonged to Sharon Marshall or at the white Cape Cod on the other side of Edison Hall's house.

We walked back to the SUV.

"Sarah, do you have an address for Teresa Reynard?" Mr. P. asked once he was settled in the backseat.

I was buckling my seat belt and I half turned to look at him. "Don't tell me you can lip-read at that distance?" I said.

He frowned and looked a little confused. "I can't lip-read at all, my dear," he said. "Although I can read upside down, which has proved very useful a time or two. Why do you think I was lip-reading?"

Rose was smiling. "The little one told you, didn't she?"

Mr. P. smiled back at her, the puzzled look gone from his face now. "And her father told you," he said.

"Yes, he did," Rose said. "He's a pleasant young man, but I'd forgotten how literal-minded he could be." She gave Alfred an inquiring look.

He held up a hand before she could speak. "And before either of you worry that I interrogated that lovely child, I didn't. I just happened to notice that she had one of those little old wooden toy jeeps that you"—he tipped his head in my direction—"bought from Teresa about two weeks ago. All I did was ask her where she got it."

"Teresa gave it to her," I said.

He nodded. "She said the nice lady with the rolly hair gave it to her."

"Rolly" was a good description of Teresa's mass of

dark curls. I checked for traffic and pulled away from the curb.

"Then she asked me if I liked to play hide-and-seek," Mr. P. continued.

"Children that age have a very short attention span," Rose said. Rose had been a teacher for a lot of years. Not only did she know a lot about kids, but she also knew pretty much every scheme or scam a kid between the age of five and eighteen could come up with.

"Alyssa is very bright for her age," Mr. P. said. "And very observant."

I glanced in the rearview mirror and he gave me a Cheshire cat smile. "For example, she noticed Teresa, over at the Hall house the morning of the murder, playing hide-and-seek. Or to be more exact, hiding by the side of the garage."

Chapter 5

"We have to talk to her," Rose said at once. I could feel her eyes on me. "Sarah, where does Teresa live?"

"I don't know," I said. "Somewhere just outside town, I think."

"It doesn't matter, dear," she said. From the corner of my eye, I saw her pull out her phone. "I'll Google her address."

"I'm sorry," I said. "I need to get back to the shop and . . ." I hesitated, not wanting to get any more involved than I already was and, even more important, not wanting to insult either one of them by pointing out the obvious.

"And what?" Rose asked.

I stopped at the corner, checked the traffic in both directions and took the opportunity, while we were stopped, to look at both of them. "And have you considered the fact that your information came from a four-year-old?"

"She's very bright," Mr. P. said immediately, leaning

forward and placing one hand on the back of my seat. "She has the vocabulary of a much older child."

Rose turned partway round to look at him. "Sarah was the same way," she said. "She could read before she started school. Isabel used to get her to read everyone's horoscope out of the newspaper."

I flashed to sitting at my grandmother's table in a red plastic booster chair with a cookie in one hand and the newspaper spread out on the round wooden table.

"I remember that," I said, smiling at the memory as I turned left.

"I don't doubt that you do," Rose responded a tad tartly. "You were a very bright child, too."

"And I'm smart enough now to see you're trying to play me like a piano."

"I'm disappointed that you would think that," she said. I didn't have to look over at her to know she was sitting at attention in her seat, her shoulders squared, chin jutting out just a little. The tinge of self-righteousness in her voice told me that.

"Because I'm right," I said lightly. I did shift my gaze right for a moment then.

Rose blushed and ducked her head.

"We need to go back and talk to those other neighbors," Mr. P. said from the backseat. "Which doesn't mean I think Alyssa made up what she told me. No offense, Sarah."

"None taken," I said. "And for the record, I don't think it's a bad idea to talk to Teresa. I just don't want to see her ambushed."

"She won't be," Mr. P. promised.

When we got back to Second Chance, Rose and

Alfred went into their sunporch office and I walked through the workroom to the store. While we were gone Mac had brought in two blue rattan egg chairs that we'd picked up at the curb of a house two streets over from the store the night before the spring-cleaning pickup Paul had spoken about. Jess had made cushions for them with heavy, dark blue canvas removable covers. Elvis was sitting on one of them, methodically washing his face with one black paw. My brother, Liam, was sitting on the other.

He grinned when he saw me, got to his feet and wrapped me in a hug.

"What are you doing here?" I asked, leaning back to look up at him. Liam was Nick's height—six-foot-plus, with blond hair he kept fairly short these days, blue-gray eyes and a little boy grin that most women couldn't resist.

"Business," he said. "I'm consulting on the new proposal for the harbor front."

"That's great," I said. "How long are you here?"

"Couple of weeks, probably."

I smiled up at him. "I'm glad."

He snaked an arm around my neck and pulled me against him. "That's because you can't feed yourself and you know I'll cook for you."

"I can cook. Sort of."

"Yeah, right," he said with a roll of his eyes as he let me go.

"Rose is teaching me," I said with an edge of self-righteousness to my voice.

"How's that going?" he asked dryly.

"Merow!" Elvis proclaimed loudly.

Liam looked at the cat, raising one eyebrow. "That's pretty much what I thought."

"No one asked you," I stage-whispered to the cat.

"Mrrr," he said, seemingly making a face at me before going back to washing behind one ear.

"I talked to Gram this morning," Liam said, "and she told me I can stay at her place. She said you have a key."

Strictly speaking, Liam was my stepbrother, and wasn't related to Gram at all, but to her Mom was family even though my dad, Gram's only child, had died when I was five. So when my mom had married Liam's dad, they became family, too.

I nodded.

"Or I could just live with Rose for the next two weeks," he said. He swung around and swooped Rose—who had been quietly sneaking up on him—into a hug.

"It's so good to see you," Rose said, grinning from ear to ear.

"It's good to be seen." Liam took both of her hands, took a step backward and looked at her. "You look as beautiful as ever."

"And you're as full of it as ever," she said sternly, but she was smiling even as she shook her head at him.

Charlotte came downstairs then carrying a mug of coffee. She handed it to Liam.

He turned his smile on her. "Thank you. I left early this morning and I'm down by at least three cups." He took a long drink and Charlotte, just as Rose had, beamed at him.

I pulled my keys out of my pocket, slid Gram's off the ring and held them out to him. "The gold one is for the front door and the silver one is for the apartment."

"Thanks," he said. He took another sip of the coffee.

"There's nothing to eat," I warned him. "The fridge is empty and so are the cupboards."

"In other words it's like staying at your place."

I stuck my tongue out at him.

Liam looked at his watch. "I have a meeting downtown and I need to get going or I'm going to be late." He drained his mug and Charlotte took it from him.

"How about dinner at Sam's?" I asked.

Liam shook his head. "Can't," he said. "But I shouldn't be late, so I'll talk to you later."

I nodded. "All right."

He gave Rose and Charlotte that little boy grin that had been getting him out of trouble with women—and into some as well—since grade school. "It's really good to see you both," he said.

"Come for dinner some night you're here," Charlotte said.

He nodded. "Give me a day or two to get a schedule worked out and I'll let you know what works." He looked at me again. "Later."

Liam disappeared out the door and Rose and Charlotte exchanged smiles.

"It's good to have Liam here," Charlotte said.

Elvis murped his agreement and settled himself a little more comfortably in his chair.

"I think he looked a little thin," Rose offered, slipping off her jacket.

Charlotte frowned. "Maybe a little," she said. "I expect he's as bad as Nicolas, working all the time. It would be nice if he could meet someone."

I took the empty cup she was holding and leaned in to kiss her cheek. "I'll be in my office if anyone needs me," I said.

Upstairs I set the empty cup in the sink and poured myself coffee, taking it back to my small office. Elvis was there, sitting on my desk chair.

"I thought you were staying downstairs," I said. He blinked his green eyes at me. I picked him up, sat down and settled him on my lap. That involved some grumbling and poking my legs on his part.

It was good to have Liam in town for a while. We hadn't lived in the same house for years and even though he knew how to drive me crazy better than anyone else, sometimes I missed seeing him every day.

I knew how lucky we were to be so close. Most people who didn't know assumed that we were biological siblings and were surprised to find out that we weren't, a tribute to Mom and Dad—and Gram—who knew that family was more than biology. As far as Gram was concerned, Liam was just as much her grandchild as I was.

And a bonus to having Liam around for the next couple of weeks was that Rose and Charlotte and Liz would have someone else's love life to ask loaded questions about instead of mine and Nick's.

I wondered if Liam had let Nick know he was in town. Probably not, since he hadn't let me know. I put a hand on Elvis to steady him and reached for the phone. The cat gave me the stink eye for disrupting his nap.

"Hi, Sarah, what's up?" Nick asked when he answered the phone.

"Liam's here," I said, leaning back and carefully propping my feet on the edge of the desk. "I figure since he didn't call me he probably didn't call you, either."

"No, he didn't, but it's great he's in town," Nick said. "How long is he staying?"

Elvis lifted his head, nudging my hand. I took the hint and began to stroke his fur. He closed his eyes and purred. "He could be here for a couple of weeks. He's consulting on the new development proposal."

"Good. That must mean it's a go."

"According to Liz, it is," I said. "After the North by West deal fell apart, she got involved with the group that was looking for another developer."

"Why do you know that and I don't?" he asked.

"Probably because I make it to dinner at your mom's more than you do."

Nick laughed. "Speaking of dinner, can you and Liam meet me at Sam's tonight?"

On my lap Elvis stretched, yawned and then looked expectantly at me. He made an exhalation that sounded a lot like a sigh of contentment.

"Sorry," I said. "Liam had plans." I realized my brother hadn't told me what his plans were.

"So just you and me?" Nick said.

I couldn't keep mooching meals from Rose—well, maybe as far as she was concerned, I could—and I didn't feel like going grocery-shopping after work. "Sure," I said. "But there's something I need to tell you first. You might want to rescind that invitation."

"Mom already told me that they've started their investigation."

"And you're surprisingly calm about that," I teased.

I heard him exhale slowly. "I give up," he said.

I had a metal image of Nick holding up both hands in a gesture of surrender.

"They just ignore me," he continued. "They smile sweetly, pat my cheek and do what they damn well want."

I laughed. "Welcome to my life," I said. "And by the way, what took you so long?"

He started to laugh as well. "I don't know. I guess I'm a slow learner."

I heard other voices in the background. "I have to go," Nick said. "How's six work for you?"

"That's fine."

"Do you want me to pick you up?"

"I'll meet you there," I said.

We said good-bye and I ended the call. "Time to get up," I said to Elvis. I gave him one last scratch behind his left ear and then I picked him up and set him on the floor. "Go see if we have any customers."

He shook himself, took a quick pass at his face with a paw and disappeared around the half-open door. Elvis knew customers generally meant lots of attention for him, especially if he did his Sad Kitty face and made sure the long scar that cut diagonally across his nose was in the right light.

I stood up and brushed cat hair off my pants. Seeing Liam and talking to Nick had distracted me, albeit briefly, from dealing with what we'd learned from Paul Duvall and his adorable daughter.

It was easy for people to feel a little uncertain about trash pickers like Teresa. Both Teresa and Cleveland, the other picker I bought from regularly, lived pretty much outside the conventional work world. They bartered, traded, scavenged and Dumpster-dived for everything from furniture and car parts to clothes and food. They were both quick to make a deal if it would make them a profit and equally quick to share whatever they had with anyone who needed it. Cleveland and Teresa had always been fair with me and I'd tried to do the same with them.

I thought about Teresa. She was quiet and serious, but she had a good eye for small things like clocks, jewelry and old general store fixtures. I ran my hand over the cigarette case on my desk that I used to hold pencil leads and paper clips. I'd bought it from Teresa because it had reminded me of a similar box my dad had used to hold guitar picks and extra strings.

I couldn't put Rose and Mr. P. off forever. They were going to talk to Teresa sooner rather than later and I hadn't exactly been straight with them. It wasn't that I was afraid she'd get railroaded, because I knew there was no way she would have been sneaking around Edison Hall's house looking for something to take. It was because I knew there was at least a possibility that she had been.

Chapter 6

When I went downstairs Elvis and Charlotte were with two women who looked to be interested in an old card file cabinet that Avery had found in a Dumpster behind the library. Mac was in the workroom with the parts of . . . something spread across the workbench.

"I take it you saw Liam," I said.

He held a small metal gear up to the light and frowned at it. "I did. He's going to give me a hand with the rest of the drywall out in the workshop, probably on Sunday."

I'd had plans to turn the old garage into a workshop from the very beginning. Aaron Ellison, who plowed the parking lot in the winter, also owned a roofing company and he'd given me a good deal on a new roof after Mac got his mother's old grandfather clock working again. We had a woodstove for heat and several massive shelving units that had come from an old warehouse Liam had been renovating for storage.

Mac and I had insulated and drywalled three of the walls. All that was left was the fourth and part of the ceiling and now it looked as though that would be finished soon as well.

"How did the detecting go?" Mac asked, settling the gear on a piece of cloth by his left elbow and turning to give me his full attention.

"All right," I said with an offhand shrug.

He studied my face for a moment without speaking.

"Do you remember that gray Cape Cod diagonally across the street from Edison Hall's house?" I asked.

"Yes," he said.

"It turns out a friend of Josh Evans's just bought it a few weeks ago."

"Someone you know."

I nodded. "Paul Duvall." I was taking way too long to get to the point, but I knew Mac wouldn't rush me. "He saw Teresa at the house a couple of times and she was around last week as well."

"A lot of people would have been around last week," Mac said. "We were all over town. It was the spring pickup."

"I know," I said, fidgeting with a button on my shirt. "The thing is, it looks like Teresa might have been at the house the morning we found Ronan Quinn's body." I blew out a breath. "And she might have been trying to avoid being seen."

"Are you sure?" he asked.

"Yes and no."

Mac reached for a rag on the bench and wiped his hands. "Tell me the yes," he said.

"Paul saw Teresa's van driving down the street sometime before six in the morning."

"And the part that makes you not so sure?"

"The person who thinks Teresa was hiding by the garage is four." I folded my arms over my midsection.

Mac tossed the rag back onto the bench.

"You know some of Teresa's background," I said. "You know she was arrested more than once when she was a teenager. And you've seen what a black-and-white person she is."

"I'm guessing Rose wants to talk to her."

I nodded. "She does." Through Jess I knew that Teresa had had several run-ins with the police when she was younger, all stemming from Teresa taking things that she believed were rightly hers. I also knew something a lot of people didn't, that she'd spent some time in a psychiatric hospital after the death of her mother when she was twelve. Maybe it was because we'd both lost parents when we were young that I felt a kinship, a connection with her. Maybe if I hadn't had Rose and Charlotte and Liz to wrap their arms around me—and my mother and Gram—when my father died, the same thing might have happened to me.

"I don't know how much they know about Teresa's background and it's not really my story to tell," I said. I raked my hand back through my hair and watched a few strands fall to the floor. Why did it seem as if that happened a lot more when the Angels had a case?

"So tell Rose that," Mac said. He picked up a small spring between his thumb and forefinger, studied it for a moment and then set it down again. He looked at me and just a glimpse of a smile played across his face.

"Tell me what?"

Rose was standing at the far end of the workroom.

She always claimed she had ears like a wolf, and I was inclined to believe her.

I smiled at Mac. "Thanks," I said softly. I'd told Nick more than once that sometimes he underestimated his mother and her friends. Mac had just (nicely) pointed out that I was doing the same thing.

I walked over to Rose.

"What is it?" Rose asked. "It's something to do with Teresa Reynard, isn't it?"

"Yes," I said.

She looked up at me, her head tipped to one side. And then she smiled. "You're a kind person, Sarah," she said.

She must have seen the confusion on my face.

"I called Liz when we got back. When she was a girl she went steady with Teresa's grandfather. She went steady with half the male population of North Harbor, but that's not really relevant."

Rose knew about Teresa's background.

Why was I surprised about that? Between the three of them, she and Liz and Charlotte had gone to school with, taught—in the case of Rose and Charlotte, or dated—in the case of Liz, most of the male population of North Harbor over the age of twenty-one.

"I'm not saying I think you'd ambush Teresa—" I began.

"It's okay, sweetie," she interrupted. "I can be a bit of a pit bull when we're working on a case. But I promise I'll be a pussycat with Teresa."

I swallowed back a smile, leaned over and gave her a hug. "How about I get in touch with Teresa and get her to stop by?"

Rose nodded. "That'll be fine." She looked at her watch. "Heavens! It's almost time for me to get to work. What do you need me to do?"

"There are two boxes of grade school readers that I'd like to put out on display," I said. I looked back over my shoulder and frowned. "I'm just not sure where they should go."

Rose looked thoughtful, her tongue caught between her teeth. "What if I rearranged things in the hutch?" she asked, referring to one of my first purchases for the store, a monstrosity we hadn't been able to sell in almost a year. At the moment its shelves were showcasing everything from Avery's trophy candleholders to a collection of Depression glass plates. "I can spread everything else around the store."

"Sounds good," I said. Rose had a good eye for displaying things in unexpected ways like a collection of cocktail glasses on a tray next to a vintage rubber ice pack and several patent medicine bottles.

"I'll just get Alfred a cup of tea and then I'll get started," she said, bustling past me.

I walked slowly back to Mac, wondering if there were any other private investigators who drank so much tea. "I'm going to grab some lunch and do some paperwork. Would you get Avery started cleaning that silver service I bought from Helen Craig?"

"Will do," he said, rooting through the bits of metal strewn in front of him. "Did you talk to Rose about Teresa?"

I nodded. "She agreed not to go pit bull on Teresa. And I agreed to ask Teresa to stop in."

He grinned. "That's good."

I found myself smiling in spite of myself. "Well, not to overkill the metaphor, but you know what she can be like when she sinks her teeth into a case."

Mac groaned and shook his head. "Go eat, Sarah," he said. "I think you're suffering from low blood sugar."

I laughed and headed for the shop.

A black paw appeared around the side of my office door as I settled on the love seat and began to unwrap my roast beef sandwich from McNamara's. Elvis had impeccable kitty radar when it came to lunch. He stopped for a drink from his water bowl but ignored the kitty kibble in his dish, jumping up instead to sit next to me on the love seat. He leaned forward and sniffed in the direction of the sandwich on my lap, then looked expectantly at me.

I pulled a small bit of roast beef from between the slices of French bread and offered it to the cat. "You're so spoiled," I said as he ate.

He made a low, contented sound in the back of his throat. After he'd had a taste of my sandwich, Elvis was happy to sit next to me on the love seat and wash his face while I had my lunch. When I finished eating I moved behind the desk. I'd sent a text to Teresa and I knew I had about an hour before she showed up.

When I went downstairs just before one thirty, I found Rose standing in the middle of the store, head cocked to one side, hands on her hips, frowning at something.

I walked over to join her. She'd brought out an old wooden dressmaker's dummy that Mac had trash-picked. Avery had named it Francine. Rose had attached a small globe to the top of Francine's neck, topped it with an oversize hat swathed in lavender tulle and hung about half of our collection of costume jewelry necklaces around the dummy's neck.

"What do you think?" she asked, her mouth pulled to one side. "Is the hat too much?"

I studied the figure, my arms folded over my chest. "I don't think so," I said. "I think it makes her look very worldly."

Rose rolled her eyes at my pun and swatted me with the back of her hand as I started for the door to the workroom. I stopped to look at the bookshelf where she'd arranged the grade school readers along with a pair of Rock 'Em, Sock 'Em Robots, an Etch A Sketch and some other toys from the seventies that had been in a box in our under-the-stairs storage space. I turned to look back at her. "Looks good," I said, gesturing at the shelves.

"Thank you," she said, brushing off her hands. "Avery went and got the toys for me."

"I'll thank her, too," I said.

Mac and Mr. P. had their heads bent together over something in the middle of the workbench. Avery was sitting on a stool at the far end, rubbing the handle of a silver milk jug with a soft cloth. When she saw me coming she set the jug in front of her, held up her hands like a spokesmodel showing off the newest car model. "Ta-da!" she said.

The old silver had polished up even better than I'd hoped. "Nice work, Avery," I said with a smile.

She grinned back at me and pushed the stack of bracelets she was wearing back up her left arm. "It's kind of pretty. I thought maybe we could set the long table with that yellow-flowered china and put the tea stuff in the middle with maybe some plants?"

"I like that idea," I said.

"So, can I do it?" she asked. She made a motion as though she was going to flip her hair over her shoulder and then remembered that she couldn't.

Avery had cut her hair to chin length a couple of weeks before and dyed a wide strip in the front cranberry red. Both the color and the style suited her. Liz had grumbled that now they couldn't go anywhere that boys weren't looking at Avery.

"I look right back at them," Liz had said. "So they get the message, look but don't touch!"

We'd been having dinner at Charlotte's and Avery had looked up from her mashed potatoes and waved her fork in Liz's direction. "Yeah. I might as well become a nun." She'd frowned. "Do you have to be Catholic to be a nun?"

"You can date when you're forty," Liz had retorted.

Avery had regarded her grandmother thoughtfully across the table. "Do you know how old you'll be then, Nonna?" she'd asked.

"I'm perfectly capable of doing the math, thank you very much," Liz had replied tartly.

Rose had opened her mouth to say something and Liz had fixed her with a baleful look. "Say one word, Rose Jackson, that has anything to do with my age and you'll be wearing that dish of potatoes for a hat."

Straight-faced, gray eyes twinkling, Rose had held up her right index finger and written the number one hundred followed by two plus signs in the air. Charlotte had wisely leaned over and whisked the potatoes to the other end of the table.

I looked at Avery now, her enthusiasm for decorating a table in the shop evident on her face. "Yes, you can do it."

She clapped her hands gleefully together like a little kid. "Thanks, Sarah," she said.

"Thanks for getting that box of toys out for Rose," I said.

"No problem," she said.

I moved over to Mac and Alfred. They were studying the top section of what looked to me to be a wooden clock case. "Let me see what I can do," I heard the older man say. He looked up at me and smiled.

Mac turned around. "What's up?" he asked.

Before I could answer, the bell rang at the back door. I held up a finger. "Hang on," I said.

Teresa Reynard was at the door. "Hello, Sarah," she said. "It's after one thirty."

"Yes, it is," I said. By my guess it was less than five minutes after. "Please come in."

She stepped into the back entry. Her thick mass of curly hair was loose as it usually was. She was wearing work boots and her hands were jammed in the pockets of her brown canvas jacket.

"You said in your text that you wanted to talk to me about Edison Hall." Teresa was a very literal-minded person, far more so than Paul Duvall.

I gave her a small smile. "Yes. My friends are trying to find out what happened to the man whose body was found at the house."

"I didn't kill him," she said flatly.

"I didn't think you did," I said. I led her into the work-room.

"Hello, Teresa," Mac said. His eyes met mine. "I'll get Rose," he added softly as he passed behind me.

"Teresa, this is my friend Alfred Peterson. He's a private investigator."

Mr. P. smiled. "Hello, Teresa," he said.

"Hello," she said. "Sarah said you wanted to ask me some questions about the man who died at Mr. Hall's house."

"Yes, I would," Mr. P. said. He gestured at a stool. "Would you like to sit down?"

Teresa shook her head. "No, thank you." She studied him for a moment. "Are you a real private investigator?" she asked.

The question didn't faze Mr. P. "Yes, I am," he said, nodding. He pulled out his wallet and took out some kind of ID I didn't even know he had. He held it out to Teresa, who studied it carefully and then nodded before handing it back.

Rose came in from the shop. "Hello, Teresa," she said.

Teresa frowned slightly. "Are you an investigator, too?" she asked.

"I'm learning," Rose said.

"You're an apprentice?"

Rose nodded. "Yes."

The answer seemed to satisfy Teresa. "What did you want to know?" she asked. She hadn't moved. She was still standing, feet slightly apart, hands in her pockets.

"You know who Ronan Quinn was?" Mr. P. asked.

"Yes."

Alfred waited for a moment and then seemed to realize Teresa wasn't going to say anything else.

"You know someone killed him," Rose said.

Teresa's expression didn't change. "I've heard people talking. I think it's probably true." She looked at me. "I already told Sarah I didn't kill him."

"My dear, when were you last at Edison Hall's house?" Mr. P. asked.

"Tuesday, last week."

"Why?" Rose asked. She smiled at Teresa.

If Teresa was unsettled at all by the questions, it didn't show. "I was there to get what belonged to me."

Rose and Mr. P. exchanged a look. "And what was that?" he asked.

"A metal moose."

"You mean a toy?" Rose asked, frowning.

"No," Teresa said. "A metal moose." She pulled her hands out of her pockets and held them about three feet apart.

Mr. P. smiled as he seemed to figure out what she was talking about. "Like the old sign markers along the trail to Moose Lake?" he asked.

"Not like one of them. It is one of them."

"If it was yours, why was it at Edison Hall's house?" I asked.

Teresa shifted and looked at me. "Because he cheated me."

"Cheated you how?" Rose said.

"He was at a flea market, selling some gas station signs." She shook her head. "Nobody wants those anymore. I heard him tell someone that he had other signs in his garage, so I asked if I could see them."

"He said yes?" I asked.

Teresa nodded. "I picked out six signs that I wanted to buy. We settled on a price. I wrote it all down. People aren't always honest." She looked at me. "I don't mean you, Sarah."

"Thank you," I said.

"How did Edison cheat you?" Mr. P. asked.

"I didn't have enough money on me," Teresa said. "I had to go to the bank. When I got back, he had the signs wrapped in an old blanket." She pressed her lips together. "I counted to make sure all the signs were there, but I should have looked at each one."

"Bait and switch," Rose said softly.

"He replaced the moose with something else," I said.

"A sign for the Moose River Lodge," Teresa said. "He'd shown it to me. I didn't want it, but he said it was the one I picked. He lied."

"So you were trying to find it," Mr. P. said. He gave Teresa a sympathetic smile.

"It was mine," she said. "I paid for it. I tried to find it before, but I couldn't." She looked at me again. "I knew you would be starting to work at the house and I didn't have any way to prove to you that the sign belonged to me."

"Your word is enough for me," I said.

"The sign belongs to me," Teresa said. "I paid for it." She pulled a folded piece of paper out of her left pocket and held it out to me. I took it from her.

It was the handwritten receipt she'd created. The signs and the prices she had offered were listed in Teresa's square, block printing. Her signature was at the bottom. What I took to be Edison Hall's signature was underneath.

I offered the piece of paper to Rose, who looked it over, frowning, and then gave it back to Teresa.

"I believe you," I said again. "I'll talk to Stella. If we find the sign I'll make sure you get it."

"Thank you," she said.

"When you got to Edison's house that morning, what did you do?" Mr. P. asked.

"I parked my van at the corner," she said. "And then I walked back to the house." Her eyes weren't quite focused on Alfred. It was almost as though she was running down a list of what she'd done in her head. And for all I knew, maybe she was.

"I wanted to look in the garage," she continued. "There was an old folding door leaning against the side window and I couldn't see anything, so I went around to the back."

"You didn't see the moose sign," Rose said.

Teresa shook her head. "No. It was too dark inside the garage. And it didn't look like the signs were in there anymore."

"Did you get inside the garage?" Mr. P. asked.

"No," Teresa said.

Another look passed between Mr. P. and Rose. "Why not?" he asked.

"Because Mr. Quinn showed up."

"Wait a minute," I said. "It was maybe quarter to six in the morning and Ronan Quinn was at Edison Hall's house? You're certain?"

Teresa blinked at me. "Yes," she said.

"What was he doing?" Rose asked.

Teresa shrugged. "Waiting, I think."

"Waiting for what?' I asked.

"I don't know," she said.

Luckily Mr. P. was better at phrasing questions than I was. "Why did you think he was waiting?" he asked.

"Because he parked his car in the driveway, got his briefcase out of the backseat, and then he went around to the back of the house. He stood by the door and looked at his watch."

"Did you see anyone with Mr. Quinn?" Rose asked.

"No," Teresa said. "I went back to my van."

Rose sighed softly and I touched her shoulder. "Did you see anyone on your way to the van?"

Teresa nodded. "I passed a man walking up the sidewalk."

"Was he old or young?" Mr. P. said.

She thought for a moment. "Younger than you are but older than Sarah."

That was a pretty big age spread, but all Mr. P. did was nod. "Did you see his face?"

"For a moment as he walked past me," Teresa said. Her eyes darted from side to side as though she was trying to pull something out of her memory.

Mr. P. looked from Rose to me and gave his head an almost imperceptible shake. I took it to mean he wanted us to stay out of the conversation for now.

"What color hair did the man have?" he asked Teresa. At the same time I saw him reach behind himself with one hand and give Avery's arm a squeeze. She'd been so quiet I forgot that she was still polishing the tea service. She raised her head, looked around and then pulled her earbuds out of her ears.

I had no idea what Alfred was up to, but apparently Avery did. She sat still as a statue for a minute or so, then reached for a pad of paper Mac kept on the bench and pulled a pencil stub out of her pocket. Without saying a word, she bent her head over the paper. It seemed obvious that she was drawing something, but I didn't know what and with Avery's body hunched over the pad, I couldn't tell. Was she trying to draw the man Mr. P. was slowly getting Teresa to describe? If that was what he was up to, it was way too much of a stretch.

I was wrong, of course.

Teresa finished describing the man and Avery looked up from the paper maybe thirty seconds later. She slipped off her stool, walked over to Teresa and held out her work. "Is this the man you saw?" she asked.

"Yes," Teresa said, looking from Avery to Mr. P. "That's him."

Avery turned the notepad around so we could all see it. My first thought was, why hadn't I known that Avery could draw so well? My second was that the face she'd sketched looked very familiar.

"Rose, why do I know that face?" I asked, scanning my own memory trying to pull out a context for the familiarity.

Mr. P. was also looking at Rose. "It is, isn't it, Rosie?" he asked.

She nodded. "Yes, I think so."

Frowning, Avery tipped her head to one side and studied her own work. After a moment her frown turned into a grin. "Holy crap," she said. "It's that guy that keeps hitting on Nonna, isn't it?"

"What guy that keeps hitting on Liz?" I asked, totally confused.

"Channing Caulfield," Rose said. "The former manager of the North Harbor Trust Company."

Chapter 7

Mr. P. took his cell phone out of his pocket. After a moment he nodded at the screen and held out the phone to me so I could see the photo he'd found. "That's Channing Caulfield," he said.

Rose leaned over for a look and nodded.

The photo was of a man in his late sixties or early seventies. It looked like the kind of picture businesses take of their senior staff—a head-and-shoulders shot of a smiling man posed in front of a blue-gray background. The resemblance between the photo and Avery's drawing was strong.

I took the phone from Mr. P. and showed the picture to Teresa. "That's him," she said.

"After you got in your van, what did you do?" Rose asked. Elvis had wandered in. He jumped onto the bench and walked down to us, stopping next to Teresa.

"I went home," she said, reaching out to pet the cat.

Mr. P. put a hand on Rose's arm. "Which way did you go?"

"I went back down Beech Hill Road. It's faster."

Elvis was purring, looking at Teresa with a blissful expression on his face as she stroked his fur.

"Where was the man going?" Mr. P. asked.

Teresa gave another shrug. "He wasn't going anywhere," she said. "He was standing behind that big maple tree next to the curb, looking at old man Hall's house."

Teresa couldn't really tell us much more. I walked her to the door and thanked her for stopping in. I told her again that I'd do everything I could to get the sign Edison had cheated her out of.

Avery had gone back to polishing the silver teapot. I smiled at her and held out my hand. We fist-bumped and she smiled back at me. "I didn't know you could draw like that," I said.

"I haven't had any lessons or anything like that," she said. Her eyes darted over to Elvis for a moment. Rose was talking to him and he seemed to be listening intently to every word. "I have some I did of Elvis if you'd like to see them sometime."

I nodded. "I'd like that."

"I'll bring them tomorrow."

As if he'd somehow known we were talking about him, the cat came walking down the workbench. He nudged Avery's arm with his head and meowed softly.

Rose joined us. She put an arm around Avery's shoulders. "That was a marvelous drawing. Thank you," she said.

The teen's cheeks flushed with color. "It was easy," she said. "Teresa was really good at remembering details."

"And you were really good at turning it into a

drawing," Rose countered. "We wouldn't have figured out who it was without you."

"Mrrr," Elvis said.

Rose nodded at the cat. "Everyone agrees." She looked at Avery. "I think you deserve a treat for all your hard work. There are cookies in the staff room."

"Merow!" Elvis said with great enthusiasm. He jumped down to the floor and started for the door.

Rose smiled. "You can get Elvis a treat, too."

"There's a bag of those fish crackers he likes in the cupboard over the refrigerator," I said.

Avery slid off her stool and started after the cat. "Okay," she said over her shoulder.

Mr. P. was just ending a conversation on his cell phone. "She's on her way," he said to Rose.

"Who's on her way?" I asked.

"Elizabeth," he said.

I remembered what Avery had said about the retired bank manager. "You're going to get her to talk to Channing Caulfield," I said.

Alfred nodded. "One needs to use all the tools in one's toolbox," he said sweetly.

I shook my head and smiled at him. "Of course."

Rose leaned against me as the three of us walked toward the sunporch. "Teresa didn't have anything to do with what happened to that man," she said.

I squeezed her arm. "I know."

She looked up at me and smiled back. "You saw Elvis."

The jury was still out on whether or not the battle-scarred black cat could actually tell when someone was lying, but there was certainly some evidence to suggest that it was possible. More than once I'd seen him make a disgruntled face when someone was stroking his fur and not telling the truth. Mac thought maybe Elvis could somehow feel a person's sweaty palms and racing heart when that person was lying. Maybe the sour face was because it didn't feel very good to him.

"Am I crazy?" I said.

Mr. P. gave me his Mona Lisa smile. "Well, my dear," he said. "It seems to me that's a separate question from whether or not Elvis can tell if someone is lying."

I laughed. "I think I'm just going to quit while I'm ahead." I gave Rose's arm one last squeeze.

"I'll be right out," she said to me.

Mac and Charlotte were both with customers. I headed for the stairs. Avery was on her way down, a cookie in one hand with—I was pretty certain—a second one wrapped in the napkin peeking out of her shirt pocket. Elvis trailed behind her, licking his whiskers.

"Do you want me to stay in the shop or go back to the silver?" Avery asked.

"Would you stay in the shop just until Rose comes out?" I asked.

"Sure thing," she said, pushing her bracelets up her arm. "I'll straighten up those place mats and runners."

"Thank you," I said.

Elvis had stopped on the third stair from the bottom. "Are you coming up?" I asked.

He cocked his head to one side and after a moment's thought turned and walked up with me. I went into the staff room for a cup of coffee and one of Rose's cookies.

"Mrr," Elvis said, doing the head-tilt thing again because he knew it made him look extra adorable.

I got three kitty crackers from the bag and held my hand out to him. His nose twitched as he sniffed them. He looked past me to the cookie can on the little stretch of counter.

"Like you didn't already have part of a cookie with Avery," I said.

He made a huffy noise, grabbed all three crackers in his mouth and stalked out, flicking his tail at me so I knew just how miffed he was.

I was answering Web site e-mail when Mac tapped on my door about half an hour later.

"Your presence is requested in the Angels' office," he said.

"I'm guessing Liz is here," I said as I signed out of the store's Web mail.

He nodded. "Your guess would be correct."

"Did Rose and Mr. P. bring you up-to-date?"

"Rose did," he said, leaning against the doorframe. "Do you really think it was the former bank manager Teresa saw?"

I shut off the computer and stood up. "Mr. P. found a photo of the man online." I stretched my arms out in front of me. "It's him, Mac. The sketch, Teresa's description, they match the photo."

"So what was he doing skulking around Edison Hall's house before six o'clock in the morning?"

I gave him a wry smile. "I'm pretty sure that's where Liz comes in."

Liz was standing in the middle of the porch, arms crossed over her chest. She was wearing a jacket the color of butter toffee and her nails were flame orange. "So basically you want to pimp me out," she was saying.

Mr. P.'s eyes widened.

"No!" Rose exclaimed, shaking her head. "No one is expecting you to . . . do anything." She looked shocked at the implication. "We just want you to invite him for lunch and see what you can find out."

I came up behind Liz and wrapped my arms around her. "All they're looking for is your very considerable charm," I said.

She turned her head and glared at me. "That giant sucking sound you hear in the room is you, Sarah," she said.

"You know that Channing Caulfield has always had a soft spot for you," Rose said. "And don't tell me you never noticed that. I wasn't born yesterday. You know you'll get a lot more out of him a lot faster than either Alfred or me."

"She's right," I said before Liz could say anything. "Remember Royce?" Liz had managed to get information out of the retired mail carrier when the Angels were investigating Arthur Fenety's murder.

"I wasn't born yesterday, either," Liz retorted. "But I'm not so old that I don't recognize that the three of you are trying to flatter me into going along with this ridiculous scheme of yours." She paused for a moment. "Luckily for all of you"—she raised a finger and made a loop that included Alfred, Rose and me—"flattery works on me."

Mr. P. beamed at her. "Thank you, Elizabeth," he said.

I pressed my cheek against her face. "Thank you," I said softly. "I'm sure Channing Caulfield's pants aren't nearly as low-hanging as Royce's were." The older man's trousers had sat so low on his hips that I'd been a little afraid that if he sneezed they'd end up at his ankles.

"Oh no, missy," Liz said in a low voice. "You're not getting off that easy. You're coming with me." She turned her head and gave me a gleeful grin. "Channing Caulfield may like me, but he likes younger women even more." She raised one eyebrow. "Make sure you wear something that shows some leg. And when I say some, I mean lots."

I had the sinking feeling that it wasn't Liz who had just been played, it was me.

Chapter 8

Channing Caulfield might have been retired from the bank, but he was still working, at least part-time, for an investment firm in town. Liz called the office and set up a lunch appointment for the next day.

"You see?" I teased. "There's no way we'd be able to see him on a Saturday if it wasn't you he was going to be having lunch with."

"Us," Liz said firmly. "And remember what I told you: wear a dress. Short is good. Tight is better."

I stuck my tongue out at her back as she headed for the door. "I saw that," she said with a dismissive wave of one hand. "One of these days your face is going to freeze like that."

Charlotte was at the cash desk. She laughed and walked over to me. "I see you got drafted to have lunch with Liz and Chucky Caulfield."

I rolled my eyes. "Liz wants me to wear something short and tight."

Charlotte folded her arms over her aproned front.

She narrowed her brown eyes. "Do you still have that blue-gray wrap dress?" she asked.

"Not you, too," I said.

"Chucky always did like the ladies." Charlotte smiled. "And you look so pretty in that dress." She reached over and straightened my collar.

That dress met all of Liz's requirements. It was short and tight and I wasn't a hundred percent sure I'd be able to breathe, let alone eat, if I wore it.

"Why do you call Channing Caulfield Chucky?" I asked.

Charlotte smiled. "We were in the same first grade class. In those days Channing was the kind of name that would get you beaten up on the playground. The teacher very wisely called him Chuck. In a classroom full of Bobbys and Tommys, that very quickly became Chucky and it stuck."

She shrugged. "I'm not sure he liked being called Chucky once we got a few years past first grade, but the name stuck."

I put a hand on the back of my head and stretched my neck. I could use a cup of coffee and one of those peanut butter cookies, assuming there were any left in the staff room. "So don't let Liz call him Chucky if we want to get any information out of him," I said.

"Good grief, yes," Charlotte exclaimed. "If she gets her knickers in a knot over something, she's apt to do that."

"I'll try to keep her in line," I said. "But I'm not making any promises."

"I understand, dear," Charlotte said with a smile. "Liz can be stubborn."

I raised an inquisitive eyebrow at her. "As opposed to you?"

"I'm not stubborn," she said, nudging her glasses up her nose with one finger. "I'm determined."

I laughed. "So, what did they call you in first grade?"

"Charlotte," she said. "Not Lottie. Not Charlie. Charlotte." A sly smile crept across her face. "I was determined back then, too."

I had just set the timer on TV so Elvis could watch *Jeopardy!* when Nick knocked on my door after work. "C'mon in," I called. It was about a minute before six o'clock. I leaned down and scratched the top of the cat's head. "You're so spoiled," I said to him.

He licked my hand and wrinkled his nose at me.

I went back out into the living room. Nick was standing just inside the front door. "I'm in," he said.

"I just have to grab my jacket and I'm ready," I said.

He was holding his phone and he glanced down at it. "Are you waiting for a better offer?" I asked.

He shook his head. "No. I was hoping I'd hear from Liam. I sent him a text to see what his plans were and if he could maybe join us after all."

I grabbed my red plaid jacket from the closet. "He's probably working late." I picked up my keys and bag from the chair by the door. "I'm leaving," I called to Elvis.

"Why do you do that?" Nick said with a laugh. "You're talking to a cat. He doesn't know what you're saying."

I held up one hand. "Wait for it."

The answering meow came from the direction of the bedroom. The cat had impeccable timing.

I gave Nick a smirk and went out into the hallway.

"That doesn't prove anything," he said as he followed me out.

"Yes, it does," I said as I locked the door. "It proves that my cat is smarter than you—"

"Careful," he warned, his dark eyes gleaming. "You don't exactly have a lot of options for dinner at the moment."

"—might expect," I finished.

Nick laughed. "Good save!"

His SUV was parked at the curb. "Is it okay if we drive?" he asked.

I nodded. "Sure. Are you on call?"

He shook his head. "No. But I may need to stop at the station later to talk to Michelle."

"About the Quinn case?" I asked as I climbed in.

"I can't tell you that," he said. He shut my door and walked around the front of the vehicle.

"Sure you can," I said when he opened the driver's-side door. "You just don't want to because you're afraid whatever you say to me I'll share with your mother and Rose."

"And how is the investigation going for the state's newest licensed private investigator and his merry band of senior citizens?" Nick countered.

"I can't tell you that," I said, deadpan.

He laughed and slid behind the wheel. "Truce?" he asked.

I nodded. "All right. No talking about your case."

"Tell me about your cooking lessons," Nick said as he pulled away from the curb.

"New rule," I said. "No talking about your case or my cooking lessons."

"Oh, c'mon," Nick said, darting a quick look in my direction. "You must have learned something by now. When are you going to make dinner for me?"

I settled back against the seat with a smile. "When you lace up a pair of sneakers and come running with me."

Nick didn't run. He played hockey. He biked. He swam. I'd never seen him run. Jess claimed it was because he looked as if he were being attacked by a swarm of bees when he ran. For all I knew, she was right.

"New rule," Nick said after a moment, his eyes fixed on the road. "No talking about my case, your cooking or anybody running."

I laughed. "Deal," I said.

I didn't ask Nick where we were going for supper. I was sure we were headed for The Black Bear, so I wasn't surprised when he turned onto the street by the waterfront.

"You're not going to find a parking spot down here on a Friday night," I said.

As soon as the words were out of my mouth, almost as if Nick had some sort of magical powers, a car pulled away from the curb just two doorways from the pub. "Good, clean living," he said, backing smoothly and expertly into the spot.

The pub was busy, no surprise, since it was a Friday night. Sam was talking to a server by the bar. He looked up and smiled when he caught sight of us, heading across the floor to meet us. "Hey, kiddo," he said, wrapping me in a bear hug.

Sam was tall and wiry with salt-and-pepper hair and a close-cropped beard. He'd been my father's best friend and even though I'd eventually gained a wonderful dad in my stepfather, Sam had played a fatherly role in my life, too. He was always ready to listen and he never said, "I told you so," no matter how badly I messed up.

He pulled out of the hug and offered his hand to Nick. "We missed you last night," he said.

"I missed being here," Nick said. I noticed that he didn't offer an explanation for where he'd been.

"Liam didn't say you were meeting him," Sam said, looking toward the back corner of the restaurant.

"Liam's here?" I said.

Sam looked a little surprised. "Yeah. They got here about five minutes ago."

They. Nick looked at me. He'd caught the word as well. It probably meant my brother was using his considerable charm on some business associates.

I looked around Sam and caught sight of Liam in one of the back booths. He was leaning forward, one arm propped on the edge of the table, having an animated conversation with someone I couldn't see seated opposite him. I knew that body language. He was definitely charming someone, probably a woman.

"We're just going to say hi," I said to Sam.

"Sure," he said, giving me a look that could best be described as amused.

Nick and I started across the restaurant. I gestured toward Liam, who was so focused on his companion that he hadn't noticed us yet. She—because I knew it had to be a woman he was with—must have said something funny, because Liam was laughing.

I looked up at Nick over my shoulder. "You know what he's doing, don't you?" I said.

He grinned back at me. "Of course I know what he's doing. Who do you think taught him how to do it?"

I laughed. "I'm not even going to dignify that with a snappy comeback."

One eyebrow went up. "In other words, I've left you speechless."

I poked him gently in the ribs with my elbow.

Just as we got to the table Liam finally looked up and noticed us. "Hey, what are you doing here?" he said, getting to his feet and sliding out of the booth. He wrapped Nick in an enormous bear hug, clapping him on the back the way guys did. "It's good to see you, man."

"You, too," Nick said.

Liam turned to me.

"We just came for supper," I said. "I called you. Twice."

He shook his head and put a hand to his pocket. "I'm sorry. I turned my phone off when my meeting started and then I forgot to turn it back on."

"How long are you going to be here?" Nick asked.

Liam smiled and pulled a hand over his neck. "Looks like a couple of weeks."

"That's great," Nick said. "We're still playing shinny and I could probably scare up a pair of skates for you."

My brother grimaced. "I haven't been on skates since last winter. It would probably be pretty ugly."

"You pretty much just described the entire team," Nick said with a shrug.

"You're in the middle of something," I said, smiling at Liam. "We're going to get a table. I'll see you later, right?"

"He's not in the middle of anything," a voice said behind me.

I turned slowly around to see Jess, leaning out of the booth.

"What are you doing here?" I said. Liam was having dinner with Jess? She hadn't mentioned it early when she stopped by the shop to look at the wooden church pew. Liam was turning the charm on *Jess*? They'd known each other since she and I became roommates in college. As Avery sometimes said, *What the frack?*

"In about thirty seconds, eating mac and cheese," she said, leaning sideways and pointing in the direction of a waiter approaching carrying an oversize-serving tray on each arm.

"We'll let you get to it," Nick said, taking my arm. He looked at Liam. "Give me a call when you have a minute."

"Absolutely," Liam said. He put an arm around my shoulders for a moment and kissed the side of my head. "I'll probably see you at the house later."

I nodded. "Sure."

"I'll call you tomorrow," Jess said to me, turning to give the waiter her own megawatt smile.

Nick looked around, spotted Sam and pointed questioningly at a table near the middle of the room. Sam nodded and Nick led me toward it.

I took off my jacket and hung it on the back of a chair, using the opportunity to look back at Liam and Jess. "Is she feeding him?" I asked.

Nick picked up my chair and moved it around the table so my back would be toward their booth. "We don't care," he said, enunciating each word carefully.

I made a face at him and sat down, taking the menu a waiter had just brought over.

"Thank you," Nick said to the young man. "We're going to need a few minutes."

"I don't care that Liam is having dinner with Jess," I said. "It's just that he's not her type and she's not his."

Nick pulled out his chair, sat down and opened the menu the waiter had left at his plate. "The clams and chips look good," he said.

"I'm serious," I said. "They can't be on a date, can they?"

He shook his head. "Who are you, Sarah? The person who writes the couple-matching algorithms for Match-dot-com? Leave it alone."

"Fine," I said. I bent my head over my menu and watched him under my lashes. As soon as he dropped his own head, I turned to look over at Jess and Liam again.

A crumpled paper napkin struck me on my right temple. I turned back to Nick. "Hey! What was that for?"

"Stop looking at them," he said. "What the heck is wrong with you?"

I propped an elbow on the table and leaned my forehead against the palm of my hand. "I don't know," I mumbled. I turned my head and looked over at Nick. "What are you having?"

"Bear burger and fries," he said.

"That's sounds good," I said, closing the menu and setting it on the table. I resisted the urge to glance over at Liam and Jess again.

The waiter came back for our order. After he'd taken it and headed for the kitchen, I looked at Nick. "What the heck *is* wrong with me?" I said. "Jess has known Liam since she and I were roommates in college. How many times have we all had dinner together?"

"I don't know," Nick said. "A lot."

"So why does it feel all . . . weird seeing the two of them over there having dinner?"

He studied me for a long moment. "I don't know," he finally said, reaching out to set his knife spinning in a circle on the wooden tabletop. "You tell me."

I pulled a hand back through my hair and sighed. "Liam was doing that thing he does."

"That thing?" Nick asked, just a bit too casually, frowning across the table at me.

"That guy thing." I made a circular motion with both hands. "You know, where he leans forward, smiles and tips his head to one side the way Elvis does when he's trying to wrangle a bite of cookie from someone. That thing that you just said you taught him."

"Oh, that thing," he said, and his cheeks flushed with a bit of color.

"Jess is my best friend. I don't want her to get hurt," I said.

Nick actually laughed.

"Not funny," I said, glaring at him.

He leaned against the back of his chair, still laughing. "Yes, it is, Sarah. Jess is probably the only person in the state, heck, maybe on the entire East Coast, who won't fall for Liam's charm."

When I didn't immediately say anything, he raised an eyebrow at me. "Because he is good. I did teach him well." He leaned to one side and the balled-up napkin I pitched at him sailed over his shoulder.

Sam caught it before it hit the floor and lobbed it back into the middle of the table. "Play nice," he said as he passed the table.

I looked at Nick. "Okay, new rule. No talking about the case, my cooking, you running or Jess and Liam doing anything." I ticked each one off on my fingers.

He nodded. "Deal."

We looked at each other in silence. "So, what do you think of the Sox's chances this year?" he said finally.

This time I was the one who laughed. "We're going to talk about the Red Sox?" I said. "What is there to say? You know they don't have any depth in their pitching this year?"

Our waiter arrived then with our burgers. Nick waited until he'd refilled our coffee mugs before he spoke. "You're right about the pitching roster," he said. "I don't like it, but you're right. So how about we don't talk about the Sox or cooking or running or Jess and Liam, but"—he held up one finger—"how about this one time, which won't be construed as a precedent of any kind, we do talk about what Alfred and his merry band of angels have been up to? It's pretty much the safest topic I can come up with."

I looked at the plate in front of him. "Can I have some of your fries?" I asked. My burger had come with onion rings because Sam knew they were my favorite.

"As long as you don't complain about me eating them with tartar sauce," he said, grabbing two fries, dunking them in the little bowl of tartar sauce the waiter had brought to the table.

"Tartar sauce is for fish," I said, picking up an onion ring with my fingers. Nick opened his mouth and I held up my hand and smiled sweetly at him. "Ketchup is for french fries. But if you want to eat them wrong, it's okay with me."

Wordlessly he pushed his plate toward me. I used my fork to take eight or nine fries and slid a couple of onion rings in their place on his plate.

"So, what's happening with the Angels' investigation?" Nick asked.

"Rose and Mr. P. are talking to most of the people the police have already questioned." I took a bite of my burger. It was good, not that I'd expected anything else. Sam was particular about everything that came out of his kitchen.

"Did they find anything the police missed?" he asked. There wasn't any condescension in the question as far as I could hear.

"Maybe," I said.

He looked up at me. I filled him in on how Edison had cheated Teresa out of the metal moose sign and how she'd gone back to look for it and seen Ronan Quinn the morning of the day he was killed.

"You're sure it was Quinn she saw?" he said, wiping a dab of mustard off the side of his mouth.

"Positive," I said. "She'd talked to him once. She knew him on sight. I keep wondering what he was doing there so early. You think he was meeting Ethan?"

"I think Ethan would have mentioned that."

I lifted the top of the bun and stuck two small onion rings on top of the burger patty. "Maybe Quinn was getting another opinion on the wine," I said.

Nick shrugged, his mouth full.

"What was the old man like?" I asked, reaching for

my coffee. "Based on what everybody's said about him, I have to say he didn't sound like a very nice person."

Nick looked around for our waiter and, when he spotted the young man, held up his cup. He waited to answer my question until it had been topped up and then he leaned back in his chair with his hands wrapped around the mug. He'd demolished about three-quarters of his burger already.

"Edison Hall was a hard, rigid man," he said. "Although he wasn't quite so bad when his wife—Ethan's mom—was alive. I think I said that already."

I nodded.

"For all that, everything he did, everything was for Ethan and his grandchildren."

"You mean the wine collection."

"The old man worked hard all his life. The house had been paid for and he didn't have any debt, but he didn't have any savings, either. Stella said he got a little obsessed with leaving an inheritance after his wife was gone."

I reached over and speared another two fries from his plate. "I understand that. Gram was the same way for a while. Finally Mom and I got together and told her if she kept going without things so she could leave money to us we'd take it all and donate it to the Future of Swift Hills Coalition."

Nick laughed. "The group that wanted to build a condo development along the side ridge of the park? Didn't Isabel and my mother work on some sort of campaign against them?"

I shifted sideways in my chair and reached for my own coffee. "They did. Once Gram realized we were serious, that pretty much put an end to all her talk of leaving an inheritance."

"I told my mother that if she was foolish enough to leave anything to me I'd rent this place out and offer beer and chili to everyone as long as the money lasted."

"What did Charlotte say to that?" I asked, swiping another fry while his attention was diverted.

Nick gave a snort of laughter. "You know my mother. She told me she wanted her urn set up on the bar and to make sure Sam and the guys played 'You Can't Always Get What You Want.'"

I laughed, too. It was pretty much impossible to get the better of Charlotte.

Nick set his coffee on the table. There were two onion rings left on my plate. His hand snaked out and snatched the larger of the two.

"I saw that," I said, shaking my fork at him.

"And I saw you steal those fries," he countered.

I glared at him. "That onion ring is twice the size of the one you left for me."

Nick pressed his free hand against his chest. "Oh, I'm sorry," he said, his tone making it clear that he wasn't the slightest bit remorseful. "Would you like to share this one?" He held up his fork with the onion ring speared on the tines.

"Yes," I said. The moment the word was out of my mouth, I knew what he was going to do. But it was too late. He licked it. And smirked at me.

I definitely didn't want that onion ring anymore, so I took advantage of the moment and snagged the last french fries from his plate.

We stared at each other for a long moment like a

pair of Old West gunfighters with fast food instead of six-guns.

"Do we look as silly as I think we look?" Nick asked after a moment.

"Probably," I said.

"Truce?"

I nodded. "Truce."

I dipped the fries into the last bit of ketchup on my plate and thought about Edison Hall, determined to leave something for Ethan and his family. I straightened up in my chair. "Wait a minute," I said. "You said the house 'had been paid for.' What do you mean by 'had'?"

Nick's expression grew serious. He set his fork down and leaned an elbow on the table. "I'm sure Stella will tell Rose and her cohorts if she hasn't already, but keep this under your hat anyway, please?"

I nodded.

"Edison mortgaged the house and borrowed money against his life insurance to buy more wine."

"Aw, crap!" I exclaimed softly. "Stella told us he'd borrowed money, but I didn't know it was that bad."

"The real estate market is better here, because of the tourists, than it is in other places. Even so, once the house is sold and the bank is paid back, there won't be anything left." Nick hesitated for a moment. "Did Stella tell you about Ellie?" he asked.

"She did. So there isn't going to be any money at all for her surgery?" I tried to imagine what it would be like to have small children and be losing the ability to walk. I couldn't. "What about some kind of fund-raiser?"

Nick made a face. "Aaron told me that Ellie has a thing about taking charity. To her it's like begging."

"When people want to help, it's not begging," I said. "And even if it were, I don't see it as a bad thing."

"I know, but she does. She doesn't even want people to know there's anything wrong." He sighed. "You know, we're talking about thousands of dollars. A bake sale or two would only be a drop in the bucket."

I sighed softly. "If those bottles of wine had been the real thing . . ."

"It could have made all the difference," Nick finished. "You know, it turns out finding the people who've been putting those fakes out there had become a bit of a cause for Quinn. It's where he'd been putting most of his time and effort in the last six months. He was pretty much the best chance—maybe the only chance—to see these fakers brought to justice." He swiped a hand over his chin. "It doesn't seem fair."

It didn't, and I found myself wanting to do something about that.

Chapter 9

Nick and I spent the rest of the meal talking about the new guitars I had in the shop. More customers were coming in specifically just to see what we had and I'd even sold several, sight unseen, via the Web site. I told Nick the story behind my latest estate sale find, a beautiful Gibson guitar packed in a trunk in the hayloft of an old barn. An irate rooster, annoyed at my disturbing his "love nest" had chased me across the yard and into the porch of the old house. I'd actually had to toss the guitar to Mac as I sprinted past him.

"What kind of shape was the guitar in?" Nick asked. "If it's playable it can't have been outside that long."

"I was almost attacked by vengeful poultry and you want to know about the guitar?" I said in mock outrage.

"You're pretty good at that running thing," he said, trying and failing to hold back a smile. "The rooster never really stood a chance."

Nick dropped me off a little after eight. "I'm not on

call next week," he said as he leaned against the door-frame. "Will you be at Thursday night jam?"

"I wouldn't miss it," I said.

"Save me a seat," he said. He leaned over and kissed the top of my head and left.

Elvis wandered out from the bedroom. I bent down and picked him up. "How was your night?" I asked.

He wrinkled his nose at me.

"Liam was at Sam's with Jess."

Elvis didn't seem the slightest bit interested in that piece of information. I sighed. Who was I to judge my brother's social life when I was sitting at home talking to my cat on a Friday night?

Elvis squirmed in my arms. I set him down and he shook himself and then climbed to the top of his cat tower and looked expectantly at me. When I didn't immediately move he meowed loudly.

I knew what he wanted. The last couple of times he'd been sitting at the top of the polished wooden tower Mr. P. had made for him, I gave him a few little fish-shaped bits of kibble. Now he seemed to think he should have one every time he climbed to the top.

"You don't need any fish crackers," I said firmly. Two treats and he was already conditioned to expect one every time now.

The cat's response was to hang his head but at the same time manage to tip it to one side so his scar was clearly visible.

"Not going to work," I said, getting my laptop out of my briefcase and setting it on the counter. Since I was home I could check to see if there were any new Web site orders.

Elvis made a sound like a sigh. He stretched out on the curved platform and put one paw over his nose.

I watched him for a moment while he watched me but pretended not to. After what felt like several minutes but probably wasn't, I slipped off my stool, went into the kitchen and got him three pieces of the fish-shaped kibble.

Elvis took the paw off his nose. He sat up, sniffed his treat and then leaned over and licked my hand. "Mrrr," he said.

I leaned over so our faces were inches apart and scratched the top of his head. "I already told you, don't get used to this. We're not doing this every night."

He blinked his green eyes at me and licked his whiskers. Then he licked my nose.

I straightened up and headed back to the computer. I heard a soft "merow" behind me. "Still not doing this every night," I said without turning around.

I sat down at the counter again and looked at the screen. On a whim I pulled up my favorite search engine and looked for "counterfeit wine." I was surprised by the number of hits I got.

I spent the next half hour reading, fascinated by what I was learning. Counterfeit wine, like dealings in other types of fraud, was big business. Most of the dealers in those fake vintages had begun business as legitimate wine brokers. I read about one whose own, legitimate collection had sold at auction for close to forty million dollars.

The fact that these were oenophiles with knowledge of the wine-making business and educated palates made it easier for them. They carefully blended inexpensive wines to mimic the color, the taste and the character of some very rare and expensive vintages and decanted them into empty bottles that had once held the real thing, bottles that came from restaurants, wine-tasting events and other less reputable sources. They added counterfeit labels and even had ink stamps made to mark the corks.

It was a remarkably sophisticated con, one that someone like Edison Hall, who knew nothing at all about wine, could easily have fallen prey to. I still didn't like the way he'd cheated Teresa out of the old moose sign, but I also didn't like the way he'd been cheated, either.

Ronan Quinn, I learned, had impeccable credentials. He had a degree in chemistry and had worked and studied in France and Italy. He'd been an advocate for more tracking of legitimate wine sales. It had made him popular in some circles and from the half dozen articles I'd looked at, surprisingly unpopular in others. Just like the way I didn't always want to advertise that my supper was half a container of mint chocolate chip ice cream, wine collectors didn't always want word to get around that they'd purchased a particular rare bottle.

I straightened up and pulled both hands through my hair. Ronan Quinn's death had to be connected to Edison Hall's worthless wine collection. Nothing else made sense.

I was about to go to the store's Web site when there was a knock at the door. Elvis lifted his head, meowed loudly as if he were calling, "Come in."

"It's locked," I told him, getting up to see who was there.

It was Liam, smiling at me. "Hi," he said. He brought one hand from behind his back. He'd brought me a hot chocolate from McNamara's.

I took the cup from him and lifted the cover. It had just the amount of whipped cream that I liked on top. I narrowed my eyes at him. "Is this a bribe?" I asked. "I'm going to drink it whether it is or isn't. I'd just like to know."

"It's not a bribe," he said, shaking his head just a little. He looked over my shoulder. "Are you going to ask me in?"

"Maybe I have someone here with me," I said.

Liam laughed. "Right. Green eyes, hairy, about this big." He held up his hands about eighteen inches apart.

Right on cue Elvis meowed. We both laughed.

"C'mon in," I said, moving to one side to let him pass. "Although I want it on the record that it's Friday night and you're hanging out with your sister."

He made a face at me. "Touché." He pulled off his jacket, tossed it over the arm of the couch and then dropped down onto the sofa. "Hey, I'm sorry I didn't call you back."

Elvis jumped down from the cat tower and padded over. He launched himself up and settled next to Liam. The two had been great buddies from the first time Liam visited after I got Elvis. Liam claimed it was a guy thing. Sometimes I thought he was right.

Liam reached over and began to stroke the cat's fur. "I was headed down to Sam's after my meeting and I swear I was going to call you. Then I met Jess and we started talking and I just . . . forgot."

I looked at Elvis. He was purring, a contented look on his face. As far as he was concerned, Liam was telling the truth. It was good enough for me.

I sat down on the stool again, pulled the top off the hot chocolate and took a sip. It was delicious, as usual. I'd tried more than once to wheedle the secret of his hot chocolate out of Glenn McNamara, but he'd just laugh and say, "If I told you I'd have to kill you or marry you."

I wiped a smidge of whipped cream from my upper lip.

Liam looked at me and grinned. "So, am I forgiven?"

"I haven't decided," I said.

"How about I take you out for breakfast tomorrow?"

Elvis licked his whiskers at the word "breakfast."

"You've always been my favorite brother," I said.

"I'm your only brother," he retorted.

"Then things worked out pretty well for you." I smiled at him over the top of the take-out cup.

Liam slid down a little on the sofa so he was sitting mostly on his tailbone and yawned.

"So, how was your meeting?"

"Not as long as I expected. I think the people on the ground here are going to be pretty easy to work with."

I leaned back against the counter. "You said you're going to be evaluating the properties the developers are interested in buying."

He nodded.

"But I thought everything in those whole two blocks was going to be torn down."

Elvis had stretched out beside Liam, his front paws on Liam's lap. Liam was still absently stroking his black fur. "Oh, that's still the plan," he said, scratching the golden stubble on his chin with his other hand.

"My job, for the most part, is to see what can be salvaged and reused," he continued. "That kind of thing adds character to the new buildings, and there are financial benefits as well."

"Remember me telling you about the chandelier we bought when Doran's in Portland closed?" I asked, swirling the contents of my cup so the last bit of whipped cream mixed into the cocoa.

Liam nodded. "You were going to sell it to Jon West for the hotel in the old North by West project."

"Right." I leaned forward again. The edge of the counter was digging into my back. "The short version of the story is that after the North by West deal fell apart we were going to sell it to a builder who was working on a restaurant in Bangor and that fell through as well."

"Don't tell me you sold it to Jason Cavanaugh?" Liam said. Jason Cavanaugh owned Seaward Properties, the developer behind the new harbor-front development proposal.

I nodded. "Mac did, actually. Assuming the sale goes through."

Elvis rolled over onto his back and Liam shifted his hand and began scratching his furry black chest. The purring got louder.

"So, how's it working out with Mac living over the shop?"

I drank the last of the hot chocolate and set the cup behind me on the counter.

"It's working out really well," I said.

It was Avery who had originally suggested that we

renovate the extra space upstairs that we used for storage, into a tiny apartment for Mac. I was putting the rent he was paying into paying down the mortgage my grandmother held on the building a little faster.

Liam gave me a sly smile. "So, anything going on with you two?" he asked.

I made a face. "No. Anything going on with you and Jess?"

He wasn't at all perturbed at my question. "No," he said. "Not yet, anyway."

"Liam, Jess is my best friend," I began.

He held up a hand. "You don't have to give me the speech," he said. "We were just having dinner." He folded his arm behind his head. "Are you going to give Jess the speech about not breaking *my* heart?"

I shook my head. "I don't need to. I have no idea how she does it, but she's managed to stay friendly with everyone she's gone out with. And no one has said she'd go out with you, anyway."

Liam looked around. "So, what are you doing here on a Friday night?"

"I live here," I said.

"You know what I mean," he said. "You work too much. I saw Rose and her gentleman friend earlier. She has more of a love life than you do and she's more than twice your age."

"I know," I said. "Mr. P. is crazy about her. When she got kicked out of Legacy Place, he wanted her to move in with him. He even proposed."

"I take it Rose said no?"

"Uh-huh. That's how she ended up here, although I have to say that's worked out pretty well, too."

"It's probably kept you from starving to death," Liam said. He gave Elvis one last belly scratch and got to his feet. He came over to me, leaned against the end of the counter and put an arm around my shoulder. As usual he smelled liked baby powder. "Why don't you lay a big wet one on ol' Nick? Or if he doesn't float your boat, on Mac? This all-work-and-no-play stuff has gotta be dull."

I poked him with my elbow, but all he did was laugh.

"I can't do that," I said. "Not that I want to anyway. What if things didn't work out? Mac works for me and so does Charlotte. How messy could that get?"

"Yeah, blah, blah, blah," Liam said. He leaned in and kissed my cheek and then headed for the door.

"My life is not dull," I called after him. Saying that out loud was probably just tempting fate.

Chapter 10

I thought Liam had forgotten that he'd said he'd buy me breakfast, but he knocked on my door about twenty-five after seven the next morning. We drove over to McNamara's and after he and Glenn had talked about the Red Sox we spent the rest of the meal talking about the new harbor-front development proposal. I dropped him back at the house and picked up Elvis and the clothes I was going to wear out to lunch before I headed for the shop.

Michelle pulled in behind me in the store's lot. Elvis jumped down from the seat and instead of heading for the back door walked over to her. I followed.

Michelle leaned forward and held out her hand to Elvis. "Good morning," she said.

He sniffed her with curiosity and then rubbed his cheek against her fingers. She began to stroke his fur and he seemed to smile at her.

Michelle looked up at me and smiled. "Hi, Sarah," she said. "I just came by to let you know we released the

Hall house. You'll probably hear from Stella sometime today."

My phone buzzed then. "Excuse me a second," I said, pulling it out of my pocket. It was Stella with the news Michelle had just given me. She wanted us to get back to work as soon as we could.

"I think we might be able to get there this morning," I said.

"Thank you, Sarah," she said. "If you find anything that . . . might be worth something . . ."

"I'll call you first thing," I promised.

Michelle talked to Elvis while I was talking to Stella. When I ended the call she gave the cat one last scratch on the top of his head and straightened up. He meowed softly at her and started across the parking lot toward the back door.

"That was Stella, as you probably guessed," I said.

She nodded. "You're going to start again this morning?"

I slid the strap of my carryall up on my shoulder. "I'm going to try. I promised Stella we'd get the place cleaned out as quickly as we could once you were done."

She gave me a thoughtful look. "Stella told you about Ellie."

I sighed softly. "About the operation? Yes, she did."

"Any chance there're some valuable antiques in that house?"

I gave her a wry smile. "I don't think so. Mac and I did a walk-through before we said yes to Stella, and nothing we saw looked like it was worth much. We didn't see everything, though, so maybe we'll get lucky."

"I hope so," she said. Her expression changed. "If you find any more bottles of wine, will you call me, please?"

"Of course," I said. I studied her face for a moment. "Michelle, do you think that wine collection had anything to do with Ronan Quinn's death?"

She shrugged. "Right now everything's a possibility. And we're looking into the fraud as a separate case."

"I'm glad to hear that," I said. "Whoever took advantage of Edison Hall like that is despicable."

She stuffed her hands in the pockets of her black jacket. "You'd be surprised how many scams there are that target seniors. I don't mean small potatoes, either. These are sophisticated cons."

I nodded, remembering what I'd read the night before about faking the bottles of wine and how those fakes had fooled more than one expert.

"I'd like to put together an information session for people," Michelle said. "Just to go over some of the more popular cons out there. Do you think Rose and Alfred Peterson would be willing to get involved?"

"Yes," I said slowly. I wasn't sure exactly what to say next.

Michelle smiled as though she could read my mind. Or maybe it was my face that was giving me away.

"You're thinking I'm crazy," she said.

I shifted from one foot to the other. "No," I said. "Not crazy. Just . . ." I hesitated. "Okay, yes. Crazy. But just a little."

Michelle smiled. "You know what they're like, Rose, Nick's mom, Alfred Peterson. Do you really think they're going to listen to me telling them about the Big Bad Wolf?"

"No," I said.

"But they will listen to their friends, people their own age." She rolled her eyes. "And I'm sure Mr. Peterson has come across a scam or two during his travels down the information superhighway."

I laughed. "I'm guessing Nick told you that Mr. P. is a licensed private investigator now."

"I already knew," Michelle said with a smile. "He did tell me that Stella hired them to look into Mr. Quinn's death." She pulled her cell phone out of her pocket, glanced at it and put it back again. "Rose called me yesterday and told me about Teresa Reynard seeing Quinn at the house the morning he died. It gives us more of a window around when he was killed."

"Do you think he was there to meet someone about the wine collection?"

She opened her mouth, but I spoke again before she could. "I know, you can't answer that."

"I have to get going, Sarah," she said. "Be careful and if you find anything at the house call me or even Nick."

"I will," I said. I hugged her and headed for the back door. Elvis was waiting, not very patiently. He made a huffy noise as I unlocked the door, stalking through the workroom, the tip of his tail flicking back and forth.

Mac's feet were sticking out of the storage space under the stairs. Elvis meowed at him and then poked his head in the opening next to him.

"Sarah, are you there?" Mac's muffled voice asked.

"I'm here," I said. "What are you looking for?"

"That little box of glass doorknobs."

"Top shelf on the right at the back out in the garage."

Elvis pulled his head back and shook himself. A couple of dust bunnies floated to the floor. He batted at one with his paw before stopping to wash one side of his face.

Mac backed out of the slanted storage space and stood up, brushing dust off the front of his long-sleeved blue T-shirt. Another dust bunny, cousin probably to the ones that had been clinging to Elvis's fur, was on his shoulder. I leaned over and brushed it away. "I think I should get Avery to run the vacuum in there," I said.

"Good idea," Mac said. "I think the dust bunnies may be amassing an army so they can try to take over the building."

"Michelle was here and the police have released the Hall house. Do you think we could get out there today?"

He smoothed a hand over his hair. "I don't see why not. But don't you and Liz have that lunch thing with the former bank manager?"

I held up the garment bag that I was carrying. "We do, but not until one o'clock."

Mac pushed a box back into the storage area with one foot. "Do you want me to call Rose and see if she can come with us?"

"Please," I said. "Charlotte and Avery should be able to handle things here for the morning. I'm just going to put this stuff in my office." I started up the stairs.

I thought about Liam's suggestion to make a move

on Mac as I hung up the garment bag. It was a really bad idea. He was more than my employee, he was my right hand and my friend. I wasn't willing to do anything to mess that up.

"It would make more sense to get involved with Nick," I said.

Elvis stopped washing his chest and looked at me, green eyes narrowed almost as though he'd understood my words and wanted to know if I was kidding or serious.

"I don't mean I would," I said. "If Nick and I were going out, both Charlotte and Gram would be picking out baby names." The image of Nick holding a baby popped into my mind.

The mental picture was so funny I laughed out loud. I'd actually seen it happen a few weeks previous when Nick and I went to meet Jess at her shop before Thursday night jam. One of the paramedics he'd worked with when he was an EMT was in the shop and somehow, before he knew what was happening, Nick was holding her little girl. The eight-month-old had looked befuddled and Nick had looked terrified, holding her out as if she were a bag of snakes.

My cell phone rang then. It was Jess. Elvis was settled in my desk chair having another bath. The cat had a bit of a fetish about being clean, even for a cat. I dropped onto the love seat.

"Hi," Jess said. "Are you going to be at the shop all morning? I have a new bootie design I want to show you."

"Sorry," I said. "I'm going out to the Hall house."

"Drat!" Jess was the only person I'd ever met who could say that and not sound silly.

"Was that all you wanted?" I asked.

There was silence for a moment and then she said, "So it was weird, me having dinner with Liam last night?"

"No . . . Maybe." I let out a breath. "It's just that Liam is my brother. And you and I have always talked about the guys we were dating."

"*We* were dating?" Jess said. I could hear an edge of laughter in her voice.

"We," I repeated. "Although mostly you lately."

Jess did laugh then. "I'm not dating Liam, but would you be okay if I wanted to?"

I couldn't say no and I realized that I didn't really want to. "Yes, I would be okay."

"Then if it happens you'll be the first to know."

"Just maybe with a little less detail than usual," I said.

Jess laughed again. "I promise."

We said good-bye, and I grabbed my stainless steel travel mug and laced up my work boots. Then I pulled on my old paint-spattered sweatshirt.

"You're in charge," I told Elvis.

"Mrrr," he said without looking up from the knot he was working out of his tail.

Charlotte had arrived when I got downstairs and Avery was bringing out the vacuum cleaner.

"Hey, Sarah, you want me to make a list of what's under there?" she asked, pointing at the storage space with the end of the vacuum cleaner.

"Yes," I said. "There's a list taped to the wall just inside the door on the left, but it's really out of date."

Avery smiled. "Okay. I got this." She looked at my

coffee mug. "I could make you a smoothie some morning, you know, for a change."

Avery was trying to get Liz to eat healthier. Liz, whose blood pressure, blood sugar and cholesterol were amazingly low for a woman her age, was quite happy with the way she'd been eating. "If the good Lord had wanted me to eat tofu, he would have made it less disgusting," she liked to say.

On the other hand, some of Avery's stir-fries and drink concoctions looked pretty good.

"Okay," I said.

She looked around uncertainly. "Really?"

I nodded. "Yeah, really."

A smile stretched across her face. "Cool."

Mac was at the cash desk. "We can pick Rose up in fifteen minutes if that works for you."

"It does," I said. "By the time we get what we need and drive down to get her, it'll be fifteen minutes."

"I'll start loading boxes," he said.

I walked over to Charlotte. "Good morning, sweetie," she said. She was wearing a bright blue apron over her skirt and sweater. Nick had her eyes and her smile.

I put my arm around her shoulder. "Avery is going to clean under the stairs and do inventory. Could you freshen up the front window?"

"Of course," she said. "And Liz asked me to remind you about lunch."

"I haven't forgotten," I said. "My dress is upstairs." I raised an eyebrow. "And let me guess—she also told you to tell me to show some leg."

"Let's just say among other things, and leave it at that," Charlotte said, giving me a hug.

I laughed.

"I'd love to tell you she's wrong about Channing Caulfield," she began.

"But she's not," I finished.

The always pragmatic Charlotte shook her head. "No, she's not. And he didn't get where he is because he's a softie."

"Liz will eat him for lunch," I said.

Charlotte smiled again. "My money's on her."

I patted the pocket of my jeans. "Phone's on and I'll be back in time to change," I said.

Rose was standing at the bottom of the driveway when I pulled up to the house, carrying one of her big totes as usual. She climbed into the backseat. "Good morning, dear. Good morning, Mac," she said. She smiled at Elvis, who was sniffing the bag she'd set next to him on the seat. "Good morning, Elvis," she added.

I smiled at her in the rearview mirror. "Good morning, Rose," I said. "Thanks for coming."

"Oh, you're welcome," she said as she fastened her seat belt. "I know how important this is to Stella."

Mac turned in his seat. "Hi, Rose," he said. He looked at me. "So, are we still going to work the same way?"

I nodded as I pulled away from the curb. "Uh-huh. We'll start in the kitchen and work out to the front of the house. Remember, Stella wants the dishes."

He nodded.

"And those colored Pyrex bowls," Rose added.

Mac and Rose talked about our plan of attack as we drove out to the house. Elvis watched them both as though he were actually following the conversation.

As I pulled in to the driveway I glanced over at Paul

Duvall's house on the other side of the street. There was no sign of him or his daughter.

"Want to check things out before we start lugging in boxes?" Mac asked.

"I do," I said.

We all got out of the SUV. Rose carried Elvis. I unlocked the front door and stepped inside the house. Rose set Elvis down in the entryway. He sniffed the air and wrinkled his nose at me.

I could smell bleach. Stella had told me on the phone she'd wiped up the kitchen floor. It was better than the scent of blood and death that had been here before.

I hesitated for a minute, remembering Ronan Quinn's body crumpled on the floor. Mac gave my shoulder a squeeze and eased past me as if he could read my mind. He stepped into the living room and looked around. "We're taking that bookcase, aren't we?" he asked, pointing at a tall, glass-fronted set of shelves to the left of the big window overlooking the street. It was piled with stacks of old newspapers and issues of *National Geographic*.

"Yes," I said, walking over to join him. "Along with the sideboard and the hutch." I pointed to the heavy wooden pieces against the end wall. "And a friend of Mr. P. wants to buy all those *Geographic*s."

"You're kidding?" Mac said.

Elvis had started for the kitchen with Rose. She turned to look at Mac. "Oh no," she said. "Elwood and his brother, Jake, have a little side business selling old books and magazines. They'll take every one of those *Geographic*s and keep your eyes peeled for any copies of *The Saturday Evening Post*. Elwood will take those, too."

"Elwood and Jake?" Mac whispered. "The Blues Brothers? She's messing with me, isn't she?"

I grinned at him. "It's Rose, Mac. There's no way to know for sure."

We followed Rose and Elvis out to the small kitchen. The smell of bleach was stronger. Elvis walked around gingerly sniffing the boxes piled by the windows where a table and chairs should have been. "That's the wine," I said. "It stays where it is."

"Got it," Mac said. He and Rose were already walking around looking in the cupboards. Rose would pack the dishes Stella wanted to keep while Mac did an inventory of everything else on his iPad so we'd know what we had when it came time to have the in-house estate sale I was planning.

"I'm going to do a walk-around," I said.

Mac waved at me over his shoulder. I walked back out to the living room. Along with the pieces of furniture, there were a couple of framed paintings that I was taking back to the shop to sell on commission for Stella. I hoped to get more money for them by putting them on our Web site.

Elvis wandered out from the kitchen. "Let's go take a look in the bedrooms," I said.

We went down the tiny hallway. The master bedroom was the starkest room in the house with just a double bed and two dressers. Someone—Stella probably—had long since taken Edison Hall's clothes. The room had an air of sadness about it. I'd noticed a couple of blankets folded at the end of the living room sofa the first time I was in the house. I suspected Edison Hall had been sleeping there and not in this room.

The next bedroom was almost as large as the master and it was jammed full of stuff. If there was logic or a pattern to what was stored there, I couldn't see it. At least most of the stuff was in boxes. The downside was that none of them were marked. I looked in the top of one of them. It held six cans of Spam and a large jug of water. Supplies in case of a natural disaster? I wondered. I carried the box out into the living room so I could go through it to see if the food had expired.

I stepped back into the room in time to see Elvis jump onto the seat of a low rocking chair, balance and leap from there to some boxes.

"Hey! Where are you going?" I said.

He meowed at me and started making his way across the stacked cartons. I reached for him, but he was already more than an arm's length away. He turned and looked over his shoulder at me and then jumped down, out of sight, onto a lower pile of boxes. To the right there looked to be just enough space to squeeze around the piles and get the cat.

The boxes had a musty smell about them and the room was full of dust. I sneezed as I lifted a garbage bag out of my way and dust motes rose in the air. "I hope you're not back there with anything that has fur and a long tail," I muttered.

Eventually I worked my way to the back wall of the room. Elvis was sitting on the window ledge. I had dust in my nose, on my shirt and—I was pretty sure—in my hair. There didn't seem to be a speck of it on Elvis's sleek black fur. In fact, he almost looked smug. On the window-sill next to him sat what looked to me to be an old model train engine. I picked it up while the cat watched me.

The steam cylinder was painted a dark brown with the word ROCKET stenciled on the side in gold letters. A black stack of a smaller diameter rose maybe four inches above it. The only model train items I recognized were Lionel, and I knew this wasn't.

"Let's go ask Mac about this," I said to Elvis.

His response was to launch himself onto the nearest stack of boxes. The flaps were folded down, not taped shut, and Elvis pawed at one edge.

"Leave that alone," I said sharply.

He completely ignored me, scratching at the edge of cardboard again.

"Fine," I said. "I'll look, but if anything in there is alive I'm tossing you inside and closing the lid."

"Mrrr," he said, and it almost seemed as if he shrugged.

I set the train engine back on the window ledge and gingerly opened the box. As soon as I'd pulled the flaps apart, Elvis was poking his nose inside.

"Let me see," I said. I couldn't hear any noises that suggested anything had set up home in the carton.

Inside the box I found four more train cars. They looked to be the right size and vintage to go with the steam engine.

"Nice work," I said to Elvis. He blinked his green eyes at me, then began making his way toward the door.

I picked up the engine again and squeezed through the maze of boxes and bags. I left the box with the other train cars behind. I knew I couldn't squeeze through the narrow space if I was carrying it.

Elvis was already headed to the kitchen, so I followed him. Rose was humming softly while she wrapped a china cereal bowl in newspaper and Mac was standing in front of the large pantry cupboard typing on his iPad.

"Mac, do you know anything about model trains?" I asked, holding up the engine Elvis and I had found.

"Not really," he said. "Is it Lionel?"

I shook my head. "No. It's old, whatever it is. I think it might be a replica of some kind of steam engine." I showed him the word ROCKET lettered on the side of the cylinder.

Rose tucked the paper wrapped bowl into a box at her feet and joined us. "Alfred knows a little about model trains," she said. "Would you like me to call him?" She pulled her cell phone out of her pocket and held it up.

Mac looked at me and shrugged.

"Why not?" I said.

Mac took the engine from me, turning it over carefully in his hands. "It looks old, but it's in decent shape. Where did you find it?"

"That little bedroom, the one that's piled with stuff."

Elvis meowed loudly and jumped up onto the only kitchen chair that didn't have a box on it.

"I'm sorry," I said, "it was actually Elvis who found it. And there's a box with several cars that I think probably go with it."

Rose was nodding at her phone. She ended the call and rejoined us. "Alfred thinks it may be a Marklin engine," she said. "Could we take a photo and send it to him?"

Mac cleared a space on the counter. He set the engine down and Rose snapped a picture of it. It might have been another minute after she sent it to Mr. P. that her phone rang.

"What do you think?" Rose asked. She listened for a moment. "Oh, that would be lovely." She looked at me and held out the phone. "Alfred would like to speak to you."

I took it from her. "Good morning," I said.

"Good morning, Sarah," Mr. P. replied. "Rose said you found some additional train cars. Could you describe them to me?"

I shared what I remembered from my brief look inside the box.

"Splendid," Mr. P. exclaimed.

"Does that mean you know what this engine is?" I asked.

"I believe I do," he said, and I could hear an edge of excitement in his voice. "I think what you have is a Marklin S Rocket, which is a replica of Stephenson's Rocket, one of the most advanced steam locomotives of the early eighteen hundreds. It wasn't a big seller in its day for Marklin. A complete set with all the cars would be a very rare find. It sounds as though that's what you have."

I looked at the tin engine. "Does rare equal valuable?"

"Indeed it does, at least in this case. The last set, minus one car, sold for more than twenty-five thousand dollars about eighteen months ago."

"So this set could be worth more than that?" I said.

"To a collector, yes," he said. "And I should caution you that I'm no expert on this kind of thing. You need to get the train evaluated by someone who knows model trains."

"I will," I said. "Thank you."

"You're welcome, my dear," he said.

I handed the phone back to Rose.

"You're smiling," Mac said.

I crossed my arms over my chest and leaned against the rounded edge of the counter. "If Mr. P. is right, that engine and the train cars I saw in the box could be worth twenty-five thousand dollars."

"Wow."

I smiled even wider at him. "Exactly."

By noon Rose and I had packed all the dishes that were going to Stella, and Mac had finished the kitchen inventory.

"I'll check with Stella about getting these boxes moved before the estate sale," I said to Mac, indicating the cartons of wine. "Unless they turn out to be evidence."

"What do you mean, evidence?" he said.

"Michelle told me that the police are looking into the fraud with the wine," I said quietly.

"As part of this investigation or as something separate?"

"Both," Rose said, looking up from the box she was taping shut.

"How do you know that?" I said, rubbing a knot out of the back of my neck with one hand.

Rose looked at me unblinkingly. It was disconcertingly like the look Elvis often gave me.

I shook my head. "This falls into the category of things I'd probably be happier not knowing, doesn't it?"

Rose just smiled.

"Do you know how Edison Hall got interested in

collecting wine in the first place?" Mac asked. "Did Stella say anything about it?"

"Not to me," I said. I looked inquiringly at Rose.

She shook her head. "She didn't say anything to me, either."

Mac raised an eyebrow. "That might be useful information to have," he said.

Rose nodded slowly. "Yes, it might," she said. She glanced at her watch. "Sarah dear, don't you need to get back and get ready for your lunch date?"

I straightened up. "Yes, I do. Are you two coming back here after lunch? I don't need the SUV."

"I brought lunch for the two of us," Rose said, smiling at Mac and tipping her head in the direction of her tote bag sitting on the one bare space on the counter. "We could just stay here and you could come back for us."

Mac shrugged. "Fine with me."

"Why don't you drive me down to the shop?" I said to him. "Then when you're ready, you and Rose can leave. I have no idea how long this lunch of Liz's is going to take."

"Do you mind staying here by yourself?" he said to Rose. "It won't take me very long to drive Sarah back to the shop."

Elvis meowed loudly and it seemed to me, just a bit indignantly.

"As Elvis just pointed out, I won't be by myself," Rose said with a smile. "Go ahead. I'll start packing up those *National Geographic* magazines while you're gone."

Rose seemed to have an unlimited amount of energy. She could work someone half her age under the table.

"There are a couple of plastic bins in the living room," Mac said. "You can use those, but don't lift them. I'll move them when I get back."

"All right," she said in the tone of someone who was just humoring him. She patted my arm as she passed me. "Don't let Liz get off-topic, dear," she said. "You know how she can be."

"I'll do my best," I said, pulling down my shirt-sleeves. "But I'm not promising anything, because I *do* know how she can be."

"I'm just going to grab the toolbox," Mac said as we pulled in to the lot at the store. "I think I'm going to have to take the hutch and the sideboard apart."

"Put in a couple more hours and call it a day. I'll be back . . . when I'm back."

"All right," he said. Then he smiled. "Good luck with Liz."

"Thanks," I said. "I think finding that model train was a good omen."

Of course I was wrong.

Chapter 11

Liz was standing by the front door talking to Charlotte when I came down the stairs. I was wearing the dress Charlotte had suggested with heels that were probably too high and lipstick that was probably too red.

Liz looked at me and made a circular motion with her index finger. "Twirl."

I did a slow pirouette for her.

"Perfect," she said.

"You look lovely," Charlotte said with a smile.

I stuck out one foot. "Are these shoes too much?" I asked.

Liz gave a snort of laughter. "No, they're not. Those shoes make a statement."

"I'm just a little nervous about what they're saying."

One perfectly groomed eyebrow went up. "What they're saying is 'Look at these legs,' which is exactly what I want them to say and exactly want I want Channing Caulfield to do. While he's distracted by you, I can get the answers I'm looking for."

"That's rather sexist, Liz," Charlotte said.

Liz nodded. "Of course. It's totally sexist. So is Channing Caulfield. That's why it's going to work." She looked at Charlotte. "Don't shake your head at me, Charlotte Elliot. You know I'm right." She held her car keys out to me.

Charlotte tried to hide a smile but wasn't quite successful.

"Mac and Rose will be back in a couple of hours. I'll be back when Liz is finished dangling me in front of Mr. Caulfield like I'm a fly and he's a trout."

Liz laughed and put her arm around my shoulders. "Okay, Sarah," she said. "Let's go dangle you in the water and see what we can catch."

I looked back over my shoulder and waved at Charlotte.

"Where are we going?" I asked as I slid behind the wheel of Liz's car.

"The Hearthstone Inn."

"Fancy."

"It's all about setting the right atmosphere," she said, smoothing the skirt of her black suit over her knees.

"And what reason did you give Mr. Caulfield for inviting him to lunch?" I asked as I pulled onto the street.

"We're both interested in the new development proposal for the harbor front. I'm thinking of investing some of the Emmerson Foundation's portfolio and you're thinking of moving your business."

I shot a quick glance in her direction. "Will he buy that?"

Liz nodded. "Yes. Channing was—is—very good

at his job. I've talked to him several times about investments over the years. He's always given me excellent advice."

I stopped at the corner, waited for traffic to pass and then turned left. "Is Rose right?" I asked, keeping my eyes on the road. "Is Mr. Caulfield interested in you?"

"How would I know that?" Liz retorted.

I stifled a smile. "So that would be yes."

She didn't say anything.

"Have you perchance been putting up with Mr. Channing's ongoing interest in you because of his excellent advice?" I asked.

"Perchance?" Liz said, an edge of sarcasm in her voice.

"It's a perfectly valid word."

"If you're Shakespeare."

I sent another quick glance in her direction. "You're avoiding the question."

"I'm not avoiding it. It was such a preposterous question I didn't see the point in answering it."

"So that would be another yes."

There was silence for a moment; then Liz laughed. "You've been spending way too much time with Rose, missy," she said.

I nodded, keeping my eyes on the road. "Guilty as charged."

Out of the corner of my eye, I saw Liz shift a little in her seat. "When I took over the Emmerson Foundation, do you know how much money was actually going to programs?" she asked.

We were almost at the inn. I slowed down and put on my blinker. "Since you're asking the question, I'm guessing not enough."

"Fifty-four percent."

"Ouch."

"Expenses were ridiculous, especially our investment costs," she said. "I hired Channing to rebalance the foundation's portfolio, and his guidance helped us get through downturns in the market. His expertise was worth every cent we paid him. And by the way, he donated half the money back to the foundation."

I pulled in to the driveway of the Hearthstone Inn.

"Last year we spent eighty-eight percent of our funds on programming," Liz continued. "Channing Caulfield had a lot to do with that. And just to be clear, I offered to pay for his time today. He turned me down. I'm sending him a box of his favorite cigars even though I think they smell like burning tires."

I backed the car into a parking spot and turned to look at Liz. "Have I told you lately that I love you to pieces?"

She gave a dismissive wave with a manicured hand. "Everybody does," she said. "Let's get this show on the road."

We were shown to a table near the center of the main dining room at the inn. Silverware gleamed against the crisp white napkins and pale blue tablecloth. Liz had timed our arrival so we'd be at the table when Channing Caulfield arrived.

He was right on time. After I'd agreed to join Liz on this luncheon fishing expedition, I did some online research on Caulfield. He was a self-made man who'd gone to college on scholarship when he was sixteen.

Channing Caulfield was of average height, although he walked with the presence and confidence of a much larger man. He had silver hair—lots of it—combed back from his face, a ready smile and blue eyes that it seemed petty to call beady, although that was the first thought that came to my mind.

Liz got to her feet as he reached the table.

"Liz, it's good to see you," he said, leaning in to kiss her cheek. "You look beautiful, as always."

"Thank you for coming," she said. She turned and smiled at me. "This is Isabel's granddaughter, Sarah Grayson."

He inclined his head in my direction. "Please call me Channing," he said. "It's a pleasure to meet you, Sarah. How's your grandmother?"

"She's well, thank you," I said.

Liz made small talk while we looked at our menus and ordered. I took advantage of the opportunity to study Caulfield. He was very much a gentleman— smooth, polished and polite. I noticed that he was watching us and everything else that was going on in the restaurant's dining room.

I had no doubt that this was the man Teresa had seen watching Edison Hall's house the morning Ronan Quinn died. The hair was right, and so were the eyes and the slight jowls along his jawline. As he smiled pleasantly across the table at me, I had the sudden urge to lean over and ask him directly what he'd been doing that morning. Then I remembered that the whole reason I'd come along was to stop Liz from doing something exactly like that.

Caulfield added cream to the coffee our waiter had brought. I noticed that he didn't have the soft, smooth hands you'd expect to see with someone who had worked in an office. His were lined with prominent joints. "So you're interested in the harbor-front development from an investment perspective?" he said, directing his question at Liz.

She nodded, reaching for her tea. "If this proposal comes to pass, those two buildings we own the mortgages on will be sold. I've been thinking about putting some of that money back into the development. Seaward Properties is still looking for investors."

"Have you read their prospectus?" he asked.

"I have," Liz said. "It looks solid, but I know very little about Jason Cavanaugh himself."

I let them talk while I watched and listened and marveled at how knowledgeable Liz was. I suspected she could easily have turned the Emmerson Foundation's finances around without Channing Caulfield's help.

When our food arrived Caulfield turned to me. "I'm sorry, Sarah," he said. "I've been ignoring you."

"No, you haven't," I said. "I've learned a lot listening to you and Liz talk." I smiled at the waiter who had just refilled my cup.

"You're interested in moving your business downtown if the development goes through?"

"I've heard the pitch and I have the proposal."

He narrowed his blue eyes. "What's making you hesitate?"

"The cost. And parking. We get a fair amount of business from tour buses. They can pull off the highway and reach our current location easily. And right now I have a pretty big parking lot."

Caulfield unfolded his napkin and placed it in his lap. "Right now you're a destination shop. If you move your business you'll be one of many businesses in the same area competing for customers."

I smiled and nodded. Out of the corner of my eye, I saw Liz doing the same. He was sharp. "Yes," I said. "I'm not convinced the increased volume of people walking by our door will offset the increased competition for dollars in the same area."

"What's your weekly customer volume during the tourist season?" he asked.

I glanced at Liz, who nodded. I gave Caulfield the number. He frowned, holding up one hand as he did some kind of mental math.

My fish cakes were only half gone before he determined that moving Second Chance didn't make sense. It was the same conclusion I'd come to when I originally considered the idea, back when North by West was behind the harbor-front development idea, but it was nice to have confirmation of my calculations.

"You're going to be clearing out Edison Hall's property, aren't you?" Caulfield asked, raising a finger in the direction of our waiter, who seemed to appear at the table with a full cream pitcher almost by magic.

"We started this morning," I said, putting a little more spicy salsa on my plate. It was so good I could have just eaten it with a spoon directly from the little glass bowl, but Mom and Gram had taught me better manners than that. And I wasn't sure that Liz wouldn't smack me with her own fork if I tried it.

"If you come across a train layout, would you call me?" he asked.

"You mean a model train?" I said. I knew that he did, but I was stalling. He had to be talking about the steam engine and cars Elvis and I had found just a few hours ago. Interesting coincidence.

"What would Edison Hall have been doing with a toy train?" Liz asked. Under the table her hand squeezed my knee, her way of telling me, *Don't say anything!*

I put my hand on top of hers to let her know I'd gotten her message.

"Model train, Liz, not a child's toy," Caulfield said.

"There's a difference?" Liz said, raising her eyebrows.

"Yes, there is," I said, gently squeezing her hand. I wasn't going to give anything away, but I wasn't going to let this chance to ask questions slip by. "Model railroading is a very popular hobby. People collect engines and cars, build layouts with track and scenery and run their trains."

"So you think Edison Hall was into model railroading?" There was an edge of skepticism in Liz's voice.

Aside from the Marklin engine and cars, there didn't seem to be anything in the house to suggest the old man had been a hobbyist. There was no track, no layouts. I wondered if the pieces were part of another collection. Along with the stacks of *National Geographic* magazines in the house, there were dozens of blue glass electrical insulators in the garage and what looked to be maybe half a dozen weather vanes in the backyard. I suspected that Edison Hall was a man with the collector gene.

"I know he was into model railroading," Caulfield said, setting down his fork. "Years ago we were in a train club together."

"You're joking," Liz said.

He gave her his smooth smile. "No, I'm not. My father worked for the Maine Central Railroad. And Edison was a railroad man himself." He turned back to me. "I don't know if you know very much about model trains, Sarah."

"I recognize Lionel," I said. "That's about it."

"I'm looking for a steam engine and several cars made by a German company named Marklin."

It was too big a coincidence. Caulfield must have realized we'd find the model train cars pretty quickly. I suspected that was why he'd said yes to Liz's lunch invitation so easily and not just for the chance to charm her.

"I'm sure Ethan would be willing to sell you whatever you're interested in from Edison's collection, that's assuming we find one." I didn't like to lie, but since we hadn't found a collection yet, I told myself I wasn't. For the most part.

I speared the last bite of fish cake, dipped it in the salsa and ate it.

Then Caulfield said, "The model train I'm looking for is mine."

"So, what was Edison doing with a toy train belonging to you?" Liz asked. Our waiter appeared at her side then with a fresh pot of tea. I had no idea how he knew she needed a refill. I hadn't seen her so much as lift a finger—or an eyebrow.

Caulfield smiled, shifted sideways in his chair and crossed one gray-suited leg over the other. "Years ago I bought a steam engine and several cars from another member of the train club—Duncan Merriman. Edison also bought some pieces from him." He glanced toward the front window for a moment. "Merriman was in the early stages of dementia."

"He sold the same train to both of you," I said.

He nodded. "Yes. It was part of a club layout. When I went to get it I discovered that Edison had beaten me to it."

"But you had a receipt." The steam rose from the china teapot as Liz poured more tea.

Channing Caulfield laughed and ducked his head. "The fact that you're asking me that question tells me you know I didn't."

Liz raised her eyebrows over her cup but didn't say anything.

"What happened?" I asked.

"Edison asked me the same question Liz just did. When I couldn't show him a receipt, he gave me some nonsense about possession being nine-tenths of the law."

"The Hatfields and McCoys," Liz murmured.

"We'd been . . ." He paused, searching for the right word. ". . . discussing the issue for years. Last year Edison told me he wanted to make a layout for his grandchildren. He offered me a bottle of wine from his collection. I agreed. It seemed as though things were settled satisfactorily."

"Then you found out that Edison's entire wine collection was worthless," I said.

"Including the bottle he'd given me." Caulfield gave me a wry smile. "It was all just by chance really. I was in McNamara's and I recognized Quinn from the article in the *Boston Globe*. We started talking. He told me he was looking into another case of fraud, here in town. He didn't say who, but after he left Glenn McNamara said Quinn had been hired to appraise Edison Hall's wine collection. I put two and two together."

Liz tipped her head to one side and regarded him thoughtfully for a moment. "I don't suppose you happened to use that bottle to kill Ethan Hall's wine expert, did you?" she asked.

"Liz," I groaned.

The former bank manager didn't seem the slightest bit ruffled. "No," he said. "What would that have accomplished?"

Liz had crossed her own legs and one high-heeled foot bobbed up and down. "I don't know," she said. "And I'm not saying you did kill the man, I'm just asking if you did." She smiled at him, and I could see why Channing Caulfield, and men half his age for that matter, was captivated by her. She'd just accused Caulfield of killing someone and he wasn't at all offended. Of course she was showing a lot of leg at the moment—and she had great legs—and that was capturing at least some of his attention.

"I didn't kill Mr. Quinn," Caulfield said. "I'd never even met the man. On the contrary, I was hoping he'd be able to figure out who had defrauded Edison. Rumor had it that's why he was still in town. My attorney has advised me that it would be possible to file a civil suit if there wasn't enough evidence for criminal charges."

"So, what were you doing lurking around Edison's house the morning Mr. Quinn was killed?" Liz said.

I turned to glare at her.

"Don't give me that look, Sarah," she said. "I'm planning on having a slice of Aggie's maple custard pie in a few minutes and I'm not planning on continuing this discussion while I'm eating it."

I looked at the former bank manager. "I'm sorry," I said. "Liz and Stella Hall are friends, which I'm hoping explains her bluntness." I sent another frown in Liz's direction. She didn't look the slightest bit repentant.

He leaned over and gave me a conspiratorial wink. "It's all right, Sarah," he said. "I've known Liz for a long time. This isn't the first time she's been so . . . forthright about something." He looked over at Liz. "I heard that Sarah and her staff were going to be clearing out Edison's house. Since the wine Edison gave me turned out to be worthless, as far as I'm concerned our agreement is void. I was hoping I could find *my* train."

Caulfield had been trying to do the same thing as Teresa had: take back what he believed belonged to him.

"What happened?" I asked.

He shrugged. "Nothing. When I got to the house Quinn was standing by the back door. I waited for a couple of minutes to see if he'd leave. When he didn't, I realized I was on a fool's errand and left myself."

I picked up my cup mostly so I'd have something to do with my hands. First Teresa and now Channing Caulfield, not to mention Paul Duvall sneaking a cup of coffee behind his wife's back; clearly none of these people had ever watched Wile E. Coyote cartoons or they'd know all that sneaking around wasn't going to end well.

Liz waved our waiter over and ordered dessert. Caulfield and I both passed. "I see someone I need to speak to," Liz said, getting to her feet. "I'll be right back."

Caulfield stood up as well.

"Sit down," Liz said, waving a hand at him.

Caulfield watched her walk across the restaurant to a table by the front window before he resumed his seat. I recognized the person Liz had gone to speak to, Jane Evans, lawyer Josh Evans's mother.

I exhaled slowly. "I'm sorry Liz was so blunt," I said.

Caulfield pulled his eyes away from Liz and focused his attention on me. "She's a complex woman," he said. "I've wanted to get to know her better for years." He set his napkin next to his plate. "What do you say, Sarah? Would you put in a good word for me?"

I laughed, hoping he wouldn't be offended. "Did you not notice how much influence I *don't* have with her?" I asked. There really wasn't anything wrong with Channing Caulfield, I decided. He was just a little too slick. I had the urge to tell him to stop trying so hard, at least with Liz.

"Have you really been considering moving your business?" he asked.

I nodded. "Yes. I came to the conclusion it wasn't a good idea, financially speaking, but it was good to have you confirm my choice. Thank you."

"You're welcome," he said.

I leaned back in my chair. "I'm sorry you ended up with a worthless bottle of wine. For what it's worth, the police are investigating the fraud."

"From what I've been able to find out, they aren't going to get very far without Mr. Quinn. This type of fraud was his area of expertise."

"Maybe they'll be able to figure out how Edison Hall was scammed in the first place. That could lead them to whoever faked the bottles."

A look I couldn't read flashed across his face. "I may have an idea how that happened," Caulfield said slowly. "In fact, it may in part be my fault."

I leaned forward, propping an elbow on the table. "I . . . don't understand." Was he confessing to some kind of fraud? I needed Liz.

Caulfield looked down at his coffee cup for a moment, then raised his eyes to meet mine. "About a year and a half ago I was asked to be part of a seminar on money management for seniors that was being sponsored by Legacy Place. I had a lot on my plate at the time and I turned down the invitation. They ended up bringing in someone from out of town."

"And you think Edison was at that seminar?"

"I think it's possible. I don't know how they got our names, but everyone from the train club got an invitation, probably because we're all over sixty-five."

"And you think this out-of-town person was the one who defrauded Edison Hall?"

Caulfield wore a heavy gold signet ring on his right hand and he twisted it around his finger now. "No. But I think there may have been a plant in the audience."

I was sure my confusion was written all over my face.

"Several people told me that there was a woman at the seminar, not anyone from North Harbor, who was talking about how she preferred to invest in something tangible instead of stocks and bonds."

"You think *she* was connected to the scam in some way."

He gave a slight shrug. "It's occurred to me that it's possible."

Liz was on her way back to the table and I could see our waiter coming as well with her dessert.

"None of what happened is your fault," I said. "But I do think you should share this information with the police." I cocked my head to one side and smiled up at him, hoping I was convincing.

"I could be wrong," he said.

"But you could be right," I replied.

"Fine. I'll talk to them." He smiled at me.

Liz returned to the table just as the waiter reached us with her dessert. We talked in general terms about the plans for the harbor front while she ate her pie and I learned a lot about the project that I hadn't known before. Caulfield pushed back the cuff off his pale blue shirt and checked his watch as Liz set her fork down.

"Liz, it's been a pleasure, even with the murder accusation," he said, getting to his feet. He turned to smile at me. "And, Sarah, I enjoyed meeting you. If I can help you with anything else, please call me."

"I will. Thank you," I said.

He leaned over and kissed Liz on the cheek. "If you decide to invest in the development, call me before you sign anything," he said.

"Thank you for joining us," she said.

He smiled and headed for the exit.

Liz looked around for our waiter. When she caught his eye she nodded. He nodded in return. The two of them seemed to have some kind of code.

"I do a fair amount of Emmerson Foundation business here," Liz said by way of explanation when she caught me watching her. Once she'd paid for our meal, we walked out to the car. Liz fastened her seat belt and turned to look at me with a self-satisfied smile. "We make a good team," she said.

I fastened my own seat belt and stuck the key in the ignition. "You could have been a little more diplomatic," I said.

"What did you find out?" she asked.

"Why do you think I found out anything?"

She held up a finger. "Number one, I saw your heads together, so I know he told you something." She held up a second finger. "Number two, I did a damn fine job of setting up your rapport."

I turned to look at her. "Excuse me?" I said. "What do you mean, you set up our rapport?"

She smoothed a hand over her blond hair. "I was rude. You were appalled. You and Channing bonded. He confided in you. Stop stalling and tell me what he said."

I pointed my index finger at her, stabbing the air with it. "You did that on purpose."

She looked surprised. "Of course I did," she said. "You mean you're just figuring that out?"

"You could have told me what you were going to do," I muttered as I pulled out of the parking lot.

"I'm sorry about that," Liz said. "But I think it worked out better this way. So, what did he tell you?"

I repeated Channing Caulfield's story about the money management seminar.

"He could be onto something," Liz said.

"I had the same thought," I said. I stopped at the corner and used the opportunity to look in her direction.

She gave me a cat-that-ate-the-canary smile. "We're a good team," she said.

I shifted my gaze back to the road. "Do not try to tell me that we're Xena and Gabrielle again," I said sternly.

Liz laughed. "Fine, but I think you like the detective business."

"No, I don't," I said, keeping my eyes straight ahead.

Liz laughed again and it occurred to me that no matter how hard I tried to stay out of the detecting business, it somehow kept pulling me back in.

Chapter 12

Mac drove in behind me as we pulled in to the parking lot back at the shop. Rose got out of the passenger side of the SUV carrying Elvis.

"That cat is perfectly capable of walking," I said.

Rose stroked his black fur. "He's such a good boy. I don't mind carrying him," she said. "A couple of squirrels had set up house in the back porch. Elvis convinced them to move elsewhere."

The cat looked at me and licked his whiskers.

"Tell me he didn't eat them," I said.

Mac shook his head. "He didn't, but he did give them a pretty good aerobic workout." He reached over and scratched the top of the cat's head. "I found the hole where I think they got in and I filled it with steel wool."

"Thanks," I said.

"That's not all," Rose said. She held out a colored brochure. "He found this on one of the shelves of that bookcase in the living room and brought it right to me."

I took the folded sheet of paper from her. "It's for Feast in the Field," I said, turning the paper over in my hand.

Mac frowned. "Do you mean that wine and spirits tasting event last fall?"

"It could be a clue," Rose said.

I looked at Elvis. If it were possible for a cat to smile smugly, that was what he was doing. "I don't think so," I said. "This isn't from last fall's Feast in the Field. It's from the year before."

"It could still be important," Rose insisted.

"See what Mr. P. thinks," I said. I didn't like to point out that the brochure smelled like fish, which was probably why the cat had been drawn to it. I turned to Mac. "So the kitchen is finished?"

He nodded. "And we can bring the bookcase back on Monday. We came back a bit early today because I heard from Liam."

"You're going to finish the drywall?" I said, looking over toward the old garage.

Mac nodded. "That's the plan. He has some time. I wanted to take advantage of it. He should be here in a couple of hours."

"If you can get the ceiling done, you and I could finish the rest."

He pulled a hand over his neck. "Liam offered to help with the crack-filling, too. I told him that's between the two of you."

I laughed. "He thinks he's better at it than I am. He says it's like frosting a cake, which he also claims he's better at."

Mac smiled. "Sarah, no offense but do you know how to make a cake?"

"We're way off the subject," I said just a little defensively.

His smile got wider. "Then let's change it altogether. How was lunch?"

We started across the parking lot toward the back door. "Useful," I said. "Channing Caulfield definitely didn't kill Ronan Quinn."

Rose was in front of us. She looked back over her shoulder at me. "Why do you say that, dear?" she asked.

"Well, first of all because he told us he didn't when Liz asked him."

Rose immediately turned to look at Liz. "Oh, for heaven's sake, what did you do?" she said.

"I didn't do anything," Liz retorted. "It was all part of my plan."

"Your plan to what?" Rose asked. "Let a killer get away?"

Liz rolled her eyes. "You're overreacting, Rose," she said. "I was trying to help Sarah make a connection with Channing and I did an excellent job of that if I say so myself." She turned to look at me. "And it seems like I'm the only one who is saying it."

"Interesting," Mac said, almost under his breath. I shot him a warning look and turned my attention to Rose.

"First of all, Liz is right. Like I just said, he didn't kill Ronan Quinn."

"Sarah dear, just because he says he didn't doesn't *mean* he didn't." There was just a hint of condescension in Rose's voice, as if she were talking to a five-year-old.

Out of the corner of my eye, I could see Mac's lips twitching as he tried not to laugh.

"I know," I said. I turned my attention to Liz. "Did you notice how he went out of his way to avoid shaking hands with either one of us?"

Liz frowned. "You're right," she said slowly.

I held up one hand. "His finger joints were very swollen," I said, tapping on the second knuckle of my index finger. "I'm pretty sure he has arthritis in his hands. There's no way Channing Caulfield would be able to grip and lift the heavy wine bottle that was used to kill Quinn, let alone swing it."

"So we're back at square one," Rose said with a sigh. Mac held the door open and I let her go ahead of me.

"Not entirely," I said.

She set Elvis down on the floor. He shook himself and headed for the store. Rose looked at me, her head cocked to one side.

"Liz was right," I said.

"Well, of course I was," Liz said.

I put my arm around her shoulders and gave her a hug. "Don't push it," I said. "She did manage to create a bit of a rapport between Channing Caulfield and me. When she was away from the table, he told me that he thought he knew how Edison first got the idea to start collecting rare vintages of wine." I told her what Caulfield had told me about the money management seminar.

"I remember when they had those seminars at Shady Pines," Rose said. "I knew they were just a bunch of hooey."

"You know people at *Legacy Place*," I said, stressing the proper name of the seniors' complex where Rose had lived until she'd been evicted, basically for her attitude. "See what you can find out."

Rose beamed at me. "That's an excellent idea," she said. She reached over and squeezed my cheeks between her two hands. "I'm so glad you went to lunch with Channing." She headed for the shop.

Liz looked from Mac to me. "I was there, too," she said.

Rose was already halfway across the room.

I leaned over and kissed Liz's cheek. "Superheroes are never appreciated by the masses, Xena," I said.

She laughed. "You're an irritating child sometimes, but I love you," she said.

I grinned at her. "Everybody does," I said.

Chapter 13

I went upstairs and changed out of my dress and heels, dropping down onto the love seat to rub my aching feet before I put my Keds back on. I had no idea how Liz managed to walk around all day in spike heels.

When I went back downstairs, Avery was at the cash desk with one customer and Rose was showing a bed frame to two others. Mac walked over to me.

"Things look pretty much under control in here," I said to Mac.

He nodded. "Avery did a good job under the stairs— no more marauding dust bunnies."

I nodded solemnly. "Those critters can be very sneaky."

"She updated the list and put a copy on the door and another copy over by the cash."

I glanced across the room where it looked as though Avery was showing her customer the various bracelets that snaked their way up her left arm. "She's the only teenager I've ever met who actually likes doing that kind of thing."

Mac passed a hand back over his close-cropped black hair. "What do you think about getting her to do an up-to-date inventory when we finally get the old garage into a workable space?"

"I think that's a great idea," I said.

"If you don't need me for anything else, I'm going out to get the old chandelier from Doran's and put it in the workroom."

"Need any help?" I asked.

"You could come hold the door for me," Mac said.

I smiled. "Sure."

We started for the workroom. "Where's Charlotte?" I asked.

"Talking to someone who was at that financial planning seminar. Someone she used to teach with, I think."

"Do you think Caulfield is right?" I asked. "You think it's possible that was where the whole wine thing began for Edison?"

"It's possible," he said. "I've seen this kind of thing before." He held up a hand. "Not wine collecting, but other sorts of scams—rare coins, vacation properties in Florida. All the con needs is for one person to take the bait."

"Why does someone 'take the bait'?"

He shrugged. "My experience is pretty limited in this kind of thing, but I can tell you it's usually not greed that motivates. I think, as crazy as it sounds, it's the same kind of thing as making a wish when you blow out the candles on a birthday cake. It's hoping for something more."

"Do you think maybe Edison wanted to leave something more for Ethan?"

"I think it's possible."

"Which made him the perfect target for anyone looking to run a con."

Mac nodded. "Pretty much. And it may not have happened at that financial seminar. The reality is, Edison Hall could have been scammed in a dozen or more ways." He held the back door and I stepped out into the parking lot. Clouds were rolling in from the water.

"Including Feast in the Field?" I asked. "Rose thinks it's possible."

"You did notice that brochure about Feast in the Field smelled like tuna, didn't you?" he said.

"I did," I said. "I don't think it's important, but the more I think about it, the more I wonder about that money management seminar. According to Mr. Caulfield, Edison would have received an invitation. Maybe Charlotte will come up with something."

Mac pulled his keys out of his pocket. "So you don't think Elvis looked at that brochure and thought, *Hey, a clue?* He is a pretty smart cat."

I shook my head. "I feel pretty confident that the only thing he was thinking about was lunch."

We had a wheeled dolly that we used to move anything large or awkward from the old garage to the workroom in the shop. I helped Mac get the brass and glass light fixture settled on it. As he maneuvered the dolly into the workroom, Charlotte came out of the Angels' office, a look of satisfaction on her face.

"Sarah, is it all right with you if Rose works the rest of my shift?" she asked.

"Sure," I said. "What's up?"

"I talked to three different people who were at that

first financial seminar. They all remember a woman who said she lived in Rockport, talking about the unpredictability of the stock market and how much better tangible things were as an investment."

"Interesting," I said.

She nodded. "Maribelle Hearndon just called me back. She knows someone who knows someone—you know how those things work—and I have a name and an address for the woman. Liz and I are going to see her."

"Good luck," I said.

Mr. P. arrived about twenty minutes after Liz and Charlotte had left.

"Did you walk up the hill?" I asked. "I could have come and picked you up."

"Oh, thank you, Sarah," he said, pulling the strap of his messenger bag over his head. "I've walked that hill many times. It doesn't bother me, but I actually got a ride from your brother." He inclined his head in the direction of the old garage. "He's outside talking to Mac."

I took a couple of steps backward and looked out into the parking lot. Liam was standing beside his half-ton truck deep in conversation with Mac.

"Rose is in the shop," I said to Mr. P. "And I think there's tea upstairs."

He reached over and patted my arm. "Thank you, dear," he said.

They all did that, I realized—patted my arm, smiled sweetly at me and called me "dear." For all that I worried about them and tried to keep them from getting in too much trouble, I had the feeling, sometimes, that they were just humoring me.

Liam was dressed to work in jeans and a blue plaid shirt with the sleeves rolled back. "Hi," he said as I joined them. "I was just telling Mac I'm free for the rest of the day, so we can probably get this whole thing finished if that's what you want."

"That works for me, Sarah," Mac said.

"I'd love to get it finished," I said. I smiled at Liam. "Thank you, big brother." Emphasis on "big."

He grinned. "Oh yeah, when you're looking to get something from me, then you acknowledge that I'm older and wiser."

I bumped him with my hip. "I said you were older; I didn't say you were smarter."

"I'm smart enough not to let you cook me dinner to pay me back," he retorted.

"Are you coming to Thursday night jam?" I asked.

"Wouldn't miss it."

"Fine," I said. "I'll buy you dinner beforehand."

"And all the nachos I can eat while Sam and the boys are playing."

"Deal."

"I can eat a lot of nachos," he warned.

"You also do a lot of flirting, which cuts into your eating," I said with a grin. "I think I can afford it."

Liam and Mac went to work in the old garage and I went back to the shop. Mr. P. was in the sunporch busy with his computer. Avery and Rose were both with customers and as I stepped into the store Avery beckoned me over.

It turned out to be a busy afternoon. A small caravan of RV campers was working its way up the coast and they'd stopped in North Harbor for a couple of days. One of the RV owners bought two guitars and when I asked him about his camper—which looked like an oversize van to me—he offered to let me have a look inside. It had a tiny galley kitchen, a separate bathroom and a sofa at the back that turned into a queen-size bed.

"There's a lot more room inside than I expected," I said to the owner, who said his name was Joe. I was guessing he was in his mid to late fifties.

"Everyone says that," he said. "It's not bad on gas and it's pretty easy to park." He gestured at the store behind us. "You could travel all over the state with this and bring things back for your store. Or park it in the middle of the woods somewhere and spend the whole day playing guitar."

"I like that second part," I said with a laugh.

Joe told me that the group would be heading south again in a couple of months and he'd stop in then to see what musical instruments I had in stock.

I walked back inside to find Rose giving the driver of one of the other RV's directions to the Black Bear and Avery selling three of the bracelets she was wearing to a woman about my age. Elvis was holding court on the tub chair being fussed over by three more customers. Mr. P. came down the stairs carrying two mugs.

"I just made a fresh pot for Mac and your brother," he said. "Would you like me to get you a cup when I come back?"

I hesitated and then the phone rang.

"Go answer that," Mr. P. said. "I'll bring you coffee

in just a minute." He made his way across the room, smiling at both Rose and Avery as he passed them.

As I went to get the phone, I realized that as much as it might be fun to run off in an RV, I'd miss them all too much to ever do it. Then I got a mental image of taking them all with me, Mr. P. with his pants hiked up to his armpits driving one of the oversize vans, Liz with her heels and perfect manicure behind the wheel of another and me with Elvis riding shotgun leading the way. The thought made me laugh as I picked up the phone.

Charlotte and Liz got back about an hour before closing time. I knew from the expression on their faces that they hadn't returned with any useful information.

"That was a fool's errand," Liz said, setting her purse on one of the chairs in the Angels' office.

"I don't think it was," Charlotte said, unbuttoning her jacket. "I think we're on the right track at least."

"What happened?" I asked.

"The woman moved and no one in the building seemed to really know her or know where she went," she said. "More than one person remembers her talking about the uncertainty of the stock market. She's the woman we're looking for."

"Which doesn't do us any good, since we didn't find her," Liz said.

"But we do know Edison was at that seminar," Charlotte said. "I talked to Stella," she added as an aside to me.

I opened my mouth to point out to them that knowing Edison Hall had been at the seminar proved nothing because there was no proof that anything underhanded had happened there, but before I could speak, Mr. P. did.

"I found her," he said.

"Found who?" Liz asked. She looked over his shoulder at the laptop he was working at.

He looked up at us. "The woman from the seminar. At least based on the description Charlotte got, I think I found her."

He clicked several keys and video footage appeared on the screen. Thanks to the Angels' investigations, I'd seen security camera footage enough times to recognize that was what this was.

Mr. P. tapped the screen with one finger. "This is from the day of the seminar."

"Which was more than eighteen months ago," I said.

"I'm aware of that, my dear," he said.

The view was the parking lot at Legacy Place, taken, as far as I could tell, from the building next door, which housed offices for several doctors and dentists. I was going to ask him how he'd gotten the old security footage—how he'd even known it existed—but I thought better of it. Alfred and I had come to an unspoken agreement about this kind of thing. I didn't ask him how he got his information and he tried to keep his tactics more or less legit.

The image on the screen was of a woman in her early seventies talking to a younger man.

"I think that could be her," Charlotte said. "She looks like the woman Maribelle's friend described." She turned to Liz. "What do you think?"

Liz studied the computer. "It's her. See her purse?"

Charlotte and I both leaned in for a better look.

"Maribelle's friend said the woman was carrying a plaid purse—a beige background with white, black and red lines."

"Alfred, can you zoom in on her bag?" Liz asked.

He clicked a few keys and a close-up of the right side of the woman's body filled the screen. The image was a little blurry, but the purse did match the description Liz had just given.

"That's the Haymarket check," she said, pointing at the screen. "The bag is a Burberry. Let's just say it's not cheap. We need to find that man Alfred."

Mr. P. smiled. "I think I can enlarge his face and run it through a nifty little software program I came across to enhance the image just a little."

I cleared my throat, but they either didn't hear me or ignored me. I did it again.

"Sarah, are you trying to bring up a fur ball or did you want to say something?" Liz asked without looking away from the computer.

Charlotte, however, turned to look at me. "What is it?" she asked. Her glasses had slid down her nose and she pushed them up with a finger.

"We have to give this information to Michelle," I said.

Liz looked at me then, one hand on her hip. I knew that posture. I was in for an argument. "No, we don't," she said. "There isn't any information to give. All we have so far is a third-hand description of a woman who may or may not have been touting alternatives to the stock market at a financial planning seminar that took place well over a year ago."

Charlotte sighed softly and looked from Liz to me. "I don't like to take sides, Sarah," she said, "but Liz is right. We don't have facts. All we have is guesswork."

"You don't think it's guesswork," I said. "And neither does Liz."

"Is this because of Nicolas?" Charlotte asked.

I shook my head. "No, it isn't."

"Then are you part of our team or not?" Liz asked, holding out a hand.

"Of course Sarah is part of our team," Mr. P. said with just a hint of recrimination in his voice. "And she's right. We should share what we've learned with the police. We're both trying to find out who killed Mr. Quinn."

Liz made a sound a lot like a snort.

Mr. P. chose to ignore her. "I'd also like to show Nicolas and Detective Andrews that we know what we're doing and we're not going to disrupt their investigation."

Charlotte smiled. "Alfred, you're a very sensible, reasonable man," she said.

Liz exhaled loudly. "Yes, you are," she said. "And I like you despite that." She got to her feet. "I need a cup of tea." She headed for the door. "I'm going to bring Rose up-to-date." She caught my hand and gave it a squeeze as she passed me.

"Thank you," I said to Mr. P. once they were both gone.

"Everything you said was correct," he said. "And underneath her bluster Elizabeth knows that as well. I think she's still a little touchy over being a suspect in that whole dreadful business last winter."

The dreadful business he was referring to was the

death of Lily Carter. Liz had never been a serious suspect, but she had been questioned more than once.

"I think that's probably right," I said. "And thank you for saying I was part of the team."

He smiled. "It's true. You are part of the team, my dear."

I just nodded. I didn't know what to say because I realized that good or bad, right or wrong, I was.

Chapter 14

I went back up to my office while Mr. P. made the phone call to Michelle. I was printing out two new orders from the store's Web site when my cell rang. It was Nick.

"Hi," he said. "I was just in a meeting with Michelle and she had a call from Alfred Peterson. I sense your hand in that."

"It wasn't me," I said, sitting on the edge of my desk.

"So you know about their theory that Edison Hall met the person who sold him all those worthless bottles of wine at some money-management thing?" The skepticism was obvious in his voice.

"You don't?" I asked.

"I just don't think it has any relevance to the investigation."

"You don't think Mr. Quinn's death had anything to do with the whole wine scam?"

"That's not really my part of the case."

I reached over and took the two pages I'd just printed out of the printer tray. "It doesn't mean you don't have a theory."

I heard him exhale. "I'm not saying what happened isn't connected to those worthless bottles of wine. I'm just saying I don't think the connection is directly related to Edison Hall."

"So how is it connected, then?"

Nick laughed. "I suppose I may as well tell you," he said. "It's not like Alfred won't ferret this out if he hasn't already. Ronan Quinn was already involved in a court case over another fake wine scam."

"That's not exactly a secret, Nick," I said. "There was an article about the case in the *Boston Globe*. It's how Ethan came to hire him."

"Quinn had received death threats because of that case as recently as a week before he came to town."

"The police are looking in that direction."

"They're looking in a lot of directions, but yes, that one seems to hold the most promise."

"I hope it works out," I said. Could someone have followed the wine expert here to North Harbor just to kill him? It wasn't any more of a stretch than the angle the Angels were working on.

"Michelle said they released Edison's house back to the family," Nick said.

"She did and we've already started working out there."

"I'm really glad to hear that," he said, and I could hear the smile in his voice. "This has been hard for Ethan. Once his father's estate is settled, he'll be able to get on with his life."

"I promised Stella that we'd work as quickly as we can." I stretched my legs out in front of me, glad once again to be out of those heels no matter how good they made my legs look.

"I know you gave Stella a deal, Sarah," Nick said. "Thanks. Any chance you can find something in that old house that's worth some money?"

I thought about the Marklin train set Elvis and I had found. Even though its ownership was in dispute, maybe there was a way it could still be used to help Ellie Hall. "I'm working on it," I said.

"I gotta go," Nick said then. "Are you coming to dinner at Mom's on Sunday?"

"I am," I said. "Rose is going to teach me how to make gravy."

"Oh," he said. "Well . . . um . . . good luck with that. I'm not much of a gravy man myself."

"Nice try," I said. "I've seen you in your mother's kitchen eating gravy out of the roaster with a spoon at Thanksgiving."

He cleared his throat. "Sarah, we've known each other since we were kids and in all that time you've never made anything that was edible. Face it. You did not get the cooking gene. You're the kind of person for whom takeout was invented."

"Nicolas Elliot, I'm going to make you eat your words," I promised, feeling a little surge of competitiveness in my gut.

"It'll have to be better than eating your cooking," he said before he ended the call, laughing.

I took the orders downstairs. "Avery, would you get these started, please?" I asked the teenager.

"No problem," she said, taking the pages and heading for the workroom.

Rose was busy straightening up, putting chairs in place around a small table, fluffing the pillows on the seats. "I'm just going out to see how Mac and Liam are doing," I said. "Avery is out back if you need her."

"Take your time," she said, stepping back to survey her handiwork and then tweaking the position of a chair.

Mr. P. was in the sunporch, working on his laptop as usual. "Sarah," he called as I went past the door.

I backtracked a couple of steps, leaned around the doorframe and looked at him inquiringly.

"I called Detective Andrews," he said. "She didn't seem very interested in our information."

"I know," I said. "I heard from Nick." I paused. "I think they're wrong."

"Great minds think alike." Then he smiled. "Of course, Elizabeth would say, fools seldom differ."

"I like yours better," I said. I gestured at the computer. "Is that Feast in the Field?"

He nodded. "I thought I would go through as many photos as I could find online this weekend."

"You don't even know if Edison Hall was there," I said.

Mr. P. smoothed the few wisps of gray hair that he had. "He was. Rose called Stella and asked."

It still seemed like a waste of time to me.

Alfred must have seen some of what I was thinking in my expression. "I am aware that brochure Elvis found smelled like tuna fish, Sarah," he said. He studied my face for what seemed like a long moment. "I also trust Rosie's instincts."

He didn't need to remind me that Rose's instincts had probably saved my life the previous winter.

"Could I help?" I asked.

"I have everything under control," Mr. P. said. "I have another little piece of facial-scanning software that I think will help me."

"I'll leave you to it, then," I said. I didn't ask him where his little piece of software had come from and he didn't volunteer the information.

Mac and Liam were making great progress on the ceiling of the old garage. They had decided to keep going until all the drywall was up. I told them I'd be back later with pizza.

Liz arrived at the end of the day to pick up Avery along with Rose and Mr. P.

I gave Charlotte a ride home.

"I'll see you tomorrow," she said as she got out of the SUV. "Bring your apron."

"I'm not so sure I should be cooking anything," I said. "What if I ruin the gravy?"

"Then everyone can have ketchup instead." She waved as she started up her driveway. I watched to make sure she made it inside.

Elvis meowed from the backseat. "No, I'm not hanging over the seat to pick you up just so you can sit up here," I said. I turned to look at him. "If you want to come up here, you're going to have to jump."

He meowed again, just a little louder.

I turned the radio on and sat back in my seat, and

a tail smacked the side of my head as Elvis landed on the top of the middle section of the split front seat.

"Hello," I said.

He gave me a look of annoyance, jumped down and moved over to settle himself on the passenger side, craning his neck to look out the windshield. It didn't matter where he was sitting: The cat was a backseat driver.

I took Elvis home and then collected the pizza I'd ordered before I'd left the shop. The guys had just finished hanging the last sheet of drywall.

Mac brushed dust off the front of his T-shirt. "Thank you," he said to Liam. "I owe you for this."

Liam wiped his hands on the front of his pants. "You don't owe me a thing." One long arm snaked out and caught me around the shoulders. "You, on the other hand, owe me big-time."

I reached over and flicked his forehead with my thumb and forefinger. "Really?" I said. "I still have that video of you in the onesie Mom bought you at Christmas, wearing Dad's hat with the flaps while the two of you sing a rousing chorus of 'Grandma Got Run Over By a Reindeer.'"

Mac's lips twitched as he tried not to laugh. Liam let go of me and put one hand over his heart. "We're family," he said with mock sincerity. "You don't owe me a thing."

I laughed and hugged him.

We ate the pizza and talked more about Liam's role in the proposed downtown development. Because the previous North by West proposal had fallen apart, it seemed as though the harbor-front revitalization had been the only topic of conversation for close to a year now.

"Do you think this is really going to happen this time?" I asked Liam.

He pulled a long string of mozzarella from his slice and ate it. "Yeah, I do," he said. "I looked at the financials and the numbers are good." He nudged me with his elbow. "So I'll probably be around a lot more, at least for a while."

I smiled back at him. I liked having Liam around, and not just because he could cook. "You should come running with me," I said.

"How about tomorrow morning?"

I nodded. "That works for me."

Half a slice of pizza was on his plate. Liam rolled it up and put the entire thing in his mouth. After he swallowed he stretched and stood up. "I really need to get going," he said.

"Thanks for the help," Mac said.

"Not a problem," Liam said. "Anytime."

They shook hands and surveyed their handiwork.

When Liam turned to me I wrapped him in another hug. "Thanks," I said. "I really do owe you."

He grinned. "Don't worry. I'll collect." He pulled his cell out of his pocket, looked at the screen and put it back. "If you see Rose, will you tell her I'll look for those photos and e-mail them to her later tonight?"

"What photos?" I asked as he leaned forward and brushed dust and bits of paper out of his hair.

"From that wine- and food-tasting thing last fall," he said.

"Feast in the Field?"

He nodded. "That's it. She asked if I had any pictures. I was pretty sure I did. I just need to charge my phone and I can send them to her. I forgot to plug it in last night."

"Rose asked you for photos from Feast in the Field this past fall? *Not* the year before?"

"Yes. From this past fall. *Not* the year before."

I was confused. The brochure Elvis had found wasn't from the most recent Feast. I was trying, like Mr. P., to trust Rose's instincts. I just wasn't sure where they were taking me.

Liam reached for his jacket. "So this detective thing is legit? Alfred Peterson has a PI license and Rose is working on one?"

"It's legit."

"Good for them," he said with a smile. "I hope this helps them find the guy they're looking for." He pulled his keys out of his pocket.

I held up one hand. "Hang on a minute. You hope what helps them find who?"

He looked at me as if I was missing something, which I was. "Alfred has some video of a man from somewhere downtown, talking to some older woman. I think I have a photo of the same guy on my phone. He was working at one of the wine-tasting booths this year. If it is the same guy, Nick and I talked to him. He was there the year before, too, one of those stereotypical sales types. That's the only reason I remembered him."

I looked at Mac. He raised an eyebrow but didn't say anything.

Could Rose actually be right about Feast in the Field? Could she have found the person who defrauded Edison

Hall and had Nick, of all people, actually talked to the man? I had an almost overwhelming urge to laugh. I coughed into my elbow instead. "I'll tell her," I said.

"Seven too early to run?" Liam asked.

I shook my head.

"I'll see you in the morning, then," he said. He raised a hand. "See you, Mac."

I watched Liam head across the parking lot and rubbed my left shoulder, which had tied itself in knots while Liam was talking.

"Give Rose the message and there's nothing else you can do tonight," Mac said.

"I swear I wasn't going to get involved in this case," I said, sitting next to Mac on a paint-spattered sawhorse. "Which is what I said last time and the time before that."

"They're your family."

"Yeah, they are," I said with a smile. "So what's your excuse?"

"They're kind of my family, too." Mac shrugged. "It's been a while since I've had something like that in my life."

Mac never talked about family or his past or anything personal. I suspected from a remark he'd once made about commitment that he'd been married at one time.

"Your old life," I said.

He smoothed a hand over his dark hair. "Something like that." There was something sad in his expression, in the way he held his mouth.

"You miss it, or at least you miss the people?" The words came out as a question.

"Sometimes I missed the . . . connections," he said.

Missed. Past tense. "What do you mean?" I asked.

"You know how I take my coffee. Rose remembers that I don't like hard-boiled eggs, so she doesn't put them in her potato salad when she brings it for us."

Those were the same kinds of things I'd missed when I'd been working away from North Harbor. Now that I was back, it sometimes drove me crazy that Rose and her cohorts knew me so well. Other times it made me feel as if I was truly home, surrounded by people who knew me so well.

"You probably could have picked a little less . . . colorful family," I said.

Mac laughed. "No way. I like colorful. I don't want beige and boring."

I nudged him with my shoulder. "I'm going to remind you that you said that the next time Mr. P. hacks in somewhere he shouldn't and Michelle and a dozen burly police officers surround this building."

"Wouldn't happen," Mac said. "Mr. P. is not that careless."

"Have you ever thought about going back to see your old family?" I asked, aware that I was venturing out onto shaky ground.

The smile faded from Mac's face. "No. I made mistakes. I made decisions that can't be forgiven."

"Gram says there's very little that can't be forgiven with a little time." When he didn't say anything I knew the conversation was over. I straightened up and reached for the broom.

"It looks so good," I said, standing in the middle of the space and turning in a slow circle after we'd cleaned and put things away.

"I thought I'd start the mudding and taping tomorrow if that's okay," Mac said, taking the battery out of his cordless drill.

"It's okay," I said, "but are you sure you want to work on your day off?"

He shrugged. "I don't mind. The sooner the walls are finished, the sooner we can get organized out here." He looked toward the front corner of the space.

Mac and I had partially walled off the area. I hoped to teach classes at some point in that space. Lots of light came in through the windows. A weathered barn door we'd salvaged from an old farm on the road to Portland was waiting to be hung from a sliding rail system once the walls were finished.

"Keep track of your hours," I said. "Sailing season will be starting soon."

"I will," he said. "See you Monday."

Rose and Mr. P. were just coming down the sidewalk arm in arm when I pulled in to the driveway. I waited for them by the steps.

"Liam asked me to tell you that he'll e-mail you the photos once he charges his phone," I told the two of them.

"Splendid," Rose said. "Did he tell you he might have a photo of our suspect? That man we're looking for was at Feast two years in a row."

"He did."

"Maybe I should ask Nicolas if he has any photos on his phone from Feast in the Field."

I exhaled loudly and looked at Mr. P., who cleared his throat.

Rose rolled her eyes and shook her head. "The two

of you sound like a pair of old horses," she said. "I was joking." Her gray eyes narrowed. "Although maybe I'll get a chance to borrow his phone on Sunday." She started up the steps. Behind her Mr. P. shook his head, ever so slightly.

I followed them inside. "Rose, about Sunday," I began.

She held up a hand. "If this is about the gravy, you can do it."

"When we made Jell-O, I burned the boiling water."

"How could you burn water?" Mr. P. asked, looking a little puzzled.

"She didn't burn the water," Rose explained. "She burned the kettle."

"And I don't want to burn the gravy," I said.

"You won't," she said. "I promise."

I hesitated, shifting from one foot to the other.

Rose made a shooing motion with one hand. "Stop fretting. Everything will be fine."

I smiled at her. "How am I ever going to repay you for taking on the thankless job of teaching me how to cook?" I asked.

"It's not a thankless job, dear," she said. "And you don't need to thank me, although if you do happen to find yourself with Nicolas's phone—"

"You won't be conducting any unauthorized searches," Mr. P. finished.

"I wasn't suggesting Sarah search Nicolas's phone," Rose said, pulling herself up to her full almost five feet, zero inches height. "I was merely going to say that if the opportunity presented itself, she could ask to see his photos. That's all."

Mr. P. smiled benignly. "Of course. My apologies."

"Have a good night," I said to them, turning to unlock the door.

I was tying my running shoes the next morning when Liam knocked and then poked his head around the door.

"Hi," I said.

He was wearing gray shorts and a short-sleeve Red Sox T-shirt over a long-sleeve gray one. A gray knit beanie was pulled over his hair.

"You're going to freeze," I said, indicating his half-bare legs.

Liam beat on his chest with his fists. "I'm tough," he said.

"You're still going to be cold," I retorted as I straightened up.

"And you're going to sweat like a pig," he countered, making a face at my sweatshirt and leggings.

I grinned at him. "I've missed you," I said.

"Yeah, I've missed you, too." He grinned back at me.

We headed southwest, running a route I often used that was slightly uphill, enough to give us both a challenge, I hoped.

"So, who do you run with when I'm not in town?" Liam asked. Even though he was taller we'd been running together since we were teenagers and we easily fell into a comfortable pace.

"No one," I said.

"Mac doesn't run?"

I glanced at him but didn't see anything other than genuine curiosity on his face.

"He does some kind of Israeli self-defense workout," I said.

"Krav Maga?"

I nodded and pushed a stray piece of hair behind my ear. "I tried to get Nick to come running with me."

Liam gave a snort of laughter. "I know how that went," he said. "When we went to hockey camp, man, did he hate the running drills! He was always the last person to finish, so he always ended up with extra sprints to do." He grinned at the memory.

I'd forgotten about Liam going to hockey camp. "So you know Ethan Hall?" I said.

"Yeah, I know Ethan," he said. "Mom told me about the body you found. That's the case that Rose and the rest of them are working on, isn't it?"

"It is." We crossed the street starting a long, slow climb uphill.

"So Ethan's father got scammed?" Liam asked.

"Uh-huh. I'm guessing he thought it was a sure thing. The bottles of wine he bought were supposed to improve with age and increase in value."

"Except they were swill."

I nodded. "Basically." I pushed a little harder, trying to keep the pace and not slow down.

"So this guy that Rose and Alfred are trying to find is mixed up in this fake wine thing?" There was a fine sheen of sweat on Liam's forehead. I wasn't the only one feeling the hill, it seemed.

"Maybe," I said. "It's a giant long shot."

We crossed another cross street and the incline got steeper.

"I remember the guy said he was some kind of wine dealer or broker," Liam said. "He gave us his card. Now I wish I'd kept it."

"Did you find his face in any of your photos?" I wondered how this so-called wine dealer was connected to the woman from the financial seminar. I was sure the Angels probably had a theory.

He shrugged. "Just profile, not full-on. I did send them to Rose." He shot me a look. "You think I should ask Nick if he wants them?"

I laughed. "It's probably a waste of time. Neither Nick nor the police seem to think the Angels are onto something."

"What do you think?" he asked.

"I don't know."

After our run Liam went up to Gram's apartment to shower and I changed into an old pair of jeans and a paint-spattered hoodie, collected Elvis and went to work in the backyard. Elvis prowled around while I picked up branches and other debris.

Liam had offered to drive Mr. P. over to Charlotte's for supper so Rose and I could leave early for my gravy-making lesson. After Elvis and I finished in the yard for the day, I showered and changed.

Rose was waiting for me in the hallway. "This is not a good idea," I said.

She smiled. "You're too hard on yourself."

"You know I can't cook," I reminded her as I unlocked the SUV. "Unless you call scrambled eggs cooking."

"As a matter of fact, I do call that cooking," Rose said as she climbed in. "And I think you've created a self-fulfilling prophecy. For the next week I want you to look in the mirror every morning and say, 'I am a good cook.'"

"Like that's going to work." I laughed. Then I saw

the expression on her face and realized she wasn't joking.

"Every morning," she repeated firmly.

"Yes, ma'am," I said, slipping the key in the ignition.

"Are you just saying that to humor me?" she asked.

I looked over at her. "Not anymore, I'm not," I said.

Rose just laughed.

Nick's SUV was in Charlotte's driveway while Liz's car was parked in front of the little yellow house. The kitchen smelled like turkey and fresh bread, but there was no sign of Charlotte.

Rose set her carryall on one of the kitchen chairs. I took her coat while she started unloading her bag. Liz was putting napkins around the dining room table.

"Hi," I said. "Where is everyone?"

Liz inclined her head in the general direction of the stairs and the rest of the house. "The spare room. In a moment of what may be temporary insanity, Charlotte is testing paint colors on the walls."

"I didn't know Nick was finished in there." Charlotte had had a water leak in her extra bedroom and Nick had been slowly doing the repairs—given his schedule and the fact that he still did some paramedic shifts, it had been very slowly.

Liz frowned at the napkin in her hand, shook it out and carefully refolded it. "He laid the carpet last weekend. Avery is going to help Charlotte paint as soon as they settle on a color." She set the napkin in place and looked at me then. "Charlotte got some of those little sample pots and Avery painted swatches on the wall. Nicolas is in there giving his opinion."

"So, why aren't you in there giving your opinion?" I asked, although I was pretty sure I knew the answer.

"I already gave mine," she said, "and it was suggested that I might be happier setting the table."

"And your opinion was?"

"That dandelion wine is something you drink in the bandstand behind the library with a college boy who is way too old for you, not something you paint on the wall of your spare room." There was a challenge in her gaze that I for one wasn't going to argue with.

"Duly noted," I said.

I hung the coats in the living room closet and went in search of Charlotte and the others. I found Charlotte standing in the middle of her spare room, arms crossed over her aproned front. Nick and Avery were just in front of the end wall, looking at five different patches of paint color on the otherwise white wall.

Charlotte smiled when she saw me. I went to stand beside her, draping my arm around her shoulder. "How's the decision-making process going?" I asked.

"We're down to three choices," she said, "and I'm starting to think that I should have just gone with off-white." She turned her head to look at me. "And don't you dare tell Liz I said that."

I mimed zipping my lips shut.

Nick turned around and smiled at me. "Hey, Sarah," he said. He gestured at the wall. "Want to weigh in?"

"Go ahead," Charlotte said.

I joined Nick and Avery in front of the wall.

"The two that have tape across them are out of the running," Avery said.

I looked at the three remaining colors. "Not that one," I said, pointing to a deep green grass shade. "It's too dark. The room will seem smaller." I leaned in toward the two other shades.

Nick moved closer to me and I caught the scent of his aftershave, which usually made me feel fifteen again. "Take your time," he said.

"Hey! No fair," Avery said sharply.

"What do you mean, no fair?" I said.

She crossed her arms and glared at Nick. "He's trying to be all sexy so you'll agree with him."

"I am not," Nick retorted, but the touch of color that tinged his cheeks gave him away. Avery was right.

I turned to her. "Doesn't matter," I said, laughing. "Nick's 'all sexy' doesn't work on me."

Avery made a triumphant face at him.

Nick swiped a hand over his mouth and said, "The hell it doesn't," so softly only I heard the words.

I shot him a stink eye and went back to studying the wall. The choices were a medium gray and a very pale butter yellow. "That one," I said, touching the patch of yellow paint.

"Yes!" Avery crowed, doing a fist pump in the air. She turned to Charlotte. "Sarah likes dandelion wine, too."

Charlotte's gaze shifted to me.

"I really do like the color," I said. "It's warm. It's light. It'll make the room seem bigger."

"Then dandelion wine it is," she said with a smile.

"I could help you with the painting," Avery offered. "I mean if you want some help."

"I'd love the help," Charlotte said. "Thank you."

Avery smiled. "I have to tell Nonna what color we picked."

"I'm sure she'll be thrilled." Charlotte smiled at me over Avery's head.

"Fine," Nick said, staring up at the ceiling, an aggrieved tone in his voice. "Ignore my home decor advice."

"We're pretty much going to, dear," his mother said. She beckoned to Avery. "I need to check the turkey."

Nick turned to me. "You were supposed to back me up," he said. "Didn't you see me signaling you?" He waggled his eyebrows at me.

"Oh, that was a signal," I said. "I thought you were having some kind of face spasm. I didn't realize you were being all sexy."

He laughed. "Well, next time you'll know."

We headed back to the living room. "How's your investigation going?" I asked.

"I'm getting close to wrapping things up," he said. "How's the Angels' investigation going?"

"They have a couple of ideas that might actually go somewhere."

He shook his head. "You mean a guy they think was at Feast in the Field and a woman with a plaid purse who attended a money-management seminar?"

I nodded. "It's not as far-fetched as it sounds."

"I told you that the police are already pursuing a lead," he said.

"Liam thinks the two of you might have talked to the guy," I said, ignoring his implication that Alfred and the ladies were on the wrong track.

Nick sat on the arm of Charlotte's sofa. "I know. He

told me he sent Rose and Alfred some photos off his phone." He cocked his head to one side. "Are you going to ask to see the photos on my phone?" he teased.

"I thought maybe I could be all sexy and you'd show them to me without me having to ask."

Nick laughed. "Now I'm wishing I actually had pictures from Feast in the Field."

"You don't?" I said. I knew it was a long shot that Rose's latest suspect was actually the person who had sold Edison Hall all those fake bottles, but I'd been hoping nonetheless. That was what happened when the Angels pulled me into one of their cases. They also pulled me into their particular way of looking at things.

Nick shook his head. "Sorry. I don't have any photos on my phone. I'm kind of a dinosaur. I like a camera." He reached out and caught my hand. "Does this mean I don't get to see what your 'all sexy' is?"

I felt my face begin to get red.

Rose stuck her head around the dining room doorway then. "There you are, dear," she said. "Charlotte's taking the turkey out. We need to get started on the gravy."

"I, uh, have to go," I said, motioning in Rose's direction. Nick let go of my hand and I started across the room, almost tripping over the coffee table. I could feel Nick's eyes on me.

"Did I interrupt something?" Rose asked, looking up at me.

"No," I said. "Let's go make gravy."

Everyone other than Nick seemed to be in the kitchen. Liam and Mr. P. had just walked in. The turkey was on a large platter, tented with foil. The roast pan was straddling one of the stove burners. Rose had a whisk, an odd-looking measuring cup, and a Mason jar of something on the counter next to the stove. I remembered Charlotte's remark about ketchup and fervently hoped she had some in her refrigerator.

Rose clapped her hands. "Everybody out," she said. "Sarah doesn't need an audience while she's cooking." She looked toward Mr. P. and made a move-along gesture with her hand.

He started for the dining room. "Rosie's right," he said. "Let's give them some space to work."

"You'll do just fine," Charlotte said as she passed me.

Mr. P. held the door open and once everyone else was out of the room, he smiled at me. "Don't worry, my dear," he said. "You have a good teacher." He looked at Rose. "I'll keep them in the living room."

She beamed at him. "Thank you, Alfred," she said.

He disappeared into the next room and Rose turned to me.

"Sarah darling, you know I love you like you were my own," she said solemnly, taking my hands in her own.

"I love you, too," I said, wondering where this was going.

She looked over her shoulder seemingly to make certain no one was spying on us and then took a step closer to me. "I'm going to share with you the secret of my perfect gravy, but you have to swear that you won't tell anyone. Ever." She looked back over her shoulder again.

I would have laughed except she was so deadly serious. "I swear," I promised, crossing my heart with one finger for good measure and hoping the secret wasn't something like fried turkey livers or brains or something.

Rose took a deep breath and pulled two red packets out of the pocket of her apron.

"A mix?" I said.

"Shhhhh!" she hissed, putting her index finger to her mouth.

"I thought you could cook everything," I whispered.

"Well, surprise. I can't make gravy from scratch. Or pineapple upside-down cake."

I frowned. "Wait a minute. I've eaten your pineapple upside-down cake."

"You've eaten *a* pineapple upside-down cake," she said. "And we really don't have time to talk about that right now."

"Okay," I said. "What do I do?"

Rose walked me through the instructions on the back of the mix packet and in five minutes actual turkey gravy was simmering in the roaster. She handed me a spoon and I took a taste.

"It's good," I said in surprise.

"Of course it's good," she said. "The company would have gone out of business by now if it wasn't."

Charlotte poked her head around the door then. "How's it going?" she asked.

I smiled at her. "Good. Really good."

She came up behind me and leaned over my shoulder to look into the pan. "It smells wonderful," she said.

"It tastes wonderful, too," Rose said, handing Charlotte a spoon so she could take a taste.

"Um, that is delicious," Charlotte exclaimed. Behind

her Rose tucked the empty gravy mix packages in the pocket of her apron. Charlotte straightened up and smiled at me. "I knew you could do it," she said. "Now, could you help me dish out the food?"

I smiled back at her. "What would you like me to do?"

"Put some hot water in the gravy boat to warm it and then put those rolls on the table." She pointed to the counter behind me. Then she reached for the turkey platter, glancing over at Rose at the same time. "You did get Sarah to make two packages of gravy, didn't you?" she asked.

Rose's expression didn't change, but her shoulders went rigid and the hand in her pocket froze. "I don't know what you're talking about," she said, a tad stiffly.

Charlotte moved the bird to the counter, pulled off the foil that had been loosely covering it and finally looked at her friend full-on. "Rose, you haven't made gravy completely from scratch since the seventies. Do you have one empty gravy mix in your pocket or two?"

Rose slowly withdrew her hand from her apron pocket. She was still holding the two empty packets.

"Good," Charlotte said, leaning back to regard the golden brown turkey for a moment. "That should be enough." She glanced over her shoulder at me. "Sarah, are you warming the gravy boat?"

"I'm on it," I said.

"How long have you known?" Rose asked, somewhat indignantly, one hand on her hip.

"How long have you been buying those packages?" Charlotte countered.

"A while," Rose hedged.

"Nineteen seventy-three," Charlotte said, picking up the knife. She seemed to have planned her attack on the turkey.

Rose's lips moved as she did the math. "What gave me away?" she asked, indignation replaced with genuine curiosity.

"No offense, but before 1973 your gravy tasted like burned shoes."

"How do you know what burned shoes taste like?" Rose asked, slipping on a pair of oven mitts.

Charlotte glanced over her shoulder at her friend. "You ate my mother's cooking. You know the answer to that," she said. "And the potatoes are in the green casserole dish."

Rose nodded as if it all made sense. "Are you going to tell?" she asked.

"Nothing to tell," Charlotte said.

They both looked at me. I held up the hand that wasn't holding the gravy boat. "Hey, I just made gravy that people can actually eat. The how doesn't matter. It could have been leprechauns."

"I think that's cookies, dear," Rose said helpfully.

We were about to go way off on a tangent. I smiled at her. "Either way, your secret's safe with me."

Dinner was delicious as usual. It was fun to watch both Nick and Liam take a tentative taste of the gravy and then try to hide their surprise that it was edible. After we'd eaten I caught Nick's eye across the table and tipped my head, ever so slightly, in the direction of the kitchen.

He nodded, set his napkin next to his plate and then

pushed back his chair. "Mom, that was delicious. Thank you," he said. He grinned at me. "And, Sarah, good job with the gravy."

I ducked my head and smiled.

Nick swept his finger from Charlotte to Liz to Rose and Mr. P. "Now go sit."

Charlotte was already getting to her feet. "Don't be silly," she said.

Nick looked at Liam. "Please escort my mother to the living room."

Liam jumped up, grinning. He moved around the table and offered his arm to Charlotte with a bow.

Charlotte took it and turned to look at Nick. "Yeah, I know I'm stubborn," he said with that charming little boy smile. "I've heard it's hereditary."

"It is," Avery chimed it. "I get it from Nonna even though she says she's not stubborn at all."

"I'm not," Liz said, setting her napkin next to her plate. "I'm determined."

"Yes, you are, Elizabeth," Mr. P. said warmly. Then he got to his feet and smiled across the table at Nick. "Could I help, Nicolas?" he asked, effectively ending the stubbornness discussion.

"Yes," Nick said. "You can tell Avery if you'd like another cup of coffee."

Mr. P. tipped his head to one side. He reminded me of a balding woodchuck or a groundhog with high-water pants. "I think I would like another. Thank you," he said.

"I'll get it," Avery said. She looked at her grand-mother. "More tea, right?"

"Please," Liz said.

"I'll get some for Charlotte and Rose, too," Avery said to no one in particular.

I cleared the table while Nick put the food away in the kitchen. Then I started on the pots and knives that I knew Charlotte always washed by hand while Avery and Liam loaded the dishwasher.

"Thanks, guys," Nick said when the kitchen was almost back to rights. Liam and Avery headed for the living room, each with a slice of pie—his second and her third.

"Want a cup?" Nick asked, holding up the coffeepot as I wiped the counter by the sink.

"Um, yeah," I said.

He poured, added cream and sugar and handed the mug to me.

I leaned against the counter and took a sip.

"You know, if we stay in here very long, my mother and her cohorts are going to get ideas," Nick said.

"They already have ideas," I said. "Rose pointed out that you have lots of hair and there are no bald men on either side of your family."

Nick laughed. "That's a bald-faced fabrication, pardon the pun. My grandfather McPhee had hair, but it spent the week in a box and only came out Sunday for church." He tipped his head and pointed at his own head. "This hair is man-made, but it's made by this man." He tapped his chest with two fingers.

"Good to know," I said.

He leaned against the counter beside me. "Apparently one of your selling points is that you have very few cavities."

I laughed. "Please tell me you're kidding."

He shook his head. "What can I say? Good dental hygiene is important to my mother."

"We should go see what they're doing," I said.

"Talking about us or talking about their case would be my guess," Nick said, pushing away from the counter.

They were talking about the case. Mr. P. was sitting on Charlotte's sofa with Rose on one side, Liam on the other, and Avery hanging over the back. They were all looking at his laptop. Liz was in the big overstuffed chair, one elbow propped on the padded arm. Charlotte was sitting opposite in a brown leather club chair, writing in an old-style steno notebook I hadn't known they made anymore.

I took my coffee and went to sit on the footstool in front of Liz. "What are you doing?" I asked.

"Making a list of people who were at Feast in the Field who may have taken photos," Rose said. She looked at Liz. "Celeste?"

Charlotte looked up from her notepad.

Liz shook her head. "No. She doesn't have a cell phone and the last camera she would have used was an Instamatic."

Nick had walked around the sofa to stand next to Avery. I saw him look over Mr. P.'s shoulder at the laptop balanced on his knees. Then something in his body language changed. He stiffened, then leaned in slightly.

I watched out of the corner of my eye. Something had clearly caught his attention on the computer screen. I waited for him to say something, but he didn't. He swiped his free hand over the back of his neck, came around the end of the sofa and sat on the arm next to

Liam. "What's happening with the development?" I heard him ask. "Have you started looking at those old warehouses?"

Liam shifted in his seat and I leaned forward to see what was on the screen before Mr. P. moved to another photo. The image was of a fair-haired man, arms caught animatedly in the air, in front of one of the booths. There had to be a dozen people around him, but he was the only one facing the camera. I was betting it was him Nick had recognized.

By the time Mr. P. had gone through all the pictures, Charlotte had written down twenty-one names of people who might have taken photos at Feast in the Field. Rose and Mr. P. were hoping for a better shot of the mystery man.

Liz and Avery left at the same time I did. I'd hoped to get a chance to talk to Nick and maybe find out what had caught his attention on that computer screen, but he was talking to Liam and since I was giving Rose and Mr. P. a ride, I couldn't really stall.

When I got home I found Elvis sprawled on his back on the top of his cat tower. After I'd stowed the leftovers Charlotte had sent me home with in the refrigerator, I went over to him. He eyed me upside down and I scratched the black fur under his chin. He sighed and began to purr. For a moment I wished all it would take was a scratch under my chin to make me relax.

I was sitting on the couch about an hour later going through a pile of old home-reno magazines when there was a knock on the door. "That's Liam," I said to Elvis, who had been stretched out across my legs. I moved him to the floor and went to let my brother in.

Except it wasn't Liam. It was Nick.

"Hi," he said. "Do you have a minute?"

"Sure," I said, opening the door wider. "Come in."

He stepped inside. "I can't stay for long."

"What's up?" I asked.

He put a hand in his pocket and held out a business card. "Here," he said. "This is the man Rose and Alfred are looking for."

I took the cardboard rectangle from him. "You recognized him. In the photos."

He studied me, dark eyes serious. "You knew."

I nodded. "I know your tells, remember? That's how I kept gas in Gram's truck the summer I learned to drive."

Nick gave me a sheepish grin. "I remember."

"Thank you for this," I said, turning the card over in my fingers. It was made from heavy, cream-colored card stock with a streamlined font—Century Gothic, I thought—in black. I remembered Liam saying the wine dealer had been handing out business cards.

"This doesn't mean I think they're right," he cautioned.

"Doesn't mean you think they're wrong, either."

"I didn't say that, Sarah," he said. He shook his head and gave me a wry smile. "Look, when I saw that photo I remembered the guy. There wasn't anything shifty about him. He was personable and well-spoken."

"But," I finished.

"Just between us?" he asked, raising an eyebrow.

I nodded.

"I noticed that he was just a little faster handing those out to anyone who looked to be a senior. At the time I chalked it up to him just targeting people who seemed more likely to have money."

"Or maybe he was targeting people who'd be a little more open to his pitch." I looked at the card again. "Thorne Logan," I said. "You think that's a real name?"

Nick shrugged. "It could be. I had a chemistry class with a girl named Peaches." He looked at his watch. "Do me a favor? Try to rein them in if they do find the guy."

I laughed. "Right. Because I've done such a good job in the past."

He rolled his eyes. "They listen to you more than they listen to me."

"I'll do what I can," I promised.

"Thanks," he said. One eyebrow went up and the corners of his lips twitched. "Nice shirt."

I put a hand on my chest and looked down at my tee. It was a Power Rangers shirt. Nick had bought it to replace the similar one I'd had as a kid that he'd wiped his nose on—an act he claimed was one of social commentary but that I thought was just him being a boy.

"I never asked, where on earth did you find it?"

"EBay. I've been watching for a Samurai Pizza Cats shirt for Liam's birthday."

I laughed. "He'll kill me for telling you about that, but it would be worth it."

"I'll warn you if I find it," Nick said. He looked at his watch again. "I've gotta go. Will I see you Thursday?"

"Wouldn't miss it," I said.

I locked the door behind him and went back to the sofa, where Elvis was waiting. I sat down beside him and he craned his neck over my arm to look at the business card. The only thing on it was Thorne Logan's name and a phone number. Any connection between him and the fake wine was spiderweb thin at best. And what about the woman with the plaid purse? Were they connected? Was she involved at all? The only thing we had to go on was Rose's gut feeling.

The cat cocked his head to one side and gave me a quizzical look.

"I'm not really sure what this means, either," I said to him.

Mac and Rose went out to work on the Hall house Monday morning. Charlotte and I stayed at the shop. I was expecting Cleveland, the other picker I bought from regularly, to stop by with his haul from the weekend.

I spent a chunk of my time outside working on an old metal cabinet that Jess and I had found in the ditch along an old woods road. I could still see the look on Mac's face when I'd asked him to help me lift it out of the back of the SUV.

"Let me get this straight," he'd said. "You found this in a ditch?"

"People dump their garbage out on a couple of those woods roads because they don't want to pay the fee at the landfill," I'd said, pulling on a pair of canvas work gloves before grabbing one side of the cabinet. "It's disgusting."

"So you decided to bring it here? How exactly did you get this . . . thing from the ditch to your car?"

"Jess and I carried it."

Jess had actually been the one who climbed down

into the mud and heaved the metal cabinet up onto the trail.

Mac had tried to swallow down a grin and pretty much failed. "I don't know, Sarah," he'd said. "I think you may have jumped the shark this time."

"O ye of little faith," I'd said as he'd help me carry the cabinet into the old garage. Now, standing on a tarp, scraping who knew how many years of blistered, peeling paint off the old metal, I wondered if he was right. Not that I was willing to admit defeat yet.

Cleveland showed up midmorning. I bought a couple of paintings, three potato baskets and an armless upholstered chair that looked as though it had been used as a cat scratching post.

Avery and Mr. P. showed up at lunchtime. Avery's progressive school only had morning classes, so she worked most afternoons for me. Liz grumbled that there was no way she was learning anything only attending classes in the morning, but from what I'd seen of Avery's homework, they seemed to be using the time well. I had no idea what exactly had happened at home or at her previous school, but being in North Harbor had been good for the teen. And living with Liz, for all they squabbled about kale smoothies and Avery's driving, had been good for both of them. I sent her out to the garage to work on a set of old kitchen cabinets I wanted to eventually use for storage out there.

After lunch of a turkey sandwich made with Charlotte's leftovers, I went out to the porch. Mr. P. was at his computer.

"Hello, Sarah," he said. "How was your morning?"

"I started working on that old cabinet," I said.

He smiled. "I'm sure it will be lovely when you're done."

I smiled back at him. "I hope you're right."

"I'm confident that I will be."

I held out the business card. "I think this is the man you're looking for," I said. I'd thought about giving the card to Charlotte and decided against it. I didn't know why Nick hadn't just given it to his mother and I didn't want to cause a problem between them. "I tried the number, but all I got was a very robotic leave-a-number message."

"Thank you," Mr. P. said.

He didn't seem surprised, I realized.

"It occurs to me that it might be better if I didn't ask you how you came to get this card," he added.

I wasn't the only one who could read Nick's tells, I realized.

"You're a very observant man," I said, choosing my words carefully.

The old man adjusted his glasses and smiled at me again. "Over the years I've discovered that being observant has its advantages."

"Yes, it does," I agreed. I looked over at his computer. "I'll let you get back to work."

"Thank you, my dear," he said.

I spent the next half hour returning phone calls in my office. I came downstairs to see how Avery was doing packing parcels just as Ethan Hall came into the shop. I'd called Stella and told her about finding the train and about Channing Caulfield's claim on the rare model cars. She'd told me she'd talk to Ethan and promised one of them would get back to me.

"Hi, Sarah, do you have a minute?" Ethan asked.

"Of course," I said, walking over to him. It was like standing next to Nick. Even in heels I felt short.

"Aunt Stella told me about the model train," he said. There was a day's worth of stubble on his chin, blond, like his short hair. "Do you think Caulfield has a claim on it?"

"Possibly," I said. "There's that bottle of wine that changed hands because of it."

Ethan blew out a breath. "Damn it," he muttered.

"I have an idea," I said.

"I hope he doesn't expect me to pay for that bottle of wine," he said. "I'm sorry he got conned, but so did my dad."

"Don't worry about the wine," I said. "Stella told me about Ellie needing surgery on her back."

His blue eyes clouded over. "Then she probably also told you that the surgery is considered experimental."

I nodded. "I think Channing Caulfield might be persuaded to relinquish his claim on the model train so it can be sold with the proceeds going into a fund for Ellie's surgery." I raised an eyebrow. "He gets to look good."

"And we get the money," Ethan finished. "I might be able to convince Ellie to go for that. She has some very strong opinions on anything she sees as being a handout."

"We need to do a little more research into the value of the layout," I said. I raised a cautionary hand. "And it's not going to cover the cost of the surgery by a long shot."

"But it will help me." Ethan smiled. "Thank you,

Sarah. The stress from all this has been eating me alive."

"You're welcome," I said. "I wish it were more."

He wiped a hand over his mouth. "You and me both."

Mr. P. came in from the sunporch then and walked over to us. He was carrying a sheet of paper in one hand. "Excuse me, Sarah," he said. "Would you mind if I made a copy of this?" He held up the page, which was a photo of Thorne Logan that he'd probably printed at home.

"Go ahead," I said.

He patted his pockets and I knew he was looking for a quarter. Charlotte, who kept the Angels' books, insisted that they pay for copying and printing. Arguing the point had done me no good. They'd also started paying me rent for the sunporch. When I'd tried to argue against that, Rose tartly informed me that if I didn't take the money they'd rent office space somewhere else. I couldn't see how that would be a good idea, so I'd relented. Every month half the money went to the Friends of the North Harbor Library and the other half to the Mid-coast Animal Shelter. It made me feel better about taking the money in the first place and since they didn't know they couldn't argue with me over it.

Mr. P. found the twenty-five cents and held it out to me. The photo slipped from his grasp. Ethan reached out and caught it before it could hit the floor. He glanced at the picture and frowned. "Wait a minute," he said. "Do you know this man?"

"Do you?" Mr. P. asked.

Ethan nodded. "He contacted me a couple of weeks

ago. He wanted to buy a bottle from my father's wine collection."

"Just one bottle?" Mr. P. said. Like me, he'd noticed that Ethan had said "a bottle."

Ethan glanced at the photo once more and handed the piece of paper back to Alfred. "Yes."

Mr. P. and I exchanged a look. "Why did he want a bottle of wine that isn't worth anything?" I asked.

Ethan swiped a hand across his mouth again. "Because he thought maybe it was."

Mr. P. and I stared at him.

Ethan shrugged. "I mean he was wrong. Ronan talked to some other contact he had and whoever it was agreed that the bottle was a fake." He exhaled loudly. "Just like all the other bottles in the old man's collection. I don't know why he did that to me." It was impossible to miss the edge of bitterness in his voice. Then he shook his head and gave us a wry smile. "I don't know how people can sleep at night, taking advantage of someone who's old."

Mr. P. tipped his head back and regarded Ethan thoughtfully, it seemed to me. "There's an old saying," he said quietly. "What goes around comes around."

"Well, excuse me for hoping you're right," Ethan said.

Mr. P. nodded and started up the stairs. Elvis was on his way down. The old man stopped for a moment to stroke the top of the cat's head. Elvis made a soft murp and came purposefully down the rest of the steps. He eyed Ethan through narrowed green eyes, walked around us in a wide curve and headed for the workroom.

"Ethan, do you have Mr. Logan's contact information?" I asked. I'd tried the number on the business card Nick had given me. All I'd gotten was voice mail.

He made a face. "I'm going to sound like the stereotypical absentminded professor, but I don't. He contacted me. After I told Ronan about the phone call, he took care of it after that." He smiled. "I'm sorry."

"It's not a big deal," I said. "The police are looking into the fake wine angle as far as Mr. Quinn's death is concerned."

"Well, I can tell you that Logan is a reputable dealer. At least that's what Quinn said."

The phone rang over at the cash desk and I saw Charlotte head over to answer it.

"I'll let you get back to work," Ethan said. "Will you let me know what Caulfield says about the train set?"

I nodded. "I will."

"And would it be a problem if the wine collection stays where it is for now?" he asked. "I moved everything into the kitchen so Quinn could go through the bottles."

I smiled. "We can work around them for now, but it would be nice to have the space for the sale weekend."

He pulled his keys out of his pocket. "I'll talk to Detective Andrews. If the collection is evidence of . . . something, maybe she'll want to take all of it to the police station. Otherwise I'll just have to find a way to dispose of it." He sighed softly.

"Thanks," I said.

Ethan headed out and Elvis came back from wherever he'd gone. He rubbed against my leg and I bent down and picked him up and went upstairs to my office. Mr. P. was just turning off the printer/copier.

I picked up the original photo that he'd just copied and studied it. Elvis poked his head around to have a look as well.

"We're not wrong," Alfred said.

"No, I don't think you are," I said slowly.

Elvis meowed his agreement. "It's unanimous," I said. "Ethan said Ronan Quinn told him your suspect is a reputable wine broker."

Mr. P. hiked his pants up a little higher under his armpits. "Reputable is as reputable does," he said, raising an eyebrow at me.

Chapter 15

I walked back downstairs with Mr. P. "Sarah, what exactly do you know about Ronan Quinn?" he asked.

"Well, he was extremely knowledgeable about wine. He had the designation of *Maître Sommelier* from the *Union de la Sommellerie Française*. And he'd been an expert witness in several court cases."

"I don't suppose Nicolas has said anything to you about the man?"

"Where are you going with this?" I asked, leaning back and studying him. He might have looked like an unassuming little old man, but there was a sharp intellect underneath his mild expression.

"I've just been thinking, what exactly do we know about Mr. Quinn's character?"

"Are you asking if he was like Caesar's wife?" I teased.

His eyes twinkled behind his glasses. "Above reproach?" he said. "Yes. I guess that is what I mean."

"You're thinking maybe he wasn't?" We were stopped in the middle of the store.

Mr. P. looked thoughtful. "I'm not exactly sure, my dear," he said. "So if this sounds off-the-wall, I won't be offended by you pointing it out."

"I somehow doubt anything you're going to say will be off-the-wall," I said. For the most part Alfred could be counted on to be the voice of reason, especially when Rose got her mind set on something. "What are you thinking?"

"We know that Mr. Quinn was also a broker, a dealer who sold wine to collectors."

"Yes."

"And we know that he was investigating the con artists who had defrauded Edison Hall and other people."

I nodded.

Mr. P. cocked his head to one side. He reminded me of an inquisitive baby bird. "What if everyone is wrong about Mr. Quinn?"

I rubbed the space between my eyes. I was beginning to get a headache from trying to follow Mr. P.'s reasoning. "What do you mean by wrong?"

"Well, not to speak ill of the dead, but what if *he* got involved in the fraud investigation to protect himself? Do you see where I'm going?"

I reached over and straightened the pillows on the nearby tub chair. "I do," I said. "You think that maybe Quinn could have been part of the original con. That maybe he was involved in some way with selling those fake bottles of wine."

Mr. P. nodded. "We've all been assuming he was completely aboveboard." He held up one veined, wrinkled hand. "And maybe he was."

"But maybe he wasn't," I finished. I pointed to the photo Alfred was still holding. "So how does Thorne Logan tie in to this? You do have a photo of him talking to that woman who seemed to be promoting exactly the kind of thing Edison ended up losing his money in."

"What if Mr. Logan is the one in the white hat?" Mr. P. asked. "What if he was talking to that woman because he was trying to get more information about the con? What if he wasn't part of it at all?" He held up the photo. "What if he was trying to catch the people who were? He was at Feast in the Field twice and he tried to buy a bottle from Edison Hall's collection. We're just assuming he's part of the con. That doesn't mean he is."

It didn't seem like a good time to point out that *I* hadn't assumed anything. "I don't know," I finally said.

It was far-fetched. But there was also a vein of logic that ran through the old man's reasoning. I pulled a hand over the back of my neck. The headache had crept up over the top of my scalp. "I can't tell you you're wrong."

"I think it's worth doing a little more digging into Mr. Quinn's background," Mr. P. said.

I let out a slow breath. "I think it is."

He smiled. "I'll let you know what I find out." He headed for the sunporch, moving quickly like a man with a purpose, which in fact he was.

Charlotte walked over to me. She held out a blue message slip. "Someone from Seaward Properties called. They want some measurements off the chandelier from Doran's."

She was referring to the chandelier that Mac and I had brought into the shop. It had once been the focal point of the Portland department store. I'd bought it back in the fall along with several mannequins and a few other things. It had almost been sold twice.

I held up my crossed fingers. "Maybe third time's the charm."

"Oh, I hope so," she said. "I hate to think of that beautiful old piece ending up out of the state or even worse."

"Not going to happen," I said. "I think Mac's made the sale, but if we can't find a home for that light here in town, I'll twist Sam's arm until he lets me hang it down at The Black Bear."

Charlotte laughed. "I think a chandelier is just what that place needs."

I went up to my office and called the Seaward office. We set up a time for someone to come take some measurements.

Elvis had come back upstairs while I was on the phone, settling himself on my desk directly in front of the phone so that when I went to hang up I had to reach around him to do it.

"Mrr?" he said in what seemed—at least to me—to be an inquiring tone.

"If this newest development proposal actually goes ahead"—I held up my crossed fingers—"we may finally have a home for that big brass chandelier."

His response was to yawn.

"You may not be impressed, but I thought I was going to have to coerce Sam into hanging it down at the pub."

I looked at my watch. "Mac and Rose should be back

anytime now," I said to the cat. His ears twitched and he lifted his head to look around.

I wondered what Rose would think of Mr. P.'s new line of inquiry.

Then in some kind of unexplainable thinking process, my brain lined up the last things I'd said to Elvis. When I didn't immediately say anything, he nudged me with his furry head.

I reached over to stroke his fur. "I'm stupid," I said to him.

He murped softly.

"Thank you for the vote of confidence," I said, "but I am. We could have called Sam."

Elvis blinked his green eyes at me. He had no idea what I was talking about.

Sam knew everyone and he ran a bar. The odds of him knowing someone who knew someone who could tell us more about the two wine dealers had to be good. I didn't know Ronan Quinn, but I wanted the person who had killed him caught. And I wanted the person who had scammed Edison Hall caught. I wanted whoever it was to pay—hopefully financially so Ethan's wife, Ellie, could have that operation she needed. I liked it when the world was fair, when the bad guys got what was coming to them. Even though it didn't always happen, I wanted it to.

Sam answered the phone on the third ring. "Hey," he said. "What's up?"

"I need to pick your brain," I said. I leaned back in the chair and Elvis took that as an invitation to climb down and settle himself in my lap.

Sam laughed. "Whatever I have is yours."

"What do you know about wine?" I asked.

"Box or bottle?"

I laughed. "Very funny."

"I'm more of a beer guy, but I like a good California merlot," he said. "Does that help?"

"I was thinking about something a little more high-end," I said. I explained about Ronan Quinn.

"That's the guy whose body you found at Edison Hall's old place."

Elvis laid his head on my chest and I began to stroke his fur. "That's him. We'd like to know a little more about him. Do you maybe know someone?" I didn't finish the sentence.

"We?" Sam said.

"Stella Hall hired the Angels to look into Quinn's death. She thinks it might be connected to all those bottles of wine that Edison bought that turned out to be worthless."

"So you're in the detective business again?"

I could picture him behind his own desk in his office, feet propped on the corner of the desk.

"No, I'm helping, that's it," I said. I leaned back a little in my chair and Elvis gave a small sigh of contentment. "I like Stella."

"So do I," Sam said. "I can think of a couple of people I can call. Can you give me some time?"

"Take all the time you need," I said. "I appreciate this. Thank you."

"Hey, I'm happy to help."

I pictured him smiling because he was the type of person who really was happy to help anyone.

We said good-bye and I leaned over and hung up the phone.

"Sam is on the case," I told Elvis. He started to purr, which probably had more to do with the fact that I was scratching behind his right ear than his enthusiasm for Sam's help, but I decided to rationalize it as the latter anyway.

I spent the next hour downstairs in the shop helping Charlotte with customers. We sold another guitar, a wooden rocking chair and a bread pail. Charlotte spent several minutes explaining the bread-making process to the young man who bought the pail, even writing out her favorite recipe on a piece of paper.

I put my arm around her shoulders once we were alone in the shop. "I'm so glad you were here," I said. "The only thing I could have told him about bread was to read the best-before date on the little plastic tag before you buy it."

Charlotte shook her head, smiling at the same time. "You can't use that 'I can't cook' line anymore. Your gravy last night was very good."

"It came from a package."

"So does my angel food cake," she said. "There's nothing wrong with using some shortcuts."

"True," I said. "But you make the strawberry/rhubarb sauce. You even grow the berries and rhubarb yourself."

She smoothed the front of her apron. "And at Thanksgiving I chopped a few dried-up leftover cranberries from the bottom of my vegetable crisper, microwaved them with half a bottle of marmalade that was in the gift basket I won at the animal shelter fund-raiser and added what juice I could squeeze out of half a wizened lemon, and you all thought I spent half the afternoon in the kitchen." She smiled at me. "Things are seldom as perfect as they appear, and that includes cooking."

I was at the workbench taking the paintings I'd bought from Cleveland out of their frames when Sam called back.

"Linda Fairchild," he said, reciting a telephone number. "She's a lawyer in New Hampshire—Manchester, I think—and she's been involved in a couple of civil lawsuits over all this fake wine business. She's expecting your call."

I leaned against the workbench and pushed my hair back out of my face with one hand. I should have called Sam much earlier. I'd had no idea it would be so easy. "Thank you," I said. "I owe you big-time."

"You don't owe me anything," he said. "You owe Vince, although I don't think you need to give him a kidney or anything. I think if you buy him a beer next time you see him, he'll call it square."

"Wait a minute," I said. "Vince? Vince Kennedy?"

"How many other Vinces do you know?" Sam asked.

"Uh, none, but I didn't know he knew anything about wine."

I heard the creak of Sam's old desk chair. "Neither did I, but it turns out he actually knows a little. And more important, he knows a lot about playing guitar."

"And the two are connected, how?"

"Vince put some learn-to-play-guitar videos up on YouTube. They've turned out to be pretty popular. This lawyer found them, thought they were great and got in touch with Vince to say thank you. They struck up an online friendship and maybe a little more. He didn't say. I didn't ask. I know they've met in person several times."

"I had no idea Vince was seeing someone," I said. "Let alone a lawyer."

Sam laughed. "Yeah, well, I'm not sure how much of her he's seen and I don't think I really want to know."

"You and me both," I said. "Tell Vince thank you and I'm buying next time I see him."

"I will, kiddo," Sam said. "I hope you get what you need."

I had scribbled down the phone number on the back of an old envelope that Mac had left on the workbench. Sam had said the lawyer was expecting my call. Mr. P. would say "no time like the present."

I decided this was a call best made from my office. I went back into the shop. "Can you handle things here for a little while?" I asked Charlotte. "I need to make a phone call."

"Go ahead," she said. "Rose and Mac are on their way back and I can always get Avery to come in if I need help."

I called Linda Fairchild's office and when I gave the receptionist my name I was put directly through to her office.

"Hello, Sarah," she said. "Vince said you have some questions about Ronan Quinn." She had a warm, husky voice. I knew Vince well enough to know he would have been intrigued by the woman the first time he heard her speak. He wasn't the first musician I'd met to have a thing about voices.

"I do," I said. "I appreciate you talking to me." I explained how we were clearing out the house for Stella and how all of Edison's savings had gone into his wine collection. And I told her about Ellie's need for surgery without going into too many details that would violate her privacy.

"I don't mean to make it sound like some hokey old movie in which the widow with the six kids is going to lose the farm unless everyone pulls together and puts on a show," I said. "But I know the family was hoping Mr. Quinn would be able to put together enough of a paper trail for them to go after the people that defrauded Edison Hall."

"I'm sorry," Linda Fairchild said. "Ronan told me about Mr. Hall's wine collection. I've heard stories like that before—and worse. But it could take years for a lawsuit to move through the courts and there's no guarantee the family would end up with anything. These people can be very . . . creative at hiding their money. I'm surprised Ronan didn't explain that."

"Maybe he did," I said. "I didn't ask a lot of questions." I hesitated. I wasn't sure how to ask her if there was any chance Quinn had been involved in any sort of scam. I settled for asking her what kind of person the man had been.

"Ronan was a straight arrow," the lawyer replied. "He was the kind of person who did what he said he would do when he said he would do it." She went on to talk about how much work Quinn had put into building the case that she'd taken to court. "In that case we were able to get some money for the woman who had been defrauded. And now the police are looking at bringing criminal charges against the two people involved. They didn't sell any wine to Mr. Hall, by the way."

I flashed to the image of Ronan Quinn's body on the kitchen floor of the Hall house. I had the feeling I would have liked the man. And I also had the feeling that Mr. P. was on the wrong track.

"So he was one of the good guys?" I said.

"He was." Now it was her turn to hesitate. "Sarah, are you thinking that Ronan might have been involved in something illegal?" she asked, almost as though she'd read my mind.

"That was a possibility," I admitted. "That's why I wanted to talk to you, but from what you've said, he just doesn't sound like that kind of person."

"He wasn't. I worked with the man for months and I can promise you that all he wanted was to catch the bad guys. He wasn't one of them. In fact, when I spoke to him last week he seemed to think that he was onto something."

My office door swung partway open, seemingly by magic. Then in a moment Elvis jumped onto my desk. He walked over and sat down next to the phone. "Something to do with Edison Hall's wine collection?" I asked.

"I think so," she said. "In the case I mentioned, the fraud involved just a few faked bottles. Ronan said this seemed to be deception on a larger scale. He was planning to drive down and see me a couple of days after he was killed." She cleared her throat. "I'm sorry I couldn't be any more help."

"You've actually helped more than you realize," I said. The first thing I was going to do after I hung up was go tell Mr. P.—gently—that his idea that Ronan Quinn had been involved in conning people was off base. "I have one more question."

Elvis leaned against my shoulder and looked expectantly over at the half-open office door.

"Do you know a wine broker named Thorne Logan?" I asked.

"Yes, I do. His real name is Thornton Logan."

Mac slipped around the door, set a steaming cup of coffee on my desk, smiled at me and left again.

"Would you say he's the same caliber of man as Ronan Quinn?"

She hesitated, cleared her throat again. "I have no personal knowledge of Mr. Logan being involved in any illegal endeavors," she finally said.

That was about as close to a no as I was going to get. I thank Linda Fairchild for her help and we said good-bye. I leaned back in the chair again, wrapping both hands around my coffee cup. "How did Mac know I needed this?" I asked Elvis. He craned his neck to look at my cup and then almost seemed to smile at me.

I thought about Liam, urging me to make a move on Mac. I shook my head. Mac and I had way too good a relationship for me to do something like that.

I took another sip of my coffee. "I have to go tell Mr. P. and the others that we're on the wrong track as far as Ronan Quinn is concerned. It wasn't any lack of honor among thieves that led to his death." On the other hand, it seemed as though it was worth taking a closer look at Thorne, formerly Thornton, Logan.

I pulled a hand back through my hair. "You know what Nick would say?" I said to Elvis, who was looking over the side of my desk at the left drawer where he somehow knew I'd put a box of kitty kibble that morning.

The cat looked up and cocked his head to one side. I'd seen him do that enough times to know he was faking an interest in what I was saying because he thought it would get him a treat.

"Nick would say this is what I get for getting involved in something that is really none of my business." I opened the drawer, fished out half a dozen tiny bits of the dry cat treats and lined them up in a row on my desk.

Ever polite, Elvis meowed his thanks before starting to eat.

I took another sip of my coffee. Aside from the information about Ronan Quinn, one other thing had stuck in my mind from my conversation with the lawyer: the fact that she'd stressed that there was no big payout in a lawsuit against these con artists. Ethan had told me that he wanted the people who had defrauded his father punished. What had he said, quoting Ronan Quinn? *If the law can't get them, then at least we can hit them in their wallets.* Had Quinn really said that or had Ethan misinterpreted his words. Each time I talked to Ethan I couldn't help noticing that he was a little self-absorbed.

Elvis was crunching away happily on a star-shaped piece of kitty kibble. "You know what?" I said, lowering my voice so the cat would be the only one to hear me. "I like Stella a lot. But there's something about Ethan . . ." I didn't finish the sentence.

As if he'd understood my words, the cat turned and glanced at the doorway before bending down for the last treat on my desk. "I know," I said with a sigh. "That's probably not something I can share with anyone else."

Chapter 16

Rose was in the Angels' office with Mr. P. when I went downstairs.

"Hello, dear," Rose said. "Did Mac tell you we're finished in the living room and one bedroom?"

"I haven't had a chance to talk to him yet," I said, "but that's good to know. Thank you." I looked at Mr. P. "Do you have a minute? I have some information I think you might find useful."

"Of course," he said. "Go ahead. Rosie is up-to-date."

I leaned against the doorframe. "It occurred to me that Sam might know someone who could tell us more about Ronan Quinn, so I called him."

"Of course," Rose said. "We should have thought of that sooner. What did he say?"

"He put me in touch with a lawyer who had worked on a couple of lawsuits over the fake wine with Quinn. I just got off the phone with her."

"I was on the wrong track, wasn't I?" Mr. P. said, pushing his glasses up his nose with one finger.

I nodded.

"I've been looking into Mr. Quinn's background and he really was what he appeared to be, a decent man trying to stop whoever was taking advantage of people like Edison Hall."

"I did learn one thing that might be helpful," I said. "I told you that Sam's contact was a lawyer, so she was pretty circumspect about what she said, but she didn't seem to have a very high opinion of Thorne Logan, and by the way, his real first name is Thornton."

Mr. P. reached for a pencil and wrote the name on the pad of paper next to his laptop. "Thank you, Sarah," he said. "So far we've been hitting a dead end trying to find contact information for the man. I tried the number on the card as well. I got the same message you did. This will help."

"There's something fishy about this man," Rose said. "Who runs a legitimate business and doesn't have a proper voice mail message?"

"Any luck on tracking down our mystery woman?" I asked.

Mr. P. shook his head. "Whoever she is, she's very good at covering her trail."

"Charlotte and I have a few more people to talk to," Rose said. "We'll find her."

I smiled at her. "I have no doubt about that."

Mr. P. was frowning at his laptop.

"Problem?" I asked.

He shook his head, his eyes never leaving the screen. "Sarah, look at this photo of our unidentified woman."

He'd found another angle from the security footage. I could see her fully face-on. "What am I looking for?"

Mr. P. touched the screen with his finger. "Look at her cheekbones and the angle of her jaw."

Rose leaned around me so she could see as well. Alfred picked up the photo of Thorne Logan and handed it to me. "Do you see it?" he asked.

Logan had the same strong jaw and high cheekbones.

"They're related," I said.

Rose looked from Mr. P. to me. "What?" she said.

He raised an eyebrow. "Mother and son?"

I nodded slowly. "I think so."

"I told you there was something fishy about that young man," Rose crowed.

"If you could just prove Edison had met Purse Lady, I'd say you were onto something," I said, slipping one arm around her shoulders. "Go ahead and say it."

Her gray eyes sparkled. "Charlotte found three people who remember him talking to her at the seminar."

I gave her a hug. Then I put my hand over my heart. "Rose Jackson," I said. "You are onto something."

I left them and went out to the old garage. Avery had finished priming the cabinets. As usual she'd done a good job. The teenager was meticulous with a paintbrush and Mac and I were slowly letting her work on more finishing projects.

Mac was looking at the potato baskets. "Hi," he said. "Did you get these from Cleveland?"

I nodded. "I'm thinking once they're cleaned up I may dip them."

He nodded. "Good idea. We've had a couple of designers in lately working on show homes, and those baskets are exactly the kind of thing they like."

"Rose said you're through two more rooms at the house."

Mac fished the keys to the Hall house out of his pocket and handed them to me. "The old man actually had a system to those boxes. Rose noticed that they were stacked in concentric squares, more or less. Then we realized that each—can I say ring when I'm talking about a square?"

"Sure."

He smiled. "Okay, each ring is one kind of item— books, glassware, et cetera." He smoothed a hand over his cropped hair. "And most of the boxes actually have a list of the contents inside."

I smiled back at him. "That's going to save us some time and Stella some money."

"How's the detecting going?" Mac asked.

"It turns out that Ethan knows the mystery man in the photo."

Mac's eyebrows went up.

"He's a wine broker with possibly less than stellar business practices."

"Do you think he had anything to do with Ronan Quinn's death?"

"I don't know anymore. I agree with Mr. P. and Rose that it has to be tied to those bottles of wine, but other than that . . ." I shook my head. "They did find out that Edison was at that financial seminar and that he talked to the mystery woman. *And* it looks like there may be a connection between this broker and the woman with the purse, although I don't know how they're going to find either one of them."

"Maybe the police will come up with something."

"I hope so," I said. "I'm starting to think that this is a case where angelic interference isn't going to help."

"Don't count Rose and Alfred out," Mac said. "They're like Elvis when he smells a mouse, assuming he also had computer skills."

I laughed at the mental image that popped into my head. "Yeah, I'm not sure if that's a good thing or a bad thing," I said. The keys to the Hall house were still in my hand. "Mac, can you handle things here?" I asked. "There's something I need to do."

"Sure," he said. "Is there anything you want me to work on?"

"I bought a couple of paintings from Cleveland," I said. "I started taking them out of the frames and then I got sidetracked."

"I'll take care of it," Mac said. "Shall I get Avery to start cleaning the baskets?"

"Please," I said. "And thank you for the coffee earlier. It was just what I needed."

"I thought so," he said. "You're welcome."

Mac started for the shop and I walked over to my SUV. I wanted to see the wine collection for myself. I didn't know what I was expecting to find that no one else had noticed.

The cartons of wine bottles were still in the kitchen at the Hall house. I opened the top of the closest box and looked inside. Mac had said that most of Edison's boxes had a list of the contents inside. Maybe these boxes did as well.

The box held four bottles, stored upright, which didn't really matter, since the contents were the equivalent of Kool-Aid. Taped inside was half a sheet of loose-leaf. I pulled it free and at the same time lifted out one of the bottles.

Edison Hall had listed the details about each of the bottles in cramped, spidery handwriting on the paper. I spent the next twenty minutes checking boxes, looking for some kind of clue, even though I had no idea what it would look like. In the end, all I discovered was that there were six bottles missing.

I did a quick search of the kitchen. There were no bottles on the shelves or in the cupboards. Ethan had said his father's entire collection of wine was at the house. "Maybe I misunderstood," I said. I was talking to myself, I realized. I was so used to talking to Elvis that now I was talking to myself.

I grabbed the flashlight that Mac had left on the counter and went down to the musty basement. The missing bottles weren't there, either.

Paul and Alyssa were in their front yard kicking around a couple of what looked like beach balls. When I went out to the SUV, Paul raised a hand in hello and I walked across the street to join them.

"Hi, Sarah," he said. "How're you making out in the house?"

"Pretty good," I said. "We're planning a sale in a couple of weeks. There's a very nice wooden r-o-c-k-i-n-g h-o-r-s-e." I glanced at Alyssa, whose forehead was knotted in concentration as she tried to bounce one of the balls off her knee.

Paul smiled. "Thanks," he said. "I'll try to get over and have a look. Alyssa is into p-o-n-i-e-s at the moment." He glanced over at the empty bungalow across the street and lowered his voice. "Have you heard anything about the investigation? Do the police have any idea who killed that man?"

I followed his gaze for a moment. "Nothing so far," I said. I realized that I had a photo of Thorne Logan on my phone. "Could you look at a picture?" I asked.

"Sure," he said.

I found the image of the wine dealer and held out my phone. "Did you ever see him over at the Hall house?"

Paul studied the photo. "Sorry, Sarah," he said. "He doesn't look familiar. Did he have something to do with Mr. Quinn's death?"

"I'm just fishing," I said, stuffing my phone back in my pocket. I smiled. "I better get back to the shop. It was good to see you."

I walked back across the street. It seemed that Thorne Logan or Thornton Logan or whatever he called himself was another dead end for now.

I went right up to my office when I got back to the shop. There were six bottles of wine on Edison Hall's list that weren't in the house as far as I could tell. They nagged at me. Had Quinn taken them for evidence? Did his killer have them?

It occurred to me that maybe Ethan knew. "I'm as bad as Rose," I muttered to Elvis, who was making himself comfortable in the middle of my desk.

When I tried Ethan's cell phone, the call went straight to voice mail. Then I remembered that Stella had given me Ethan's home number.

Ellie Hall answered the phone. I could hear little voices singing the ABC song in the background. "Hi,

Sarah," she said. "Ethan's teaching, that's why you couldn't reach him. Could I help you with something?"

"Possibly," I said. "We're trying to do a detailed inventory out at the house and I wanted to be sure that none of the bottles in Edison's collection get misplaced, you know, in case the police do ever need them as evidence in a case." That was true as far as it went. "You don't have any at your house, do you?"

"No," she said. "Ethan left everything at his father's house so Mr. Quinn could go through the boxes. Everything in the collection is there. And you don't need to do an inventory. I remember Ethan saying his father had a list inside one of the boxes."

"Good to know," I said. "Thank you. We're hoping to have the estate sale in about two weeks."

"That would be wonderful," Ellie said. "Ethan and I appreciate you continuing, under the circumstances. I'm sorry that you had to . . . find Mr. Quinn." She had a warm, friendly voice, laced now with a touch of apology.

"I'm just happy we can help."

"I was supposed to be there, first thing that morning," she said, "to pack those dishes Stella wanted to keep. I keep thinking that I might have walked in on the killer."

"I'm glad that didn't happen."

"I had to have a small procedure done and they had a last-minute cancellation at the clinic. I almost said no, but Ethan insisted that I go." She hesitated. "I'm guessing Stella told you about our situation, about the surgery I need on my back. I mean, it's not really a secret."

"She did," I said. "I'm sorry that collection turned out to be worthless."

"Thank you. I'm sorry that Edison was taken advantage of." She cleared her throat. "He was a prickly man, but I know he cared about Ethan and his grandchildren. What he did, buying all those bottles as an investment, that was for us."

I thought about the meticulous details kept on every bottle I'd seen in Edison Hall's kitchen. It didn't seem fair that things had ended the way they did.

"We'll do everything we can to make as much money as possible from the estate sale," I said.

"Thank you, Sarah," Ellie said. "I, uh, don't want to be a charity case. I guess I'm like Ethan's dad in that way." The little voices in the background were getting louder.

"I understand," I said, even though I wasn't sure I did.

We said good-bye and I hung up. Elvis had moved off the desk. Now he regarded me from his perch on the love seat.

"This whole thing bites," I said.

He immediately craned his neck in the direction of my desk drawer.

"No, not those kinds of bites," I said. Elvis blinked his green eyes at me and began to wash his face.

I looked around the office, hoping somehow I'd find inspiration. My old black leather phone book was on my desk. I'd had it for years, adding and crossing out phone numbers and e-mail addresses as I moved from one radio station to another in my past life, to my life here in North Harbor.

I slid the book closer, across the desk. I still knew a couple of people who worked in radio in this area. Maybe they'd be willing to help. Ellie had just said her situation wasn't a secret, so I wouldn't be violating her privacy.

"If I can't catch the bad guys, maybe I can give the good guys a leg up," I said to Elvis.

He stopped washing his sleek black fur and turned to look at me, paw paused in midair. The expression on his face seemed to say that he thought my analogy was pretty lame, which it was. I just hoped my efforts wouldn't be.

Chapter 17

I was coming back into the house in the morning after carrying out another box of sweaters I'd felted for Jess when the doorknob was literally pulled out of my hand. I stumbled, off balance, into the entryway, almost knocking Rose over.

"Oh, there you are, dear," she said. She was grinning a Cheshire cat grin, which I had learned was not always a good thing.

"What do you need?" I said, running a hand over my hair. It wasn't quite raining, but a fine mist had dampened my hair on my dash to and from the SUV. I knew Elvis would grumble when it was time to leave.

"Do you have a rain jacket?" she asked, the almost smug smile turning into a frown.

"Yes," I said. "Would you like to borrow it?" I knew Rose had a hooded yellow slicker of her own, but maybe she'd left it at the shop.

"Well, now, if I wore your jacket what would you wear?" she said, shaking her head as though I were a child. "Don't forget your boots," she added as she headed back to her apartment.

"I won't," I called after her. I might have been a grown woman who was perfectly capable or deciding whether or not I need to wear boots, but I was also smart enough to know that my morning routine would go a lot faster if I didn't have to have a discussion about appropriate footwear with Rose before we even got to the shop.

Five minutes later we were in the SUV, Rose on the passenger side wearing her boots and slicker and Elvis on the backseat looking toward the windshield. He'd already swiped his paw over his face to dry off.

"Why were you looking for me before?" I asked Rose.

"Oh yes," she said. "I got sidetracked by the weather. I wanted to tell you that I've come up with a way to find Mr. Logan." She fastened her seat belt and gave me that smile again.

"And that way is?" I prompted.

"Are you familiar with the movie *The Sting*?" Rose asked. "Robert Redford and Paul Newman."

"I know it," I said, pulling out on to the street.

"Well, that's what we're going to do."

"You're going to invite him to play poker on a train?"

"Don't get saucy," she said, but she was smiling, so I knew I wasn't really in trouble. "We're going to set up a situation that our wine broker won't be able to resist."

"And how are you going to do that?"

"Shady Pines has an e-mail newsletter that they send to all the residents."

I cleared my throat loudly.

"Oh, excuse me," she said with a slight edge of sarcasm to her voice. "*Legacy Place* has an e-mail newsletter that they send to all their residents."

"Which you aren't anymore."

"Well, their system doesn't seem to understand that, which is why I know that there's going to be another one of those money management seminars for seniors over in Rockport."

I came to a stop at the corner and took the opportunity to look over at Rose. "When?"

"Today."

"Today?" I exclaimed. "That doesn't give you enough time to set up anything."

"You seriously underestimate me," she said.

I gave a snort of laughter. "That's one thing I never do. Tell me your plan."

From the corner of my eye, I could see her smug smile. "Well, basically it relies on Alfred's innate sex appeal."

"I see," I said, unsure of what else to say. Mr. P. was a darling man, but sexy wasn't an adjective I'd use to describe him.

"I know someone your age doesn't see it," Rose said, "but to a woman of my vintage, Alfred is a chick magnet."

"I like Alfred," I said, keeping my eyes firmly fixed on the road. "And I'm going to take your word for it on the sex-appeal thing. Tell me the rest of your plan."

"Alfred will go to the seminar. He'll talk a bit about his desire to leave something to his son—and what a nice young man he is. That woman who reels in the rubes will end up hooked herself, and that will lead us to Mr. Thorne Logan."

"And what are you going to do when you find Mr. Logan?" I asked. There was a small murp of dissatisfaction from my furry backseat driver. I flicked on the wipers to clear the mist from the windshield.

"Call Detective Andrews," Rose said.

I shot a quick look in her direction.

"You didn't expect I'd say that, did you?" she said tartly.

This time I did laugh. "No, I did not."

Her expression grew serious. "We're not stupid. If this man had anything to do with Mr. Quinn's murder, the police should be involved."

I reached back with my right hand and gave her arm a squeeze. "You never cease to amaze me, Rose Jackson," I said.

I pulled in to the parking lot at the store and parked closer to the back door than I usually would in case it was raining later. The lights were on in the workroom, but there was no sign of Mac. I could smell coffee, though, which was a good sign.

"Alfred should be here in about half an hour," Rose said, stepping out of her boots and pulling a pair of shoes out of her tote bag. "And Liz will be stopping in. We have to decide on the best look for Alfred. I don't want him to turn it on too much. And he needs to look a little down on his luck."

"So that's going to be your approach?" I asked.

Rose patted her hair into place. "Hardworking father looking to leave an inheritance to his deserving son and grandchildren."

"Alfred can pull that off," I said. Then I remembered what she'd said in the car about Alfred's so-called son.

"We'll have set up what a nice young man he is." "But how exactly are you going to 'set up' what a nice young man his imaginary son is?"

With the perverse perfect sense of timing the universe sometimes has, Liam came strolling in carrying a mug of coffee. The ends of his hair were damp, but he hadn't shaved. He was wearing jeans, a plaid work shirt, work boots and a big gooney grin. He held out both arms and bowed. "Alfred Peterson Junior, at your service."

I turned and looked at Rose. "You're kidding me, right?"

She shook her head. "No. For this to work we need the patsy to buy into Alfred's character. We need her to see him with his hardworking son."

Liam smirked at me and took a sip of his coffee.

"This will not work!" I said emphatically. Rose had been watching too many old movies again.

"Thanks for the vote of confidence, baby sister," Liam said. He was still grinning. He wasn't taking this seriously enough. I was sure he wasn't taking it seriously at all.

I folded my arms over my chest. "Liam, you have the acting skills of an iguana." I looked at Rose. "When he was seventeen he was late getting home from a date and he told Mom and Dad that the road was blocked by an elephant."

Liam pointed a finger at me. "That story is not as stupid as it sounds. The circus was in town. I could have been held up by an elephant."

I shook my head, laughing too hard to speak.

Behind us someone tapped on the door. It was Mr. P. engulfed in a black-hooded raincoat. Rose turned to open the door. As she did she nudged me with her elbow. "Don't worry, Sarah. Liam doesn't have to say a word. All he has to do is look adorable, and he can do that in spades."

I sighed and walked over to Liam. "What are you doing?" I asked. "Have you lost your mind?"

"No more than you," he said.

"What are you talking about?" I asked. I reached over and took his cup from his hand, turned it around so I could drink from the other side and took a sip. Then I gave it back.

"C'mon, Sarah," he said, wiping the edge of his mug where I'd drunk with his sleeve. "You've been involved in all this private detective stuff from the beginning and don't say you haven't, because I've been talking to Nick."

"Nick's biased," I muttered.

Liam laughed. "When it comes to you, oh yeah. But that has nothing to do with this." He gestured toward the door where Rose was peering into the huge duffel bag Mr. P. had brought with him. "They're like Gram. They're going to do this no matter what you or anyone else says. At least if I'm part of things I can hopefully keep it all from going south."

I laughed then.

"What's so funny?" he asked.

"I thought that. I thought I could keep them out of trouble, on the straight and narrow as Dad would say." I leaned against him. "It's not going to happen, big brother."

Liam wasn't the least bit bothered by my words. "We'll see," he said. "And for the record, that elephant story would have worked if you hadn't pointed out that the circus was an animal-free circus."

I kissed his cheek and straightened up. "I'll be in my office if you need me," I said.

Elvis had disappeared who knew where. I went upstairs, dumped my things on the love seat and went for a cup of coffee. Based on the morning so far, I was going to need more than one cup.

Mac was in the tiny staff room. He reached for the largest mug on the shelf and handed it to me without saying a word. I poured a cup, added cream and sugar and took a long drink.

"Good morning," he said with a smile.

"Easy for you to say," I said.

"You've been talking to Liam."

I took a deep breath and let it out. "And Rose. You know what they have planned?"

He nodded.

I waited for him to say something, but he didn't.

"I worry about them, Mac," I said. "This guy, Thorne Logan, he could be a killer. At best he's most likely a con artist and Rose is trying to outcon him."

"Which is why it won't hurt to have your brother lurking in the background," he said. "I would have volunteered, but compared to Alfred"—he stuck out an arm, the sleeve pushed back to expose the smooth brown skin of his forearm—"I'm a tad toasty."

"I'm overreacting."

Mac shook his head. "No. You care about them."

I brushed a stray strand of hair away from my face. "Rose did say if they find Mr. Logan she'll call Michelle."

"You don't believe her."

I shrugged. "I want to, but it's just that Rose could do a much better job of selling an elephant blocking the road than my brother."

Mac smiled. "I'm just going to pretend that made sense and go open up."

Liz arrived about nine thirty and she and Rose outfitted Mr. P. in a pair of brown polyester pants with a green-and-brown-plaid shirt.

"Remember, you just want to leave something for your family," Liz cautioned.

"Alfred knows how to get into character," Charlotte chided gently.

Rose was nothing if not resourceful. She'd rented an old pickup from Cleveland. The trash picker's unofficial motto was *Anything for a Buck*, so he'd been happy to help.

The plan was for Liam to drive the old truck and drop Mr. P. off at the seminar, making sure to be seen, if not by the mystery woman, then at least by other people.

"She might not be the only plant," Rose said.

"Someone's been watching late-night TV again," Liz whispered to me.

Rose and Liz would follow in Liz's car, staying out of sight in case there was anyone at the seminar who recognized them.

Mr. P. was fastening a small pin shaped like a beaver to the collar of his shirt. He twisted it so the beaver was standing on all fours and then turned and clicked several keys on his laptop. An image of the back wall of the porch filled the screen.

"What is that?" I asked.

"It's a camera," Rose said, reaching up to smooth down a couple of wisps of Mr. P.'s hair. "That way Liz and I will be able to see and hear what Alfred can."

I turned to Mr. P. "Do I want to know where this came from?" I asked, thinking that I'd asked that question a lot in the last six months.

"I Spy With My Little Eye," he said.

"I don't think you play that game with cameras," I said.

"What about that game with the young man with the striped shirt and glasses?" Rose asked.

"That's not a game," Liz said. "You mean *Where's Wally?*. It's a book and it's all illustrations."

Rose frowned. "*Where's Wally?* doesn't sound right."

Liz was walking around Liam, making a face, it seemed, at his hair. "I can't help how it sounds," she said. "That's the name of the book."

We were getting way off track. Before I could try to rein them in, Charlotte clapped her hands. We all automatically turned and looked at her. She could still command a roomful of people.

"You're both right," she said, looking from Liz to Rose. "It's *Where's Waldo?* here and *Where's Wally?* in Britain." She turned her head and looked at me. "Sarah, I Spy With My Little Eye is an electronics store in Portland. The camera is perfectly legal." Finally she fixed her gaze on Liam. "Child, what did you wash your hair with?"

"I don't know," he said. "Whatever Gram has in her shower."

"Organic Burst Rosemary Mint shampoo," I said.

"You smell too good," Liz said, reaching up to run her fingers through Liam's hair. "You smell like a girl, not a carpenter."

"Nobody's going to smell his head," Rose said, hands on her hips.

"You don't know that," Liz retorted.

I turned to Mr. P. "I'm coming with you. I can run the computer."

"You don't have to do that," he said.

I nodded. "I know." I tipped my head toward Liam. The three women had surrounded him, debating what was the best way to make him not smell so good. "You're not going to make me stay here and miss all the fun, are you?"

"Of course not," he said, a smile playing around his mouth.

Mr. P. gave me a crash course on how to record and monitor the feed from his beaver cam. I had no idea whether what we were doing was completely legal or not, but I decided that was something I could ask Michelle or Nick later.

Liz and Charlotte solved the problem of Nick's great-smelling hair with something they borrowed from Avery when she showed up at lunchtime. By a quarter to one we were in the workroom pretty much ready to leave.

"Can I come?" Avery asked. She was way more interested in the beaver cam than I liked.

"I need you here," I said, putting a hand on her shoulder. "Mac can't do everything by himself."

"Is that just a line because you don't want me to go

because you think I'm a kid?" she asked, crossing her arms defiantly across her chest.

"No," I said. "It's because Mac really can't do everything by himself."

"Fine," she said after a moment, "but you owe me a big hot chocolate from McNamara's."

"Deal," I said.

Avery started back to the shop. "With extra whipped cream," she called over her shoulder.

"Have I been had?" I said to Liz.

There was a gleam of amusement in her eyes. "I think the correct term is 'well, duh.'"

Liam and Mr. P. left in Cleveland's pickup. I followed in the SUV with Rose riding shotgun and Liz and Charlotte in the back. The plan was for us to park in a lot across the street from the community center where the money management seminar was being held. The tiny digital camera had a transmit range of about five thousand feet.

"What if this woman doesn't show up?" Liz asked. "Do we have a plan B?"

"We don't need a plan B," Rose said, very confidently, it seemed to me.

"And that would be because?"

"Because she'll be there," Charlotte stated calmly.

I glanced in the rearview mirror. Liz was frowning at her friends. "What do you two know that I don't?"

"Good question," I said. "What do you two know that Liz—and I—don't?"

"Our mystery woman has shown up at five financial seminars in this area aimed at senior citizens in the last six months," Charlotte said. "Every time she talked about investing in things you can see and touch and every time she spent most of her time with someone who came to the seminar alone."

"So she'll only have to win over one person, not two or three," I said.

"That's what we think," Rose said.

"She's going to show up," Charlotte said. "This is exactly the kind of setup she likes—small town, a presentation aimed at seniors who have some money saved but not enough that they'd already have a financial adviser."

"It's despicable," Rose said. I glanced at her. Her mouth was pulled into a tight line.

"It is hard to accept that someone who is a senior citizen would be taking advantage of other people her age," Charlotte agreed.

Ahead of us Liam put on his blinker and moved over into the exit lane. I did the same.

"Maybe it's all she has," Liz said.

Beside me Rose shifted so she could look at her friend in the backseat. "What do you mean?" she asked.

"Maybe she's doing this because she doesn't have any other choice."

"There are always choices," Rose said.

"True," Liz said. "But there aren't always good ones."

Liz could be quick to judge, but the truth was she was probably the softest touch of all of us. No one said anything for a moment. Then, out of the corner of my eye, I saw Rose reach her hand over the seat toward Liz. "Elizabeth Emmerson Kiley French, I love you," she said softly.

"Yeah, yeah, everybody does," Liz said.

I looked in the rearview mirror and blew Liz a kiss. She never ceased to amaze me.

The community center was easy to find in Rockport. Liam actually found a place to pull in at the curb in front. We retreated to the back row of the parking lot across the street, according to plan.

I set Mr. P.'s laptop on my knees, turned it on and followed the instructions he'd given me. After a few moments we were looking at the dashboard of Cleveland's old truck. Rose pulled out her cell phone.

Mr. P.'s cell played the first notes of "Ode to Joy" as his ring tone, the sound coming clearly through the computer as I turned up the volume.

"Sarah has everything working," Rose said.

"Thank you, Sarah," Mr. P. said.

I gave Rose a thumbs-up.

Everything went smoothly after that. Liam played the role of the good son, walking Alfred inside, standing awkwardly around for a couple of minutes and telling him, within earshot of others, that he didn't need an inheritance and maybe they should just go home.

For his part Mr. P. was the epitome of a hardworking dad. He patted Liam on the arm and said he'd call if he needed a ride home.

Liam pulled the truck into the parking lot a row ahead of us and sprinted back to the SUV, sliding onto the backseat next to Liz.

"How was I?" he said with a grin.

"You were perfect," Rose said, beaming. Charlotte nodded.

"Good job," Liz agreed, giving him a fist bump.

He looked at me. "What do you think, Sarah?"

I smiled at him. "Good job, big brother."

Mr. P. had chosen an aisle seat and he looked around a couple of times, which gave us a good view of the small meeting room. It was about five minutes before the start of the seminar when Mr. P. said softly, "She's here. I'm going for a cup of coffee."

I looked at Rose and the hand folded in her lap gave me a thumbs-up.

Mr. P. was a born actor. He got himself a cup of coffee and managed to knock over the container of plastic stir sticks. It was all the opening our con woman needed.

"Let me help you," she said. "I don't know why they can't just put out some spoons." Then she gave an embarrassed laugh. "I'm sorry—I sound like an old fogey, don't I?"

"No, you don't," Mr. P. said. "Excuse my language, but those plastic thingamajigs aren't worth a damn. Someone can't wash a few spoons?"

That was all it took. It shouldn't have been that simple, but it was. Mr. P. carried his coffee back to his seat, and his new friend, whose name was Leila, took the empty chair next to him.

The presentation was mind-numbingly boring and from my perspective seemed to be geared to five-year-olds, not people with decades of life experience.

"Oh, for heaven's sake!" Liz exclaimed after the first five minutes. "How stupid do they think the average person over sixty-five is?"

"It is a little . . . insulting, isn't it?" Charlotte said.

Liam leaned his elbow on the back of my seat. "So why don't you do something better?" he said to Liz.

"I could," she said.

"So why don't you?" he asked. "Seriously, those two guys"—he gestured at the computer screen—"are acting like they have an audience of kindergarteners who get two quarters for an allowance. I know you could do better. Why don't you put together a program that actually gives seniors some decent advice? Because this one sure as hell doesn't."

"You know that Channing Caulfield would help you," I said.

Liz made a face at me.

"Well, he would," Rose added.

"It's not a bad idea, you know," Charlotte said. "You've been looking for a way to get Jane Evans to come work for the foundation. This might be it. She used to work for the bank."

"I'll think about it," Liz said. We all looked at her. "I promise," she added.

I held up a hand. "I think Mr. P. is getting the pitch," I said. I nudged up the volume.

"If it makes me old-fashioned, then fine, I'm old-fashioned," Leila was saying, "but if I'm going to invest in something, I want it to be something I can see and touch."

"My father used to say, 'Invest in land, boy. They aren't making any more of it,'" Mr. P. said.

"He was right," Leila agreed.

Mr. P. sighed. "I don't have that kind of money. I

just, I just want to be able to leave something for my boy. He's got an ex-wife who pretty much took him to the cleaners a couple of years ago."

Liam put a hand to his heart and tried to look wounded. I rolled my eyes.

In short order Leila had confided in Mr. P. about the money she'd made with her "tiny" wine collection and offered to introduce him to the wine broker she dealt with.

"Yes!" I said, softly, doing a little fist pump in the air.

"Does he have references?" Alfred asked.

"Of course," she said, "and I can promise you I checked Mr. Logan out very carefully. You can't be too careful with your money."

Now came the tricky part. Mr. P. had to find a way to get the meeting to take place in North Harbor, instead of Rockport. The Angels had agreed to bring the police in on their meeting, which meant it had to happen in Michelle's jurisdiction.

"I don't want my son to know," Mr. P. said. "He keeps telling me I don't need to leave him anything, but I want to. Maybe next time your broker friend is in North Harbor, he could give me a call." He tapped his chest with one hand. "I got a bum ticker, so I can't drive anymore." Then he got to his feet and held out his hand. "It was nice meeting you, Leila."

I held my breath, wondering if she would let him walk away.

She didn't. As luck would have it, Mr. Logan was going to be in North Harbor the next day—big surprise—and Leila could set up a meeting with him. Mr. P. hesitated, all according to script, so he wouldn't seem too eager and then agreed to meet Leila and Thorne Logan at McNamara's.

"It was lucky for me, meeting you," Mr. P. said.

Leila smiled. "Sometimes things work out the way they're supposed to."

"Yes, they do," Rose said softly beside me.

I didn't get to see Mr. P. face-to-face until we got back to the shop. "You were terrific," I said to him as he climbed out of the old truck.

He smiled. "Thank you, my dear. I was onstage many years ago. I'd forgotten how much I enjoyed it."

"I suspect you have many talents I don't know about," I teased.

"Indeed I do," he said with a wink. Then he headed over to Rose and the others.

Liam came around the back of the rust-pocked pickup. "You walked right into that one," he said with a laugh, putting an arm around me.

I shook my head. "Yeah, I guess I did." I looked up at him. "You were good, too."

"Thank you," he said. "It was probably because there were no elephants in this story." He ran a hand over his hair. "I'm heading over to the apartment. I don't know what this stuff is that Liz got from her granddaughter, but it smells like bear grease."

I laughed. "Admit it. You like smelling all flowery."

He waggled his eyebrows at me. "Let's just say it makes me very popular with the ladies."

I held up both hands. "I don't want to hear about your love life, especially if it involves Jess."

Liam started swaying from side to side, pulling me with him. "I haven't said a word about Jess," he teased.

"I haven't, for example, told you that she's a good kisser . . . or a bad one."

I put both hands over my ears and began to hum. Loudly.

Liam just laughed. He pulled one hand away from my head. "I'm gone," he said. "If 'Dad' needs me for anything, let me know." With that he headed for his truck.

I walked over to the others. "Where's Liam going?" Rose asked. "I have a coffee cake in the staff room."

"He had some things he needed to do. He asked me to tell you that he's available if you need him again."

"Your brother is a very nice young man," Mr. P. said.

I nodded. "Yeah, I got lucky."

We went inside.

"How did it go?" Mac asked.

"Good," I said. "I learned that both my brother and Mr. P. are very good at pretending to be someone else." I looked around. "How were things here?"

"One customer," Mac said, swiping a hand over the back of his neck. "He bought that old fiddle."

"Good," I said. "I'd about given up on selling the thing."

"And the trestle table and six chairs," he said with a grin.

I blinked at him. "You're kidding me?"

He shook his head. "No, I'm not. The table sold itself, but it was Avery who sold him on the six chairs."

I looked over at the teenager, who was clearly getting all the details of our afternoon from the others. She held up a hand and high-fived Mr. P. "I think I should give her a raise."

Mac nodded. "I agree. She's really been working hard."

"I have to make a couple of calls," I said. "I'll just be a few minutes." I smiled at him. "There's going to be cake."

"I like it when you all go on a quest," Mac said. "We always have cake."

I laughed and started for the stairs.

After some discussion Mr. P. had asked me if I would call Michelle, once we located Thorne Logan. I wasn't sure she'd be interested in talking to the man, but I'd promised both her and Nick that I'd keep them up-to-date, so I'd said yes.

I'd expected I'd have to leave a message, but she answered on the fourth ring.

"Hi," I said. "Do you have a couple of minutes?"

"Sure. What is it?"

"Well." I wasn't sure how to start. "I'm, uh, I guess you could say I'm acting as the spokesperson for the Angels."

"All right," she said. It seemed to me that I could hear just a little amusement in her voice.

I explained what had happened, leaving out some of the details like Liam masquerading as Mr. P.'s son. "So Mr. P. has a meeting with this broker, tomorrow afternoon at Glenn McNamara's."

Michelle laughed and I felt my heart sink. She wasn't taking this seriously. Then to my surprise she said, "They're good."

I wasn't sure I'd heard her correctly. "Excuse me?" I said.

"I've been looking for Mr. Logan for the past couple

of days. He's a difficult man to track down. How did they find him?"

The knot in my stomach unclenched and I leaned back in my chair. "Old-fashioned, senior word of mouth. It's faster than the information superhighway."

"I'm assuming you'll be there tomorrow afternoon," Michelle said.

"I will," I said. "Maybe I could buy you a cup of coffee."

"Coffee's on me," she said. "I don't suppose there's any way to convince the rest of them to stay home, is there?"

It was my turn to laugh. "Only if you intend to use handcuffs."

"I was afraid you'd say that." She exhaled softly. "Please, use whatever influence you have with them. No grandstanding, no theatrics."

"I'm not sure how much influence I have," I said. "They all changed my diapers and they're not afraid to point that out, but I'll do what I can."

We set up a time to meet at Glenn's and I hung up.

"I'm going to close up early," I said to Mac at lunch-time the next day.

"Then maybe I'll come with you, if that's okay," he said.

"Please."

I'd been awake half the night, having second, third and fourth thoughts about this whole enterprise. Mr. P. could be walking into a meeting with two murder-ers. They could be armed. Backed into a corner, they could take hostages.

"Rose is as wired as a five-year-old on Christmas Eve," I said. "I caught her looking up how to make a citizen's arrest when Mr. P. was upstairs changing." I slid a hand back over my hair. "And short of duct-taping her to a chair, there's no way she's going to stay out of this. I promised Michelle I'd try to rein them in, but I think they're more likely to listen to reason if the voice of reason is yours, not mine."

"They've been pretty restrained so far," Mac pointed out.

I nodded. "I know, that's what worries me. We're due for something a little over-the-top."

We were all in our places by quarter after four. Liz and Charlotte at one table, Mac and Rose at another and Michelle and I at a third. Michelle also had an officer in the kitchen and another working behind the counter with Glenn. Plus, ex–football player Glenn was, by himself, perfectly capable of popping your head off like the cap off a soda bottle.

Michelle propped her elbows on the table and bent her head over her coffee. "See the car diagonally across the street?" she asked. "I think that's them. The woman is using the last name Flaherty."

I pulled a hand back through my hair and looked out the front window of the sandwich shop. There was a silver Lexus parked on the street and I could see Leila in the passenger seat. "It is," I said. "I recognize the woman who's working with him."

Mr. P. was on his way up the sidewalk. He was wired again, this time just for sound with a tiny police-issue microphone attached under the edge of his sweater vest.

He came inside, smiled at us all and sat at a table in the corner to the left of the door. Glenn took him a cup of coffee.

Michelle looked around. "We got lucky," she said. "This place could have been filled with people."

"That's why Mr. P. decided on this time of day," I said, picking up my cup and setting it down again. Across the street Leila got out of the passenger side of the Lexus.

"They're on the move," I said softly to Michelle.

She in turn looked over at Mr. P. and nodded.

Leila and Thorne Logan stepped into the sandwich shop. I noticed that she was carrying the Burberry purse. She looked around. At his table Mr. P. stood up. "Hello, Leila," I heard him say.

"Hello, Harold," she replied. "I'd like you to meet Thornton Logan."

The two men shook hands and they all sat down.

"I like your hair like that," Michelle said.

For a moment I looked blankly at her, and then I remembered we were supposed to be having a conversation. "I've been thinking about shaving my head. What do you think?" It was the first thing that popped into my mind. I was not good at this, I realized.

"Don't you think that's a little extreme?"

I wasn't sure if she was serious with her question or if it was just part of making conversation.

"I'm thinking of training for a marathon," I said. "It would just be easier, you know, showering so much."

"Well, you could have some kind of design cut into the stubble," Michelle offered with just a hint of a smile. Now I knew she wasn't serious.

The officer working with Glenn approached the table. Both Logan and Leila ordered coffee.

The door to the little shop opened and Avery walked in. My breath caught in my chest. I should have known she had agreed far too easily to being left out.

"What is she doing here?" Michelle asked, her voice low.

"I can get her out," I said. I started to get to my feet.

Michelle caught my arm. "Sit," she said. "I don't want to do anything to draw their attention." She tipped her head, ever so slightly, in the direction of Mr. P.'s table.

Liz was shooting daggers in her granddaughter's direction.

Avery ignored the look. "Hi, Gram," she said, walking over to the table. "Sorry I'm late."

Michelle caught Liz's eye and gave an almost imperceptible shake of her head. It looked to me as though Liz nodded in return, but I couldn't be sure. She got up and headed to the counter, motioning at Avery to take her seat. That put Avery closer to the kitchen with the wall behind her.

I had to swallow hard to get the lump in my throat to go down. Why had I agreed to this? It had to be the stupidest thing I'd ever done.

Michelle squeezed my arm. "Breathe," she whispered.

I took a deep breath and then another. Panicking wasn't going to do me any good. These people were my family and I would protect them with my life if it came to that. I was really hoping it wouldn't.

Michelle and I talked about hair and running for the next few minutes. Avery bought a cinnamon roll. Liz and Charlotte seemed to be making a grocery list and from what little I could hear of Mac and Rose's conversation, she was asking questions about his love life. I sent him a smile of sympathy when he looked my way. Finally the officer turned counterperson came over to the table with the coffeepot. It was the agreed-upon signal for Michelle to make her move.

"We're good," he said almost under his breath to her.

She looked across the table at me. "Everyone stays out of the way," she said.

I nodded, hoping I wouldn't have to dramatically fling myself in front of anyone or take Rose down with a running tackle.

Michelle got up and moved toward Mr. P.'s table in one quick, smooth move. She stopped by Thorne Logan's chair, the officer positioning himself closer to Mr. P., effectively shielding him from the others.

"Hello, Mr. Logan," Michelle said. She flashed her badge. "I'm Detective Andrews. Could I talk to you for a minute?"

"I'm sorry, Detective," Logan said, smoothly confident. "As you can see, I'm in the middle of something. Perhaps another time."

A flash of uncertainty passed across Leila's face.

Michelle smiled. I'd seen that smile before. It did not mean good things were going to happen. "Mr. Logan, please stand up," she said.

He gave a sigh of annoyance. "Look, I know I have a couple of parking tickets that I should have paid." He held up both hands and gave her his best approximation of a boyish smile. It was pretty good. "I plead guilty to having a lead foot and I promise I'll come by the station and pay them as soon as I'm done here."

I wasn't sure his charm would have worked on anyone, but it definitely didn't work on Michelle.

"Get up, please," she repeated, and when he didn't she nodded to the officer beside her.

"Stand up, sir," the young officer said, helping Logan to his feet. Michelle explained why he was being arrested while the handcuffs were snapped into place.

While all the focus was on Thorne Logan, Leila had started to back toward the door. I noticed she wasn't at the table and turned to see Mac block her way. "Excuse me," she said, trying to go around him.

He stepped in front of her again. "I think the police officer over there with your friend would like to talk to you," he said.

Michelle walked over to them. "I need you to come down to the station with me, Mrs. Flaherty," she said.

Leila pressed her lips together and glowered at Michelle. "You're dumb as a stump," she hissed as Thorne Logan passed her being led out the door.

"Stop talking, Mother," he said through gritted teeth.

Michelle raised her eyebrows at me as she passed me.

"That was so cool!" Avery said, bouncing up from her seat as soon as the door closed.

"And you are so grounded," Liz said matter-of-factly. "Two weeks."

"You didn't tell me I couldn't come!" Avery scowled like a petulant child. "You just said this was no place for me."

"Three weeks," Liz said. "Want to try for four?"

"That's not fair," Avery whined.

I put a hand on her shoulder and swung her around to face me. "Avery, you scared the crap out of your grandmother," I said.

She started to argue, but I cut her off. "You scared your grandmother. You scared Rose and Charlotte and Mr. P. and Mac."

I took a deep breath and let it out. I could feel my hands shaking. "You scared *me*. And you know better." I kept my gaze locked on her face.

After a moment her lower lip began to tremble. She swallowed hard. "I'm sorry," she said, her voice raspy with emotion.

"We all love you," I said. "So you can't just do whatever you feel like doing, because if something hurts you, all of us are hurt, too."

She swallowed again. "Okay," she said in a small voice. Then she turned around to face Liz. "I'm sorry, Nonna," she said.

Liz wrapped her arms around her granddaughter and kissed the top of her head. "I love you, child," she said.

"I love you, too, Nonna," Avery said.

"You're still grounded."

Avery nodded, her head still on Liz's shoulder. "Yeah, I know."

I felt the tension drain from my body. Mac appeared at my side. "You okay?" he asked.

I nodded.

"So Leila *is* that young man's mother," Mr. P. said.

"You were right about that," I said, smiling at him.

Liz had handed Avery off to Rose, who was cupping the teenager's face with her hands as she talked to her. Liz came over to me and bumped me with her hip. "Remember what I said about that woman when we were in the car?" she asked me.

I nodded. "I remember."

"I take it all back."

Glenn McNamara was at the counter. I caught his eye. "A refill on everything, please, Glenn," I said. "And thank you for letting us stage this episode of *Law and Disorder* in here."

"You're welcome," he said, reaching for the coffee-pot. "I gotta say, though, it's going to make Tuesday afternoons from now on feel pretty tame."

I didn't hear from Michelle until after *Jeopardy!* was over. Elvis had just come out of the bedroom and jumped on my lap when my cell rang. I looked over at the screen. "It's Michelle," I said to him.

"Merow," he said, looking from me to the phone. Translation: Hurry up and answer.

Rose was right. Thorne Logan and his mother had sold Edison Hall all those fake bottles of wine. "They were falling over themselves, each of them trying to put the blame on the other," Michelle said. "That's a screwed-up family."

But Thorne Logan wasn't our killer. "He has an alibi, Sarah," Michelle said. "When Ronan Quinn was killed, Mr. Logan and his mother were up in Bangor trying to scam another senior citizen in a crowded Dunkin' Donuts with at least a dozen witnesses."

"Son of a horse," I muttered.

"Excuse me?" Michelle said.

"Nothing," I said. "Thank you for this."

"I owe you," she said. "There are four other police departments in this part of the state alone who want to talk to Mr. Logan and his mother."

"I'm glad something came out of all this."

"We're not done," Michelle said. "We *will* find out who killed Ronan Quinn. We're not even close to being done with this case."

I said good night and ended the call. "I should go tell Rose what's going on," I said to Elvis. "Want to come with me?"

The cat put a paw up over his face, almost as though he were trying to tell me it was a conversation he didn't want to be part of.

Mr. P. answered the door when I knocked. He was wearing a pair of blue knitted slippers and one of Rose's flowered aprons and holding a dish towel. "Hello, Sarah," he said. He studied my face for a moment. "You're not bringing good news, are you?"

I shook my head.

"Sarah dear, come in," Rose called.

I stepped into the kitchen. She took one look at my face, closed her eyes for a moment and sighed. "I'll be right back," she said.

"Rosie, where are you going," a clearly bewildered Mr. P. asked.

Rose had already disappeared, headed I was guessing for the bedroom. In a moment I heard the door close.

Baffled, Mr. P. looked at me. "Is she all right?"

I nodded. "She just went into the bedroom to swear because she didn't want to do it in front of me."

"Well, then," he said. "Would you like a piece of pie? It's lemon meringue."

"It could only help," I said. "Thank you."

Mr. P. got a slice of pie for both of us and we were at the kitchen table with it when Rose came back. She joined us at the table. I told them what Michelle had told me.

"Well, at least those terrible people won't be taking advantage of anyone else," he said.

Rose had a look of grim determination on her face. "Tomorrow we'll start at the beginning again. And we'll find out who killed Mr. Quinn."

"Absolutely," Mr. P. said, smiling at her.

I speared another bite of pie. It was delicious. I couldn't shake the feeling that I was missing something. I just had no clue what that something was.

Chapter 18

The Angels gathered in their office before the store opened the next morning.

"Since Mr. Logan and his mother have alibis for the time of Mr. Quinn's death, we're back to square one," Mr. P. said.

"So, what do we do?" Liz asked, tapping one pale pink nail on the arm of her chair.

"We concentrate on Mr. Quinn. We take the last week of his life apart, day by day, hour by hour." He looked at me. "Do you think the lawyer you spoke to would answer a few more questions?'

"Put them together and I'll call her," I said.

I was out working on the metal cabinet a couple of hours later when Mac came to the back door. "Sarah, phone," he called.

I set down my scraper, brushed my hands on my jeans and sprinted across the parking lot. "Do you know who it is?" I asked as I headed for the phone at the cash desk.

"She said her name was Skye," Mac said.

I smiled. Skye Reynolds was the promotions director for Tanner Media, who owned that radio station I used to work for. It was Skye I'd called to see if she could come up with some way to help Ellie Hall.

"Hey, Sarah," Skye said. "I just wanted to check in with you. Look, are you sure those people you called me about actually want help?"

"Yes," I said. "Why?"

"We have a showcase coming up next month. Half a dozen up-and-coming bands. You know how it works."

I did.

"I called the husband's office and talked to his teaching assistant. I was thinking we could turn it into a fund-raiser."

I could hear her tapping the end of her pen on her desk. "So, what's wrong with the idea?" I remembered Ellie saying they didn't want to take charity. Was Ethan so proud that he'd turn down a fund-raiser on Ellie's behalf?

"The husband's going to be away on that weekend," Skye said. It was impossible to miss the sarcasm in her voice.

"What do you mean, away?" I asked.

"Hawaii."

"That's got to be a mistake."

"It's not," she said. "Look, Sarah, I'm happy to help. You know these kinds of stories are great for us. Listeners eat this stuff up. But if this guy's wife needs surgery, what the heck's he doing going to Hawaii?"

I didn't have an answer. I told Skye I'd find out what was going on, thanked her for what she'd done so far and hung up.

"Something wrong?" Mac asked.

I rubbed the back of my neck. "I'm not sure."

"Is there anything I can do?" he said.

"I don't think so," I said. "But thanks."

I went back out to my metal cabinet. I'd taken off about half the old finish. I walked around the piece, seeing in my mind the way it would look when I was finished. Avery, I'd discovered, could do the same thing.

I'd let her work on a small side table I'd trash-picked. After sanding and priming, she'd painted it white. The front of the single drawer got two coats of lime green. She also taped off the tips of the tapered legs and painted them the same green. The sides she Mod-Podged with a bold lime-and-cobalt geometric design paper.

"I like it," I'd said when she took me out to the old garage to show me her work. "How did you decide on the design?"

"I don't know," she'd said with a shrug. "It's kind of like to me, it's what was there—at least in my head—under all the crap."

I wondered if the answer to Ronan Quinn's death was under all the crap somewhere. Just then Nick's SUV pulled in to the parking lot. Charlotte waved at me from the passenger seat. I walked over to them.

"Hi," I said. "You're early."

"I brought Nicolas over to show him that wrought-iron bed frame," she said. "Is it still in the workroom?"

I nodded. "It's wrapped in a couple of old blankets

against the end wall. Mac will get it out for you." I looked at Nick. "Does it have to be wrought iron? There's a nice dark walnut headboard that might work for you. Either way I'll give you the family discount."

"Thanks," he said with a smile. "I don't really know what I want, mainly just something to get my mattress up off the floor."

"Are you bringing either of the bedroom sets from Edison Hall's house down here?" Charlotte asked.

I shook my head. "I'd like to try to sell them on-site if we can. We don't really have the space to have everything set up here. But there is a spool bed. It needs a little work, though. A couple of the slats are cracked."

"Too small," Charlotte said. "We need something for a double mattress."

"The wrought-iron one, then," I said.

"I'll get Mac to get it out," Charlotte said, heading for the door.

"Do I get a vote?" Nick said to me.

"Probably not," I said with a grin.

He smiled back at me. "Michelle told me about your little adventure yesterday. It sounds like Alfred missed his calling."

"Can you keep a secret?" I asked.

He raised an eyebrow but didn't say anything. I told him about Liam playing the part of Mr. P.'s son.

Nick shook his head. "I don't know whether to laugh or tell you you've lost your mind."

"The first one, definitely," I said.

He grinned and then his expression grew serious once more. "Nobody's giving up, Sarah. We will find out who killed Ronan Quinn."

"I hope you're right," I said.

He smiled again. "I am." He gestured at the back door. "I better go take a look at this bed."

"I'll be there in a minute," I said.

He headed across the parking lot and I thought again how much he was like Charlotte. They had the same smile that reached all the way to their brown eyes.

I put the cabinet and my tools in the garage. As I came back out, Nick was heading to his SUV. "Work," he called to me, "but we're still on for tomorrow night. Save me a seat."

I nodded.

I went into the shop. Charlotte was in talking to Mr. P. Mac was rewrapping the iron bed frame. "Nick got a call," he said. "But I think he might take this."

"Okay," I said. "If he does and I'm not here, give him the family discount."

"Absolutely," he said.

"I need to do something," I said.

"Okay, we're good here." He studied my face. "Do you need any help?"

"No, I've got this," I said. "I won't be very long." I hadn't told Rose or Michelle or Nick about those six missing wine bottles and it was past time that I did. But before I said anything, I wanted to be certain they weren't at the house.

When I walked out to the SUV, Elvis followed me. I opened the driver's door and he hopped onto the seat. "Oh, what the heck?" I muttered. I motioned for him to move over.

"Want to come inside with me for a moment?" I said

to the cat when we pulled in to the driveway at the Hall house.

"Merow," he answered, leaning sideways to look around me. I picked him up, pulled my keys out of my pocket. Across the street Paul Duvall and Alyssa were playing hockey on their front lawn with a large neon orange ball and plastic hockey sticks. There was a makeshift net at one end of the grass made with a tarp and wooden stakes stuck in the ground. I waved and then Elvis and I headed for the back door.

Very quickly I realized that there was no way I could search for the missing bottles by myself. There were just too many boxes to check.

Elvis followed me from the living room back to the kitchen. He immediately began prowling around the stack of boxes. "There aren't any answers there," I said to him. He tipped his head to one side, seemed to consider my words and then went back to what he'd been doing.

I walked over and stood in the doorway. I looked across the floor and tried to picture Ronan Quinn's dead body, hoping somehow I'd remember something I hadn't thought of before. But there were no answers lurking in my memory. I felt my stomach turn over as I thought about Quinn's body. He couldn't have been in the house more than a few minutes when he was killed; he'd still been wearing his jacket. There had been something dark on the collar that I realized now must have been dried blood. The white mark on his left pant leg had come from the whitewashed back porch, I knew now. I'd brushed the same mark off my own pants. And the bits of black asphalt that were stuck to the sole of his shoes had most likely been deposited in the driveway outside by the tires of his car when he drove over the partially paved road and then picked up on his shoes when he walked around his car to take his briefcase from the backseat.

I crouched down and put one hand on the floor, concentrating on the image of Ronan Quinn's shoes. Elvis padded over and nudged my hand with his head. "Murp?" he asked.

I looked at him. "The person who had the best chance to take those missing bottles was Ethan. How do we even know he came from the hospital that morning? How do we know he was even there at all?" Elvis gave me a blank look.

"Exactly," I said.

I remembered the drive out to the house the morning we'd found Quinn's body. Tiny clumps of asphalt had stuck to the tires of the SUV and Elvis had made a fuss over the tar smell in the car. I reached over and stroked his fur. "If Ethan was here before we were the day of the murder, he would have parked in the garage to hide his car," I said. "He couldn't chance anyone seeing it. And if he drove over that same stretch of road that we did, there should be bits of asphalt on the floor in there."

"Mrrr," the cat said.

"Let's go look," I said.

I picked him up and went out to the garage. The sky had clouded over and it looked as though rain was close.

The key to the side door was on the ring Stella had given me. The inside of the building was dark and it took a minute for my eyes to adjust. No so for Elvis. Almost as though he knew what I was looking for, he started across the floor, sniffing the wide planks, but I was the one who found the bits of asphalt on the battered wooden floor.

Elvis made his way over to me, sniffed the tarry black bits and sneezed twice. There wasn't any doubt what we'd found.

A drop of water landed on the top of my head, followed by another and another. Obviously the rain had started and just as obviously the roof leaked. A drop of water landed on Elvis's paw. He lifted his foot, shook it and glared at me.

I straightened up and picked him up as well. "It's just a shower," I said. "The house is closer. We'll just wait it out." We sprinted to the back door. I set the cat on the kitchen floor and he shook himself and made a sour face.

I leaned against the counter and pulled out my cell phone. "We need to know if there was any other paving going on in this area either before or since," I said. "Otherwise those bits of asphalt we just found don't mean much."

"Hello, Sarah," Mr. P. said.

"Hi," I said. "This is probably going to sound crazy, but is there any way to find out where the town has been paving in the past two weeks?"

"Public Works would have a schedule," he said. "Would you like me to check it for you?"

"Please," I said. At my feet Elvis suddenly lifted his head and looked around. Was someone outside? It was probably Paul. "I'll call you back," I said.

"All right, my dear," Mr. P. said, sounding a little distracted, which told me he was already on his computer. "It should only take me about five minutes."

I looked down at Elvis at my feet. His green eyes were narrowed and his tail was twitching.

I felt the hairs rise on the back of my neck almost as though a faint breeze had blown through the old building. I turned around slowly.

Ethan Hall was standing in the doorway.

Chapter 19

"Hi," I said, hoping nothing in my face gave me away. I held up my phone. "I was just making a list of what we're going to take back to the shop."

Ethan reached over and took my cell from my hand. My heart began to pound in my chest. "I'm not finished, but hang on a sec and I'll find it for you," I said, reaching out to get the phone back.

Ethan glanced at the screen and dropped it into his pocket. "Nice try, Sarah," he said. "But we both know you've figured out that I killed Ronan Quinn."

I shoved my hands in my pockets. "Paul called you."

Ethan shrugged and gave me a smile that reminded me of nothing so much as a crocodile. "He lets me know what's going on over here and if he wants to come over when his kid's asleep and have a cigarette or a beer, I figure it makes us even."

I thought of Paul and Alyssa outside playing hockey on the lawn. "You and Paul played hockey together."

Ethan nodded. "For a couple of years. He wasn't as good as I was."

"Why did you do it?" I asked. *Keep him talking,* I told myself. *Build a rapport. Stall. Look for a way to gain an advantage.*

"Oh, c'mon," he said. "Don't tell me you haven't figured that part out yet?" He glanced in the direction of the wine bottles.

"Those missing bottles," I said slowly. "You sold them, didn't you? You passed them off as the real thing and sold them."

Ethan didn't say anything, but one eyebrow went up and he gave me a sly smile. "They belonged to me. And if people are too stupid to do their due diligence, well, that's hardly my fault."

I brushed a strand of hair away from my face and shot a quick glance to the left to see if there was anything I could use as a weapon. There wasn't. "Did Thorne Logan really approach you about buying one of those bottles, or were you just trying to steer us in his direction?"

"Both, actually," he said.

Elvis pressed against my leg, watching Ethan intently. The warmth of his small body helped keep my legs from shaking. "Quinn found out what you were doing."

Ethan sighed. "It wasn't any of his business. I hired him to tell me what those bottles were worth. That's it. He started talking about lawsuits and I thought I might get some of my money back. Then I found out the chances of that happening were pretty slim."

"The day before he was killed, that afternoon you were here, he noticed the missing bottles, didn't he?"

I could see the back door out of the corner of my eye, but there was no way I could get to it.

"I'd paid him. I *thought* he was leaving town." An ugly expression flashed across his face. "Then he wants to come out here to check on the glue that was used for the labels."

"You'd already had a plan to slowly sell all that wine to people just as unsuspecting as your father had been. You'd already started."

Ethan held up both hands. "Ding, ding, ding, ding, ding!" he said. "Give the lady a prize!"

"So why did you kill him?" I asked, clenching my hands in my pockets to keep them from shaking. "Why didn't you just tell him the missing bottles got broken?" I pretty much knew the answer, but it was another way to buy a minute or two and I was going to grab every one I could.

"Because he wouldn't let it go at that!" He sucked in a deep breath and raked his hands back through his hair. "He just would not let it go! He threatened to have me arrested. He wouldn't do what he was hired to do and just go home." He looked at me again. "Remind you of anyone?"

"He must have made you crazy," I said, ignoring his last comment.

He looked at me and gave a snort of humorless laughter. "Oh, don't pretend you understand so we can build a connection." He made air quotes around the word "connection."

I shook my head. "I really don't understand. Why couldn't you just wait to sell those bottles?"

Ethan looked up at the ceiling and shook his head. "Wait? Do you have any idea how long I've *been* waiting? I've been waiting for years to get out of this Podunkville little place, waiting for the day when I didn't have to play the dutiful son, waiting for the day when that old man who was never satisfied with *anything* I did would just die." His voice got louder and his manner more agitated with each word. "And when he did, you know what I ended up with? A wife who pretty soon isn't going to be able to walk, another freaking millstone around my neck, and an inheritance that is worth less than what I'd get for taking the bottles to the recycling center." He shook both hands in the air. "Don't tell me to wait. I was a good son. I'm a good person and the whole damn thing backfired on me!"

"Is that why you're going to Hawaii? Because you're tired of waiting?"

Something changed in his expression and the manic behavior disappeared as if a switch had been thrown in his head. "Yes," he said. "That's why I'm going to Hawaii and that's why I won't be coming back." He exhaled and smiled. "It's going to be very sad, really. I'm going to have an accident learning to surf and my body will never be found. And I'll finally get to live the life I was meant to live all along without my old man and everyone else dragging me down."

Some of what I was feeling inside must have shown on my face.

"Don't give me that look," Ethan said, a heavy edge of sarcasm in his voice. "It's not my fault. Why couldn't Quinn just stay out of it? Why couldn't you?"

"You can't kill two people in this house," I said. "People will get suspicious."

"I know," he said, "but I don't recall saying you're going to die here. I am going to kill you, but not here." He made a sad face. "You're going to have a tragic accident on the way back to your store." He put a hand to his chest. "So very tragic."

Then his arm snaked out and whipped around my neck like a rope. He pulled a small plastic bottle of ginger ale out of his jacket pocket with his free hand, managed to unscrew the cap and pressed the opening to my mouth. "Drink," he ordered.

I pressed my lips tightly together.

Ethan slapped my face. Tears filled my eyes, but I kept my mouth tightly closed.

He grabbed my nose, pinching it between his thumb and index finger.

I held my breath as long as I could, but eventually I had to open my mouth to breathe.

Ethan forced some of the liquid into my mouth. I sputtered and spit, but some of it went down. He repeated the process twice more.

"I'm going to vomit," I choked out. I wasn't, but I needed a moment to breathe, to think.

He let go of me and took a step back. "That's probably enough," he said. I was bent over, hands on my knees, trying to get my breath. "You don't have . . . to . . . do this," I managed to gasp out.

"You sound like Quinn," Ethan said. "The thing is, neither one of you gave me a choice. He was going to call the police. I would have lost my job. And he would have made all the rest of those bottles completely worthless to me. What choice did he leave me? It was him or me and I picked me."

He looked away from me again and shook his head as though he were seeing himself back in the kitchen with Ronan Quinn. "It was poetic justice, you know, him being killed with a bottle of wine that cost less than ten dollars."

Chapter 20

His attention had shifted. It was now or never. There was a stack of boxes, about shoulder height, to my left. I used my knee and one arm to knock them over between Ethan and me.

"Run!" I yelled to Elvis, and then I bolted for the living room.

Ethan hollered an obscenity and scrambled over the cartons after me. I pushed a floor lamp sideways and heard the glass shade smash as it hit the hardwood behind me. Ethan was only a few feet back.

"Get the hell back here!" he shouted.

I turned and shoved a worn leather club chair at him. It skidded across the floor and caught him in the legs, knocking him off his feet. Elvis had jumped up onto a stack of boxes. He leaped from there to the sideboard against the wall. I swept both hands at the boxes and sent them down on top of Ethan. They only held blankets and tablecloths, so they weren't very heavy, but all I needed was a few extra seconds to get to the door and get out.

There was a vintage standing metal ashtray, missing one foot on the bottom, leaning against the sideboard and hutch. When I shoved the boxes, it fell on my own foot.

I stifled a scream, kicked it out of the way and ran for the door, breathing hard. My right foot skidded on the loose bit of hall carpet. I slid into the half wall, banging my knee on the corner edge. The pain almost knocked me off my feet, but somehow I managed to stay upright. I slid along the expanse of drywall and banged against the front door.

Ethan lunged for me, catching the edge of my sweatshirt and pulling me toward him. "You stupid cow," he roared.

I tried to twist away from him and slammed into two boxes stacked on a wooden chair. At the same moment Elvis launched himself with a loud yowl from the sideboard, landing on Ethan's back, claws digging in through the man's shirt. Ethan yelled another obscenity and reached over his shoulder for the cat with one hand while the other slapped over my mouth and nose.

I couldn't breathe. I fell back against the boxes, my elbow pushing down the flaps of the top one. I felt around blindly inside for something, anything to use as a weapon. My hand touched something heavy and metallic. I grabbed and swung my arm up and out as hard as I could, making very satisfying contact with the top of Ethan's head before my left leg gave out. His eyes rolled back in his head, his hand slipped from my face and he dropped to the floor.

Elvis jumped down, shook himself and made his

way over to me. He climbed onto my chest, where he sat down and looked at what I'd just used to brain Ethan Hall. It was a can of Spam.

"Merow!" he said.

I pushed my hair back out of my face. I looked over at Ethan and nodded. "Poetic justice."

Chapter 21

I managed to get to my feet, pick up Elvis and get the front door unlocked. Ethan was out cold. I could see his chest moving, so I knew he wasn't dead, and beyond that I didn't much care.

I stumbled out onto the stoop as Nick's SUV fishtailed to a stop at the curb. Mac was already out of the passenger side running across the lawn to me before the vehicle had come to a complete stop. He caught me as my leg gave way again and I half fell down the front steps.

"Sarah, are you all right?" he asked. Nick was sprinting across the grass toward us.

I nodded.

"Where's Ethan?" Nick said.

I jerked my head in the direction of the house. "He's in there." I held up the can of Spam and grinned at them. "I spammed his scam." It struck me so funny I started to laugh. "I spammed his scam," I said again.

"She's in shock," I heard Nick say to Mac, but it seemed as though he were talking from the end of a long tunnel. "Ambulance should be right behind us."

I wanted to ask him what made him think I needed an ambulance. I had Elvis and him and Mac and a can of Spam. What more did I need?

I looked up at Nick and wondered what was wrong with his head that it had gotten so out of focus. Mac, on the other hand, looked wonderfully in focus. It struck me that laying a big wet one on him sounded like a marvelous idea, but before I could tell him that, the world suddenly went dark.

I woke up in the back of the ambulance. "What did you take?" a burly paramedic with muscles on his muscles asked me.

"I didn't take anything," I said. It was hard to get the words out. My tongue felt as if it were too long for my mouth. I made a flailing gesture with one hand in the direction of the house. "He made me drink something." The luncheon meat can was sitting on the edge of the stretcher. "I spammed his scam," I told the paramedic. I liked saying the words so much I repeated them again.

Nick appeared at the back door of the ambulance. He handed the bottle of ginger ale to the muscular paramedic. "Whatever she had, I think it's in here."

"Thanks," the hunky paramedic said. "There's another ambulance on the way for your suspect. We're going to transport her now."

I leaned sideways and waved at Nick. The straps in the stretcher were the only things keeping me from falling onto the floor.

Nick raised a hand at me and then shut the back door. The paramedic moved the can of Spam on to the floor.

"You don't have to worry," I said to him. "I would never spam you. There would be no spamisfaction in that. Spamisfaction." I said the word a few times, and then I started singing "I Can't Get No Spamisfaction" to the tune of The Rolling Stones' "Satisfaction," and much to the amusement of the paramedics, I sang it all the way to the hospital.

I spent the next several hours in the emergency room. When he came to, Ethan admitted to Nick that there was Vicodin in the bottle of ginger ale he'd tried to make me drink. I hadn't gotten that much into my system, but on an empty stomach it was enough. I'd only had the painkiller once before in my life and it had made me pretty loopy then, too.

By the time they let Liam in to see me, along with Rose and Mr. P., who had told the staff they were my parents, I was starting to feel like myself again, albeit a very embarrassed version of myself.

Mac had gone to take care of things at the shop. Before he left he caught my hand and gave it a squeeze. "I am so glad you're all right," he said.

I smiled at him. "Thank you for riding to the rescue."

He smiled back. "Anytime, Sarah."

Nick poked his head in the room about fifteen minutes after the others had arrived. Rose was fussing, fixing my pillow and sending Mr. P. to get me a warm blanket.

"How are you?" he asked.

"I'm all right," I said. "What happened to Ethan?"

"He's under arrest."

"I'd like to pound him into sand," Liam said.

Nick nodded. "You and me both." He gave me a half smile. "He crushed up some of Ellie's Vicodin in that soda he tried to get you to drink."

I made a face and shook my head. "I didn't drink very much."

Nick swiped a hand over his neck. "Yeah, well, it looks like there was enough in that bottle to drug a horse."

Rose pressed her lips together for a moment and straightened my blankets. I caught her hand. "I'm fine," I said.

"Thank heavens," she whispered.

"How did you know?" I asked Nick. He looked at Mr. P., who was just coming in carrying a flannel blanket across his outstretched arms.

"Alfred," Nick said. "I came back to look at that bed. When he called you back and you didn't answer, he got worried."

Rose looked at Mr. P. and beamed. At the same time I saw her blink away tears. I reached for Mr. P.'s hands and he came to stand next to the bed.

"Thank you," I said.

"There's nothing to thank me for, my dear," he said. "You saved yourself. And I'm very glad that you did." I squeezed his hands and he leaned forward to kiss my forehead.

"Ethan started selling those bottles of wine," I said to Nick.

He nodded. "I know." He came around the side of the bed. "I have to get back to the station to clear up some loose ends with Michelle. I'll come see you later."

"We should be able to get out of here soon," Liam said. He looked at Nick and clapped him on the back. "Thank you. This could have ended a lot differently."

Nick nodded. "I'm really glad it didn't." Like Mr. P. he leaned over and dropped a kiss on the top of my head.

I was released from the ER about an hour later. Liam, Rose and Mr. P. took me home, where Jess was waiting with Elvis. She wrapped her arms around me and hugged me. "You scared the crap out of me," she said. "Don't do anything like this again."

"I don't intend to," I said.

Elvis was sitting on the top of the cat tower. I went over and picked him up. He rubbed his face against my cheek. "You were very brave," I said to him as I scratched the side of his face. He made a sound a lot like a sigh of contentment and started to purr.

I carried him over to the sofa and sat down. Jess perched on the edge next to me. "He jumped on Ethan's back," I said, still stroking the cat's fur. "I wouldn't have been able to hit him if it hadn't been for Elvis."

Jess reached over to stroke the top of his head. "Good job, dude," she said. She looked over at Liam. "There's coffee."

"Thanks," he said, heading into the kitchen.

Jess looked at me again. "Did you really whack Ethan with a can of Spam?" she asked.

I nodded. "His father had a stockpile of food and water probably in case of a power failure."

"I almost threw that box out," Rose said.

I smiled at her. "I'm so glad you didn't."

"Alfred and I are going to make supper for everyone,"

she said. She smiled at me. "Is there anything special you'd like, dear?"

I shook my head. "Whatever you make will be wonderful. Thank you."

She blew me a kiss and she and Mr. P. left. Liam came out of the kitchen holding a mug of coffee and whistling. It took me a moment, but I realized he was whistling "Satisfaction." He sat next to me on the sofa and smirked.

"Jess, could you hand me that pillow?" I asked, pointing at the cushion on the nearby rocking chair. I set Elvis on the couch next to me, where he stretched and swiped a paw over his face.

"Sure," she said. She got up, grabbed the pillow and gave it to me.

"Thanks," I said. And then I smacked Liam with it.

"Hey!" he yelled. "What did I do?"

"Who told you?"

He tried to look innocent, which was pretty much impossible.

I whacked him again and he collapsed against the back of the couch, laughing.

"Okay, somebody tell me what's going on," Jess said, a bewildered look on her face.

Liam held his forearm in front of his face and started to sing "I Can't Get No Spamisfaction," before losing it all over again.

I stared up at the ceiling. "I didn't hallucinate that, did I?" I said.

"Nope," Liam said. He was enjoying it all way too much.

"Hallucinate what?" Jess demanded. "So help me, if

the two of you don't tell me what's going on, I'm going to get a can of Spam and smack both of you with it."

That just set Liam off again.

I looked at Jess. "I may have done a little singing in the ambulance on the way to the hospital."

"A little?" Liam said. "That's not what I heard."

Jess's expression changed as she put the pieces together. "Wait a second," she said. "You sang 'I Can't Get No Spamisfaction' in the ambulance?"

"Once in falsetto, from what I heard," my brother chortled.

To her credit, Jess tried to keep a straight face.

"Oh, go ahead and laugh," I said. "You know you want to."

"No, that would be wrong," she managed to choke out, and then she pressed a hand over her mouth, and her shoulders shook with silent laughter.

I couldn't help laughing myself. After everything that had happened, it felt pretty good.

When Liam finally got himself under control, he turned to look at me and his expression grew serious. "When Rose told me what happened to you . . ." He grabbed my hand and squeezed. I squeezed back. "It's a good thing Ethan's in jail," he said, his voice suddenly husky with emotion, "because if he wasn't I would be." He squeezed his free hand into a tight fist. "Love you," he said, and then he smiled. "Baby sister."

I put my arm around his neck and hugged him. "I love you, too, *big* brother," I said.

"Oh, crap," Jess said behind me. "You're making my allergies act up." She sniffed, took a swipe at her eyes with one hand and got up, reaching for a Kleenex on the counter.

Elvis, who hated being left out of anything, meowed loudly, took a pass at his face with a paw and looked expectantly at us.

I laughed again because it really did feel good.

We decided to celebrate the next night down at Sam's for Thursday night jam. There was a lot of good news to celebrate. I'd called Skye back and the benefit concert to raise the money for Ellie's surgery was back on. Channing Caulfield had set up an account to administer the funds. The Marklin model train hadn't been put up for auction after all. Caulfield and Stella had come to some sort of private agreement and the former bank manager had made a very generous donation to the account.

The police were satisfied that Ellie had known nothing about what Ethan had done. In fact, she'd been going to leave Ethan just before his father died, but he'd threatened to go after custody of the children if she did—he liked the image of loving son and husband he'd projected and he was afraid his father would change his will and leave everything to his grandchildren if Ethan and Ellie divorced.

She was a little shaken by everything that had happened, but she was strong and determined and I really felt she'd be all right. Stella was moving in to help with the kids for a while.

And it turned out that Edison Hall had made a new will. Elvis unearthed it at the house hidden on the sideboard he'd used as his launch pad when he attacked

Ethan. Edison hadn't spent all his savings on his wine collection after all. It turned out he had bought stock in several banks and utility companies over a long period of time. He'd put everything in a trust for Ellie and the children. It wasn't a lot of money, but it would give her something every month she could count on.

Elvis had just gotten settled in his chair in anticipation of *Jeopardy!* when I heard a knock on my door. Liam was driving us to Sam's. "He's early," I said to Elvis. I reached down and stroked the top of his head. He smiled at me and turned back to the TV. He'd received so many cans of sardines for his "act of bravery" that I wouldn't have to buy him any for at least a month.

When I opened the door, it wasn't Liam standing there; it was Nick. "Hi," I said.

He smiled at me. "Hi, Liam said I could catch a ride with you two."

"Let me get my jacket and I'm ready." Nick had stopped in twice and called me twice in the last twenty-four hours. I wasn't exactly sure how to react.

He caught my arm. "Hang on a second," he said. He handed me a paper shopping bag.

"What's this?" I asked.

"Look inside."

Inside the bag were a long-sleeved T-shirt and a pair of running shorts. I pulled out the shorts. "Uh, thank you," I said. "But these are a bit too big for me."

"That's because they're for me."

"I don't understand," I said.

"Name the time and the place and I'll going running with you." He smiled. "And my favorite meal is chicken pot pie, which by the way you need to be able to make gravy for."

I didn't know what to say. I just stood there staring at him.

"This is where you kiss me," he said, taking a step closer to me.

"Are you sure?" I asked, realizing how lame the words were as soon as they were out.

"Positive," he said.

So what else could I do?

I kissed him.

Love Elvis the cat?
Then meet Hercules and Owen!
Read on for an excerpt of the first book
in the Magical Cat series.

CURIOSITY THRILLED THE CAT

by Sofie Kelly

Available now from Obsidian.

Chapter 1

Slant Flying

The body was smack in the middle of my freshly scrubbed kitchen floor. Fred the Funky Chicken, minus his head.

"Owen!" I said, sharply.

Nothing.

"Owen, you little fur ball, I know you did this. Where are you?"

There was a muffled "meow" from the back door. I leaned around the cupboards. Owen was sprawled on his back in front of the screen door, a neon yellow feather sticking out of his mouth. He rolled over onto his side and looked at me with the same goofy expression I used to get from stoned students coming into the BU library.

I crouched down next to the gray-and-white tabby. "Owen, you killed Fred," I said. "That's the third chicken this week."

The cat sat up slowly and stretched. He padded over to me and put one paw on my knee. Tipping his head to one side he looked up at me with his golden eyes. I sat back against the end of the cupboard. Owen climbed onto my lap and put his two front paws on my chest. The feather was still sticking out of his mouth.

I held out my right hand. "Give me Fred's head," I said. The cat looked at me unblinkingly. "C'mon, Owen. Spit it out."

He turned his head sideways and dropped what was left of Fred the Funky Chicken's head into my hand. It was a soggy lump of cotton with that lone yellow feather stuck on the end.

"You have a problem, Owen," I told the cat. "You have a monkey on your back." I dropped what was left of the toy's head onto the floor and wiped my hand on my gray yoga pants. "Or maybe I should say you have a chicken on your back."

The cat nuzzled my chin, then laid his head against my T-shirt, closed his eyes and started to purr.

I stroked the top of his head. "That's what they all say," I told him. "You're addicted, you little fur ball, and Rebecca is your dealer."

Owen just kept on purring and ignored me. Hercules came around the corner then. "Your brother is a catnip junkie," I said to the little tuxedo cat.

Hercules climbed over my legs and sniffed the remains of Fred the Funky Chicken's head. Then he looked at Owen, rumbling like a diesel engine as I scratched the side of his head. I swear there was disdain on Hercules' furry face. Stick catnip in, on or near anything and Owen squirmed with joy. Hercules, on the other hand, was indifferent.

The stocky black-and-white cat climbed onto my lap, too. He put one white paw on my shoulder and swatted at my hair.

"Behind the ear?" I asked.

"Meow," the cat said.

I took that as a yes, and tucked the strands back behind my ear. I was used to long hair, but I'd cut mine several months ago. I was still adjusting to the change in style. At least I hadn't given in to the impulse to dye my dark brown hair blond.

"Maybe I'll ask Rebecca if she has any ideas for my hair," I said. "She's supposed to be back tonight." At the sound of Rebecca's name Owen lifted his head. He'd taken to Rebecca from the first moment he'd seen her, about two weeks after I'd brought the cats home.

Both Owen and Hercules had been feral kittens. I'd found them, or more truthfully they'd found me, about a month after I'd arrived in town. I had no idea how old they were. They were affectionate with me, but wouldn't allow anyone else to come near them, let alone touch them. That hadn't stopped Rebecca, my backyard neighbor, from trying. She'd been buying both cats little catnip toys for weeks now, but all she'd done was turn Owen into a chicken-decapitating catnip junkie. She was on vacation right now, but Owen had clearly managed to unearth a chicken from a secret stash somewhere.

I stroked the top of his head again. "Go back to sleep," I said. "You're going cold turkey ... or maybe I should say cold chicken. I'm telling Rebecca no more catnip toys for you. You're getting lazy."

Owen put his head down again, while Hercules used his to butt my free hand. "You want some attention, too?" I asked. I scratched the spot, almost at the top of his head, where the white fur around his mouth and up the bridge of his nose gave way to black. His green eyes narrowed to slits and he began to purr, as well. The rumbling was kind of like being in the service bay of a Volkswagen dealership.

I glanced up at the clock. "Okay, you two. Let me up. It's almost time for me to go and I have to take care of the dearly departed before I do."

I'd sold my car when I'd moved to Minnesota from Boston, and because I could walk everywhere in Mayville Heights, I still hadn't bought a new one. Since I had no car, I'd spent my first few weeks in town wandering around exploring, which is how I'd stumbled on Wisteria Hill, the abandoned Henderson estate. Everett Henderson had hired me at the library.

Owen and Hercules had peered out at me from a tumble of raspberry canes and then followed me around while I explored the overgrown English country garden behind the house. I'd seen several other full-grown cats, but they'd all disappeared as soon as I got anywhere close to them. When I left, Owen and Hercules followed me down the rutted gravel driveway. Twice I'd picked them up and carried them back to the empty house, but that didn't deter them. I looked everywhere, but I couldn't find their mother. They were so small and so determined to come with me that in the end I'd brought them home.

There were whispers around town about Wisteria Hill and the feral cats. But that didn't mean there was anything unusual about my cats. Oh no, nothing unusual at all. It didn't matter that I'd heard rumors about strange lights and ghosts. No one had lived at the estate for quite a while, but Everett refused to sell it or do anything with the property. I'd heard that he'd grown up at Wisteria Hill. Maybe that was why he didn't want to change anything.

Speaking of not wanting change, Hercules was not eager to relinquish his prime spot on my lap. But after some gentle prodding, he shook himself and got off. Owen yawned a couple of times, stretched and took twice as long to move.

I got the broom and dustpan from the porch and swept up the remains of Fred the Funky Chicken. Owen and Hercules sat in front of the refrigerator and watched. Owen made a move toward the dustpan, like he was toying with the idea of grabbing the body and making a run for it.

I glared at him. "Don't even think about it."

He sat back down, making low, grumbling meows in his throat.

I flipped open the lid of the garbage can and held the pan over the top. "Fred was a good chicken," I said solemnly. "He was a funky chicken and we'll miss him."

"Meow," Owen yowled.

I flipped what was left of the catnip toy into the garbage. "Rest in peace, Fred," I said as the lid closed.

I put the broom away, brushed the cat hair off my shirt and washed my hands. I looked in the bathroom mirror. Hercules was right. My hair did look better tucked behind my ear.

My messenger bag with a towel and canvas shoes for tai chi class was in the front closet. I set it by the door and went back through the house to make sure the cats had fresh water.

"I'm leaving," I said. But both cats had disappeared and I didn't get any answer.

I stopped to grab my keys and pick up my bag.

Locking the door behind me, I headed out, down Mountain Road.

The sun was yellow-orange, low on the sky over Lake Pepin. It was a warm Minnesota evening, without the sticky humidity of Boston in late July. I shifted my bag from one shoulder to the other. I wasn't going to think about Boston. Minnesota was home now—at least for the next eighteen months or so.

The street curved in toward the center of town as I headed down the hill, and the roof of the library building came into view below. It sat on the midpoint of a curve of shoreline, protected from the water by a rock wall. The brick building had a stained-glass window that dominated one end and a copper-roofed cupola, complete with its original wrought-iron weather vane.

The Mayville Heights Free Public Library was a Carnegie library, built in 1912 with money donated by the industrialist and philanthropist Andrew Carnegie. Now it was being restored and updated to celebrate its centenary. That was why I had been in town for the last several months. And why I'd be here for the next year and a half. I was supervising the restoration—which was almost finished—as well as updating the collections, computerizing the card catalogue and setting up free Internet access for the library patrons. I was slowly learning the reading history of everyone in town. It made me feel like I knew the people a little, as well.

ABOUT THE AUTHOR

Sofie Ryan is a writer and mixed-media artist who loves to repurpose things in her life and her art. She is the author of *The Whole Cat and Caboodle* and *Buy a Whisker* in the *New York Times* bestselling Second Chance Cat Mystery series. She also writes the *New York Times* bestselling Magical Cats Mystery series under the name Sofie Kelly.

CONNECT ONLINE

sofieryan.com

ALSO AVAILABLE FROM
NEW YORK TIMES BESTSELLING AUTHOR

Sofie Ryan

Buy a Whisker
A Second Chance Cat Mystery

Things have been quiet in the coastal town of North
Harbor, Maine, since Sarah Grayson and her rescue
cat, Elvis, solved their first murder. Sarah is happy
running Second Chance, the shop where she sells
lovingly refurbished and repurposed items. But then
she gets dragged into a controversy over developing the
waterfront. Most of the residents—including Sarah—
are for it, but there is one holdout—baker Lily Carter.

So when Lily is found murdered in her bakery, it looks
like somebody wanted to remove the only obstacle to
the development. But Sarah soon discovers that
nothing is as simple as it seems. Now, with the help of
her cat's uncanny ability to detect a lie, Sarah is
narrowing down the suspects. But can she collar the
culprit before the ruthless killer pounces again?

**"A loveable protagonist...and a
supersmart cat."**
—MyShelf.com

Available wherever books are sold or at
penguin.com

OM0170